# FEAR NO DARKNESS

## GHOST SQUADRON
## 4

## ERIC THOMSON

# Fear No Darkness

Copyright 2023 Eric Thomson
First paperback printing February 2023



Published in Canada
By Sanddiver Books Inc.
ISBN: 978-1-989314-88-3

*Turning and turning in the widening gyre*
*The falcon cannot hear the falconer;*
*Things fall apart; the centre cannot hold;*
*Mere anarchy is loosed upon the world,*
*The blood-dimmed tide is loosed, and everywhere*
*The ceremony of innocence is drowned;*
*The best lack all conviction, while the worst*
*Are full of passionate intensity.*

The Second Coming
By William Butler Yeats

# — One —

I cut the comlink and sat back, frowning. I couldn't always sense trouble coming, or if I did back in my younger days, I ignored my instinct. There was a time when I'd embodied the old saying that the Almighty looked after fools and drunkards since I'd qualified on both counts. Making colonel and taking command of the 1st Special Forces Regiment was nothing short of miraculous, as was marrying a Naval Intelligence rear admiral who'd racked up a higher body count during her career than I did.

She's the one who took over from the Almighty long ago and put me back on the path of righteousness, although not without a few interesting detours. Sometimes I wondered whether I had a touch of the gift, as some might call it. There's no doubt I could scare Sisters of the Void, many of whom could see things hidden from the eyes of ordinary mortals.

And what I was sensing now reminded me of an ancient poem by a man named Yeats called The Second Coming, especially the line which went, 'Things fall apart; the center cannot hold.' It would astonish most civilians that a Marine officer, especially one who climbed up the ranks from private to chief warrant officer before taking a commission, knew anything about pre-spaceflight poetry.

But when you spent weeks on end aboard starships between missions, you read. A lot. Most long-service Marines are self-educated to a degree that astonished even our Navy siblings. Myself, I've always been fascinated with everything historical. By the time the Corps made me a major, I could have sat the examinations for a degree in military studies and earned first-class honors. And if I'd been inclined to write a thesis, that master's degree would have been a cinch as well. But I digress.

Commanding the Fleet's premier Special Forces regiment comes with the sort of situational awareness that most generals throughout history would have envied. Of course, being married to the head of Naval Intelligence's Special Operations Division, whose blacker-than-black missions were carried out by my unit, gave me access to information few in the Armed Forces will ever see.

That's why Yeats came to mind when I heard the first rumblings of a constitutional convention to be called by the OutWorlds, those star systems colonized during the second great migration, who won their independence because of the ensuing civil war that killed countless millions. The older systems we call Home Worlds, colonized during the first great migration and who, in turn, founded colonies of their own in newly discovered star systems, had never quite reconciled to losing the latter. As a result, the

Commonwealth has been teetering on the edge of a new civil war for several generations, since before last century's drawn-out conflict with the Shrehari Empire.

And anyone paying attention to politics was aware a constitutional convention demanded by the OutWorlds could only be for one reason — to push back against the creeping centralization, which was becoming more evident by the day. It not only brought most existing colonies under direct Earth rule but threatened to strip the sovereign star systems of their power to decide their fates.

I've been fighting those Centralists, whatever they called themselves over the years, for a long time, much of it as an undercover field agent alongside my partner before we returned to more normal military careers. So I knew them, their leaders, and their intentions. Many of their operatives met a swift end thanks to my dagger or my Shrehari blaster. Or to Hera's deadly stiletto.

That constitutional convention would bring the long, undercover war out in the open like nothing else. Earth and the Home Worlds wouldn't cooperate, naturally, and would do their best to sabotage the OutWorlds' unity of purpose. By violent means if necessary. They couldn't allow a majority of star system senators, even if that majority was by one mere voice, to seize the Commonwealth Senate and turn it against the administration. Nor could they allow the OutWorld star system presidents, premiers, prime ministers, or whatever else they called their heads of government, to form a block that might, if pushed far enough, break away from Earth entirely.

As I said, a convention meant only one thing — trouble.

But that's why I had a job, one I enjoyed. If it weren't for politicians suffering from pathological narcissism, sociopathy, or other assorted derangements, my life would be tedious enough that I might just as well retire and spend my days at our seaside home, fishing, hunting, and drinking Shrehari Ale. Not that my wife, the rear admiral and former assassin, would let me sit idle while she schemed to prevent a Third Migration War.

And I just knew she'd somehow rope me into dealing with this convention. It's what she did best.

"Caledonia to Colonel Decker."

A basso profundo voice yanked me out of my private contemplation, and when I turned a gimlet eye on my open office door, I saw the smiling face of my oldest and best friend Josh Bayliss, who'd taken Ghost Squadron when they kicked me upstairs. Josh had witnessed my years as a fool and drunkard and saved my ass many times until I stepped into it so badly that even he couldn't help.

"What's up?"

Josh didn't wait for me to invite him in. He simply took one of the chairs facing my desk and made himself comfortable. There was a time when Josh outranked me, and some habits never died.

"I should ask you that, considering the worried frown on your ugly mug."

"Kal called just now, and we had a little chat."

"And what did our esteemed deputy divisional commander say that has you look like they're about to ban the importation of Shrehari Ale?"

Brigadier General Kal Ryent, another Special Forces legend, had the 1st SFR before me and was touted as one of the most promising flag officers in the Corps. I didn't doubt he'd reach four stars. He and I had worked together on some hairy operations back in the day, and he was the smartest, most capable, and most charismatic combat leader I had ever met.

"Bite your tongue, heathen. That won't happen while I'm still among the living, even if I must become a smuggler and haul it across half the galaxy myself."

"Then what? Is Kal getting his second star and announced you'd be replacing him?"

I glowered at my friend. "You're really pushing it, buddy. No."

When I finished relaying Kal's news of a possible constitutional convention and my sense that it meant big trouble in our little Commonwealth, Josh sat back and grunted.

"Damn fool politicians. Are they looking to blow everything up?"

I gave him a shrug. "It was going to happen sooner rather than later anyhow. Earth and the Home Worlds aren't doing much by way of hiding their Centralist dreams lately. Might as well bring it on."

"Then why are you worried if it's inevitable?"

"Because the OutWorlds banding together and telling Earth to stick it in the nearest black hole might trigger the proverbial antimatter containment breach. Once that's triggered, there will be no going back, and if we — meaning the Fleet — can't somehow manage the situation, it will mean civil war."

"What's the answer, then? What course of action do we take?"

Josh knew the answer as well as I did, but it was a word no one wanted to utter because even at its most benign, it meant an upheaval in the affairs of humanity like none before. But I was becoming convinced it had to happen. Between my study of human history and a spouse literally engineering the end of the Commonwealth in its present incarnation, I'd been converted.

"Ensure the politicians don't kill billions."

Josh grimaced. "A sizable chunk of the Armed Forces will obey orders to come down on recalcitrant star systems and make them repent."

"Without a shred of doubt. And I won't be in that sizable chunk, nor will ninety percent of the Special Forces community—"

"A hundred percent, Zack. We're OutWorlders to the last trooper in SOCOM."

"There are probably many Home Worlders in the MLI."

Josh waved my objection away, and I understood why. Those who joined the Marine Light Infantry regiment had broken with their pasts. Its six battalions were the Marine

Corps' own foreign legion, and the Corps' home was on Caledonia.

"They're all honorary OutWorlders by now. Especially since we took them into SOCOM."

"Granted."

"But back to the subject under discussion. Kal never wastes a word. Was he giving you a veiled warning order? Is it that what has you wondering about Shrehari Ale futures in the Rim Sector?"

I never could hide a damn thing from Josh. "Aye. It's what he does best. Our Kal could teach Commonwealth senators a few lessons about shrewdness. I'm pretty sure Hera has plans for him as well, though she won't say, and I know better than to ask. If this constitutional convention goes up the OutWorld flagpole, we'll be the ones standing guard because Earth will never allow it to go ahead, at least not quietly and without incidents."

"Did Kal say where they're holding this incendiary meet-and-greet?"

"No. But that means nothing. He might know and just isn't ready to tell. I'll ask Hera when she's at her most vulnerable this weekend." The hint of a leer in my grin must have been enough because Josh took on a stony expression. He'd been my best man at our wedding, and his respect for my wife almost crossed the line into worship.

"Did I ever mention you sometimes share too much of your personal life with me, Zack?"

"Once or twice. Why did you come to see me instead of calling, like everyone else in this regiment?"

A faint smile relaxed Josh's expression. "Are you complaining?"

"About what, that you showed up in person or that no one else does?"

"Yes."

"If we were still sergeants, I'd give you the rigid digit salute."

"Fine. Two things. Curtis wants to challenge the War College distance learning examinations. He's been spending his travel time between missions studying and writing the required essays. Should he pass, he wants leave to attend the residential portion."

Major Curtis Delgado, Officer Commanding Ghost Squadron's first company, also known as the Erinyes, was the top-rated company commander in the regiment and might easily surpass Josh and me one day. Neither of us ever bothered with the War College, and we were now too senior for it.

"He has my permission to challenge the exams. We'll discuss his taking a few months of classroom time when he's been admitted."

Josh nodded. "In that case, we should look for his replacement now because if he's off to Sanctum, he won't return to the Erinyes. I was thinking we should slot him as deputy squadron commander and not necessarily in my squadron."

"Agreed. We'll discuss it at the next command conference. What's the other thing?"

A lazy smile lit up Josh's dark, craggy features. "Are you entering the SOCOM high explosives landscaping contest?"

I smiled back at him. "You bet."

# — TWO —

Commanding the 1st Special Forces Regiment and the Marine Corps' Special Forces home station, Fort Arnhem, while being married to a Naval Intelligence rear admiral whose duty station was Armed Forces Headquarters in Sanctum, meant a lot of commuting. For me, not for Hera. After all, she outranked me by two grades and decided our family home was in one of the flag officers' quarters in the base's residential sector.

And because I didn't feel like spending hours on the road or aboard the train between Sanctum and Carrick, the town nearest to Fort Arnhem, let alone use one of the motor pool's aircars, I usually took the liberty shuttle. It left the Fort at sixteen hundred hours every Friday and returned from Sanctum on Sunday at twenty-two hundred. That meant riding with Marines from the regiment, the two MLI battalions, the Pathfinder School, and the support units, which suited me fine. There was no better way to gauge the troopers' mood than chatting them up during the quick hop between the backcountry and the big city, Caledonia's capital.

Since I had a second set of clothes and uniforms at home, I always traveled light, without luggage, and wore dark civilian slacks tucked into black boots and a collarless white shirt beneath a waist-length black leather jacket. But I carried my personal sidearm, a Shrehari blaster re-bored for human ammunition in a shoulder holster — loaded and powered, of course — and my Pathfinder dagger tucked into the small of my back, even on what was now my home planet.

Caledonia, nominally a Commonwealth colony controlled by Earth, was de facto if not de jure, the Fleet's private world, quasi-independent and self-governing to the same extent as the OutWorlds. Except the governor general was always a former Grand Admiral, the star system government was mostly staffed with retired Armed Forces officers or Defense Department civilians, especially in the more senior jobs, and there were no elected officials above the local level.

Caledonia existed solely to support the Fleet and offer its veterans a world where they could settle after leaving the Service and call their own. Even Hera and I had bought a home for our time off and, more importantly, our later years by the Middle Sea. But that didn't mean guys like me, who'd pissed off plenty of powerful and dangerous folks during an extensive career in black ops, were safe from retribution, so we went about our business armed. And that was why Hera and I lived in the flag officers' quarters on base, where security was tighter than an antimatter containment reservoir. Our home in the south was equally well equipped to repel raiders along with the occasional direct hit by a tropical typhoon.

Sure, the opposition had tried to kill us a few times over the years, but they never quite managed. Still, as we said in our business, the enemy only needed to be lucky once. We needed to be lucky every time.

When I climbed aboard the shuttle sitting in the middle of the parade square, the two hundred or so troopers aboard variously waved, smiled, and nodded as I made my way forward to one of the aft-facing jump seats against the bulkhead separating the passenger compartment from the flight deck.

"How are they hanging this fine Friday, Colonel?" The pilot asked when I poked my head through the open door to say hi. He was a Marine warrant officer from the Fleet HQ aviation battalion, which provided transportation and low-level aviation defense.

"The way SOCOM likes it, Warrant. This is your last hop of the week?"

"You bet, sir. Once I land you folks, I'm parking this baby and going home for a cold beer and a hot tub."

"That would be my plan as well, minus the hot tub. My wife doesn't believe in them."

"Can't have everything, sir. That's a fact. Say hi to the admiral for me, though."

"Will do."

At sixteen hundred precisely, the shuttle's aft ramp rose — anyone not aboard by then would need to find alternate and much slower means to reach the capital. Moments later, the thrusters spooled up, and we rose vertically into the air until the shuttle cleared ground obstacles, such as the crags surrounding Fort Arnhem, before changing to horizontal flight and a quick run down the Nestor Valley.

As soon as the seat belt notification vanished, I stood and wandered along the aisles to chat with the troopers. Though I didn't have Hera's quasi-eidetic memory and couldn't remember every name, I was good with faces and knew which unit each of them belonged to, unless they'd just been posted in or to another outfit at Arnhem.

"Off to enjoy the pleasures of the big city again, sir?" A young sergeant from the Pathfinder School asked with a smile as I neared.

"The admiral and I have experienced all of them, so it's a quiet weekend at home for both of us. Mind you, she could always have something planned that I'll only find out about at the last minute."

I winked at him and walked on as he and those around him chuckled. Everyone who'd been at Fort Arnhem when we were married in the chapel and held our reception in the Pegasus Club knew about my redoubtable spouse, and the newbies heard about it from the old-timers. It had been one of the most significant events in the Fort's history.

Sergeant First Class Jenkins, one of the 1st MLI's revenants — a Marine who'd screwed up by the numbers and ended in a prison colony on Parth before volunteering for the harshest basic training known to humanity — raised a hand as I continued my tour, exchanging a word here and there with the troopers.

"Hey Colonel, Yono here," he nudged the man beside him with his elbow, "one of our newbies fresh from Fort Erfoud doesn't believe you carry a Shrehari blaster as your personal weapon."

The newbie looked to be in his mid-thirties, which probably made him another revenant now serving under a new identity.

I stopped beside them and raised the left side of my jacket to show the huge, ugly weapon in its holster.

"There you go. My man Jenkins here wasn't lying. This isn't the original one I took from a Shrehari corsair long ago — some piece of crap pirate stole it from me — but it's just as nasty."

"No shit, sir." Yono grinned at Decker. "Any chance we'll take a prize like that from the boneheads?"

His eagerness made me smile, and though it was unlikely any MLI troopers would conduct raids in the Protectorate Zone, life had a way of changing assumptions.

"You never know."

By the time I'd finished my circuit, the pilot announced our imminent landing at the HQ spaceport, and I retook my seat. Riding the Friday liberty express had a habit of raising spirits, mine included. Once we'd settled by the passenger terminal, I watched the Marines exit with a spring in their step, then poked my head into the flight deck again.

"Have a great weekend, Warrant."

"You too, sir."

By the time I walked through the terminal's main hall, it was empty save for cleaning droids doing their duty and keeping the stone floor polished to a shine so clear you could see your reflection. The main doors opened at my approach, and I immediately saw my lovely wife, also in civilian clothes, leaning against her car, which sat in a no-parking zone by the curb.

She smiled at me in the way she never smiled at anyone else. "My fearsome warrior is finally home."

"And ready for action, Admiral, sir."

We embraced — chastely since displays of personal affection in public by senior officers were frowned upon — and climbed into the car, a dull, mass-produced gray box that contrasted with the sleek machines owned by most flag officers in Sanctum.

As we pulled away, I said, "What's new in your zoo, oh love of my life?"

"Didn't we talk last night?"

"Sure, but things happen on Fridays around the Puzzle Palace."

She turned her head to spear me with those mesmerizing dark eyes. "Why do I sense you're on a fishing expedition?"

"Because a dickey bird twittered something in my ear concerning the OutWorlds and a constitutional convention, and I immediately got a bad feeling about that."

"Your dickey bird wouldn't be named Kal, would he?"

"Yes, and because of that, I took it as an unvoiced warning order. And since this is the sort of stuff that Naval Intelligence tracks, it's a given you're already involved."

Hera raised her hand to touch my left cheek with her slender fingers. "That's why I love you so much, Big Boy. You're the perfect package — brains and good looks."

"Get us home, and I'll show you I'm much more than just a good mind in a healthy body, Honey."

"Sorry. It'll have to wait. Saga is joining us for supper."

I could feel my face light up at the mention of my only child's name. The day she followed her old man into the Corps was one of the proudest of my life. Sure, she was an intelligence analyst, not a Pathfinder or any other combat specialty. But she was bucking for a Naval Intelligence Liaison Officer job and had recently completed the basic parachute course. I'd joined her for her last and qualifying jump, and watching the CO of the Pathfinder School pin on her wings had been another proud moment.

"Excellent."

"And scuttlebutt says she'll be a captain once this year's promotion boards wrap up. Since she just has the minimum time in rank to qualify, I'd say your daughter gave an impressive performance."

"A chip off the old blockhead, eh?" I grinned at Hera. "She's a perfect package as well — her father's brains and her mother's looks. It would have been disastrous the other way around."

Saga's mother, my former spouse, may have had plenty of academic degrees and honors, but she was the perfect example of credentials not indicating intelligence beyond a narrowly focused area.

"Considering you never made captain, I'd say she's an improvement on the old blockhead."

"Not my fault. They commissioned me as a major."

"After how many years climbing up the greasy pole?"

"Touché. But in my defense, I didn't mature until later in life. Saga was an early bloomer."

When Hera gave me a sideways smile, I couldn't help but chuckle. She wasn't just the most effective field operative and assassin of her generation. She was also a master manipulator. But we'd been together for so long I could always suss out her little tricks. Eventually.

"Nice try moving the subject away from my conversation with Kal. Now talk, or I'll sleep in the spare room tonight."

"You drive a hard bargain."

"Among other hard things." I gave her a leer.

"Yes, Kal is right. Rumblings about the OutWorlds looking for a confrontation with Earth are burning up the subspace radio network. Sovereign star system high commissioners have been holding top secret meetings with each other and the governments of their host planets on every OutWorld. Even the representatives here on Caledonia are angling for a meeting with the governor general and the Grand Admiral."

"And are Larsson and the GG biting?"

"What do you think?"

"That would be a big no. They can't afford to goad the SecGen any more than they already do."

Hera nodded. "Caledonia and the Fleet are officially neutral in this matter."

"And unofficially?"

"We'll be quietly backing the OutWorlds."

"I knew it. Big trouble is coming."

"There's no way of avoiding it, Zack. All Grand Admiral Kowalski did was buy us a few decades, maybe as much as a century, and we've already used up most of it keeping the peace and preparing for the inevitable."

# — Three —

I barely had time to pop open a Shrehari Ale and mix a gin and tonic for Hera before the security system announced Lieutenant Saga Decker coming up our walkway from the quiet residential street reserved for the Fleet's highest-ranking HQ officers.

My ale forgotten on the bar, alongside Hera's drink, I reached the front door before my daughter did. She may have had her mother's looks, but she had my height, and I knew that beneath the loose, casual civilian blouse and slacks, she was as hard and muscular as any jump-qualified Marine officer. She may have the finely sculpted, blond Lagman features, but Saga was a Decker where it counted.

"Dad!"

I was treated to an enthusiastic hug from a daughter still making up for the lost years between when her mother left me to return home and raise Saga alone and the day I rescued her from kidnappers intent on overthrowing the Scandian government. I'd last seen her as a little girl and found her as a doctoral candidate ready to defend her thesis. But then, disenchanted with her mother for the umpteenth time, she took on her father's last name and career path — more or less — which made up for a lot in a short time.

"How's my Marine?"

"Doing great." She released me, and I stepped aside to let her in. "Hi, Hera."

"Hey, kiddo. Did you sort out the analysis before signing off for the weekend?"

"Yup. It's in the colonel's queue."

Saga worked on the same floor in the HQ complex as Hera, and they saw each other every weekday, or damn near. I didn't even see my daughter every weekend I came home, and sometimes, I felt a little jealous of my wife. Saga wasn't the only one who wanted to make up for lost time.

"What can I get you, honey?"

"A Shrehari Ale, please, Dad."

I grinned at her. "Excellent choice."

After I passed the drinks around and Hera checked on the autochef producing our meal, we wandered onto the covered terrace and sat around a low coffee table. As usual for this time of year, Sanctum was warm and humid, with rain coming just before sunset. Come to think of it, the city was always warm and humid, seeing as how it was in the planet's northern subtropical zone.

"Does Dad know about the rebellious rumblings along the Commonwealth frontier, Hera?"

I let out an indelicate snort. "Rebellious rumblings, eh? And how does a mere lieutenant, albeit in the promotion zone for captain, know about this when I just found out yesterday?"

Saga gave me an ironic glance. "Remember where I work, Dad? The Political Analysis Directorate?"

"Actually," Hera said, "your daughter was the first to figure it out once reports filtered in from our OutWorld listening posts."

"Was she now?" I gave Saga a congratulatory nod. "Well done."

"It cemented her position on the promotion list, especially since we could warn the Grand Admiral and the Governor General before the OutWorld representatives asked for meetings with them."

A faint smirk played on my daughter's lips. "And you figured my doctorate in political history had as much use for a Marine officer as teats on a boar hog."

"I never said that."

She raised her ale bottle and winked at me. "But you thought it."

I gave her my patented Decker frown. "Never assume. Nice traditional metaphor, though. Your grandpa would have liked it."

She gave me an innocent look. "The one who told you to never return if you joined the Corps? Or the other one who told mom to never return if she married a Marine?"

"The first one. Your Lagman grandpa was a city boy who wouldn't have known what a boar hog was. Although he referred to me as a pig more than once."

Saga shrugged. "Good thing he's not alive to see us now."

"So, he says, subtly changing the subject back to the rumblings on the subspace network, any idea where they'll hold this rebellious get-together?"

Both Hera and Saga shook their heads in precise tandem. "No, except it'll be on one of the pure OutWorlds, not one of those waffling between factions like Novaya Sibir."

"Thanks, Lieutenant Obvious. I was hoping for a bit of your incisive analysis, or do you keep that for everyone but me?"

Saga stuck out her tongue. "Grandpa Lagman might not have been totally wrong, Dad."

"And there go your chances at promotion once I tell the captain's board president you still behave like a twelve-year-old."

"Okay, okay. You want my incisive analysis. Here it is. They likely won't hold a convention in the Rim or Shield sectors. Too close to our turbulent frontiers and the Shrehari Empire. My best estimate is one of the Coalsack Sector systems other than Parth." Mischief danced in her eyes, and I immediately knew what was coming next. "Mykonos would be a good bet."

"Bite your tongue."

Saga and Hera exchanged glances. Then my daughter chuckled. "He's sometimes so easy to tease."

"Sometimes?" My beloved wife asked before blowing me a kiss.

"Okay. Let's calm down, everyone." I raised my bottle. "To your health, my dears, and confusion to the enemy."

They imitated me, and then, before the discussion could resume, the autochef signaled our first course was ready, so we trooped into the kitchen and helped ourselves before settling at the dining table with our drinks and more lighthearted conversation.

I never found out whether my daughter had inside knowledge, a touch of the second sight, or was just plain lucky. Because she'd nailed it. And they summoned me back to Sanctum the following Friday morning for orders.

***

When I reported to the office of Major General Martinson — Jimmy to his friends — Kal Ryent was already sitting comfortably in one of the chairs across from our division commander's desk.

I came to attention on the threshold and snapped off a salute.

"Colonel Decker presenting himself, sober, properly attired, and in good spirits, per the general's wishes."

"At ease and grab a seat, Zack. You came last night?"

"Yes, sir. And I came to work with Hera this morning, a rare treat. May I guess this has to do with the OutWorld heads of government summoning a rebellious constitutional convention on Mykonos in four weeks?"

The two generals looked at each other and chuckled. Then Jimmy said, "Never could hide anything from you. Yes. To say the declaration by the OutWorlds that it will go ahead despite the strenuous objections of Earth and the

Home Worlds, half the Senate, and most of the zaibatsus and their media arms has triggered a crisis would be an understatement. Late yesterday, we received word that the SecGen has declared such a convention illegitimate and would see the participating star systems sanctioned for their participation. In a way, he's right because it takes approval by two-thirds of the sovereign star systems to reopen the constitution, something that won't happen because the Commonwealth is almost evenly split. Yet denying the OutWorlds a way of effecting change to address their grievances is considered illegitimate by almost half of humanity."

"Those who make peaceful revolution impossible will make violent revolution inevitable." When Jimmy, who knew I was uttering one of the many quotes stored in my trivia-laden mind, gave me a questioning look, I added, "A man by the name John F. Kennedy who led one of the most powerful Earth nations during the twentieth century."

"Well, that fellow sure has it right. Because if the convention doesn't go ahead, we'll be one step closer to the fate Grand Admiral Kowalski foresaw if we weren't careful. Now Earth has forbidden the Fleet from getting involved in any way — no statements to the media, no naval support to carry delegates, and no providing security to the convention. They want to meet illegally? They can damn well take care of themselves. Earth won't help or recognize anything that comes from the meetings."

I nodded. "In other words, ignore the whole thing and pretend it isn't happening. Except we won't, will we?"

Jimmy shook his head.

"No. If the SecGen's henchmen try to disrupt the convention and cause casualties, we can kiss any chance of this ending peacefully goodbye. The last thing we need is aggrieved star systems making unilateral declarations of independence and launching their own FTL warships, never mind the Army and Marine Corps units stationed there supporting UDI and becoming ground forces of a hostile human polity. Sure, a few frigates cobbled together from merchant ships won't stand a chance against actual Navy units, but if we, the Fleet, begin shooting at other human naval vessels flying a star system's flag, we've lost."

"Because at this point," Kal Ryent said, speaking for the first time, "the Fleet is the only thing that can keep this from turning into an uncontrolled collapse, with everyone shooting at everyone. And our work starts on Mykonos. Which is your world of birth, isn't it, Zack?"

"Yep. So, what's my involvement? I haven't been back there since my old regiment left it long ago."

"You're taking a brigade from the division there to train with the Mykonos Regiment under Kal's overall command," Jimmy replied. "It'll be made up of Ghost Squadron, your aviation squadron, any support elements you think would be useful, and both MLI battalions designated to support your regiment. It'll be named the 1st (SF) Brigade. The Mykonos Regiment will be placed on a fully operational footing, with the reserve units called up to active duty. That'll give Kal a short division to work with."

"What about naval support?"

Kal glanced at me. "I understand a task group from the 4th Fleet will conduct maneuvers in the Mykonos system around the time of the convention. If necessary, I'll coordinate activities with the task group's commanding officer."

"Okay. Makes sense. When are we leaving?"

"In five days. We've put out orders to line up transport." Jimmy glanced at the clock on his sideboard. "And Grand Admiral Larsson expects us in ten minutes. He'll be issuing the orders and wants to look us in the eyes as he does so because he'll be openly disobeying the SecDef and the SecGen, with all the peril that entails for the Fleet."

"Just one last question, sir. Why Mykonos of all the OutWorlds?"

A thin smile lit up Jimmy's face.

"You haven't heard? President Eugenius Van Kirten of Mykonos is the unofficial leader of the OutWorld effort to reopen the constitution. He naturally offered his world as the meeting place." When Jimmy saw my expression, he frowned. "What's wrong, Zack?"

"Eugene and I went to school together. We weren't exactly friends. Last I saw him before enlisting, he threatened to make the rest of my life miserable for stealing his girlfriend in high school. And since it wasn't true, I punched him in the nose, hard enough to break it."

Surprising me, Kal and Jimmy burst out in laughter.

"Figures," the former said. "Okay, don't worry about it. Most of my job won't be riding herd on your brigade or the Mykonos Regiment but playing undercover diplomat for the Fleet inside the convention and soothing wounded souls."

# — Four —

Grand Admiral Larsson's current senior aide, a Navy captain I'd never met, stood as Major General Martinson, Brigadier General Ryent, and I entered the outer office. He gestured at the open inner door.

"Please go right in. The CNO, the Commandant, the Chief of the Army Staff, and the Commander SOCOM are with the Grand Admiral."

Great. The Fleet's top brass in a single room. This would be fun. I glanced at Jimmy and Kal, but they seemed unfazed by the news we wouldn't just be meeting with Larsson alone. As the senior among us, Jimmy led the charge through the door. He halted just inside. Kal and I lined up beside him, facing the conference table where the star-spangled quintet sat, and we saluted in unison.

Larsson, who was bareheaded, returned it with a grave nod. "At ease, gentlemen, and please join us."

He waved at the empty chairs around the table.

When we'd obeyed, Larsson, who appeared much older than the last time I saw him in person, gave us a long, hard look.

"What we're about to discuss is so highly classified that even a top secret special access designation won't suffice. You three probably touched on the subject in General Martinson's office just now, and what you discussed there is covered by this classification."

"Understood, sir," Jimmy replied.

"What we face could decide whether the Commonwealth survives intact though with changes to the constitutional order, or splinters into two or more separate star nations — Grand Admiral Kowalski's greatest fear. But no matter what happens, we must prevent another murderous civil war at all costs. Therefore, I will ensure the Armed Forces remain neutral because the alternative is unthinkable. Fortunately, unlike the eve of the Second Migration War, star systems no longer have their own navies or expeditionary capabilities, which leaves us as the sole arbiters regarding who can impose a decision by force. Now, we know the convention on Mykonos will go ahead whether or not Earth wants it to. And we're also aware Earth will try to sabotage it by any means necessary. Our stance of neutrality will extend to ensuring nothing untoward happens so that the OutWorlds can present their grievances and debate what must change to preserve the Commonwealth."

Larsson took a sip of water from the glass in front of him.

"Clearly, extending the Fleet's protection to the OutWorld convention will violate Earth's orders forbidding any involvement. So deploying a security force can trigger a crisis on its own. Make no mistake, I fully intend for you to use deadly force if necessary to ensure the delegates can speak freely and without fear of violence because silencing them through intimidation will likely trigger a chain of events we cannot control." He shook his head. "We wouldn't be in this situation if Earth and the Home Worlds hadn't done their best since Grand Admiral Kowalski's day to undermine the treaties that ended the last Migration War. But no one will listen to reason. And I'm afraid the OutWorlds will become just as intransigent if they haven't reached that point yet. President Van Kirten certainly sounds like he's had enough when he told the SecGen where he could shove his declaration that the convention is illegitimate.

"In any case, I wanted you to understand the stakes before we delve into the specifics. They cannot be more important, and the consequences of a misstep direr. What does this mean in concrete terms for you in particular? First, so that everyone can pretend the Fleet isn't getting enmeshed in this mess, officially, the designated units from the 1st SFR will train with the Mykonos Regiment under acting Major General Ryent's supervision. Congratulations, by the way, your acting promotion is effective as of this moment."

Kal nodded once. "Thank you, sir."

"Second, General Ryent is the only Armed Forces member who may interact with the OutWorld representatives and the Mykonos government."

Jimmy raised his hand. "If I may, sir?"

"Go ahead."

"Zack — Colonel Decker — is a Mykonos native and has family there. He also went to high school with Eugenius Van Kirten, though Zack says they weren't on good terms when he enlisted in the Corps."

"Very well. General Ryent may involve Colonel Decker in matters pertaining to the Mykonos government at his discretion and with the delegates, if absolutely necessary."

Kal inclined his head. "Yes, sir."

"Third, since the Constabulary will have received orders to stay completely uninvolved and leave any policing matters surrounding the convention to the Mykonos Police Service, contact with the resident Constabulary Group will be informal. If the commanding officer offers assistance, then General Ryent may decide whether to accept. It may well be that the local commanding officer will stay at a distance. But it doesn't matter since Colonel Decker's troops will be responsible for preventing any disruption by elements operating under secret orders from Earth. Fourth, you'll receive all the support you want from Naval Intelligence on a priority basis. And finally, make damn sure no one, Marines or Army, shows the slightest sign of partisanship, period. That shouldn't be a problem with Colonel Decker's troopers, but the Mykonos Regiment's soldiers are another matter. Their CO will receive orders from the Chief of the Army Staff on that subject, orders which General Ryent will reinforce upon his arrival."

Larsson glanced at the service chiefs around the table. "Does anyone wish to add something?"

When they shook their heads, he turned back to Jimmy. "Questions?"

"Yes, sir. Who signs the rules of engagement?"

"Me. Draft up what you think they should be and pass them directly to your commanding officer." Larsson nodded at the Commander, SOCOM. "Before you leave, please. I don't want them coursing through the subspace network, no matter the level of encryption. Let's hand-carry the sensitive stuff. Anything else? General Ryent? Colonel Decker?"

I had plenty of questions, but most were the sort I'd rather not get an answer to. At least not now, because it might limit my freedom of action. As a young Marine noncom, I learned that you can't get chewed out for going against the boss' wishes if you didn't know what they were. Kal was an Academy product and had never served in the ranks, but he was smart enough to think along the same lines as me because he shook his head as well.

"Very well. Please carry on with the planning and preparation. I won't wish you luck because I know you'll create your own. Make sure nobody triggers a crack-up of the Commonwealth or a civil war by interfering with the delegates."

Jimmy nodded once. "Yes, sir."

We stood, saluted, and marched out with Jimmy in the lead once more. None of us spoke until we were back in the latter's office behind closed doors.

"Congrats, Kal. Were you expecting that temporary second star?" I asked as we sat.

"Yeah. Jimmy told me this morning before you showed up."

"All right, gents. We can wet Kal's star after work at the mess. Right now, we have a lot of details to discuss. But first, did either of you find the Grand Admiral overly dramatic?"

Kal and I both shook our heads.

"Good. Because he's not in the habit of overemphasizing. The stakes are truly that high, and mistakes can resonate across this part of the galaxy for a long time."

"Problem is," I said, "the opposition doesn't care. They'll do whatever they think is necessary to keep power centralized on Earth. Heck, many of the Home Worlds would like to turn their former colonies, now sovereign star systems, back into wholly-owned dependencies. If a bunch of people must die for that, so be it. My gut tells me it'll get ugly on Mykonos before this is over."

Kal glanced at me. "Fortunately, ugly is your specialty. Okay. Specifics. Go ahead, Jimmy."

"Right. Hera is sending half a dozen undercover agents to Mykonos as quickly as possible. I've asked for a NILO with a sufficiently high-security clearance to be the liaison between you two and Naval Intelligence, including Hera's division. As for Constabulary liaison, you still have Chief Warrant Officer Kine, right, Zack?"

"Yes. She'll give us the lay of the land where the 55th Constabulary Group's views on the convention are concerned. Aleksa has a real knack for interrogating people without them realizing."

"Good. Ghost Squadron is going in wearing the winged dagger, as are you, but bring unmarked and untraceable gear. I know it means more equipment to haul, but them's the breaks. If your aviation squadron, the MLI, and other supporting elements need to look like they're not Marines, they can strip the insignia off their armor. It won't fool anyone, but as the Grand Admiral said, pretending we're not doing what we're doing will allow the opposition to back off gracefully. But the intent is to make everyone other than Ghost Squadron the visible part of the operation to distract the opposition while Josh Bayliss' crew does its thing in the darkest shadows."

"Got it." I suddenly had one of my bad ideas, the kind Hera routinely deplores but which almost always work out. "Concerning the NILO. I know a jump-qualified Marine intelligence officer with a high enough security clearance and who figured this mess out before it became public. She's on the captain's promotion list, so an acting promotion to tide her over until the boards sit would get her at the right rank."

Before I even finished speaking, Kal was chuckling with undisguised amusement.

"I think I know who Zack means, and I'm not sure the mission can stand another Decker. But he's right, Jimmy. Saga on the ground with us over there will be invaluable as an analyst, even more so than an intelligence liaison."

"Can you stand the accusations of nepotism, Zack?"

I shrugged.

"You think anyone would make them to my face? In a community where we're keen on having people we know and trust on our team? Not a chance it'll happen. If you agree, I'll ask Hera to clear it through her chain of command, and when she does, I'll want Saga at Fort Arnhem ASAP. We'll need her political insights while we plan and prepare."

"Fine. Approved. Let's discuss the timeline."

# — Five —

"Good afternoon." I dropped into my chair at the head of the regimental conference table the following Monday and placed my tablet in front of me. "Can any of you guess why I've called this assembly? Not you, Josh. You already figured it out."

"And I may or may not have speculated," he replied smugly.

"Never mind, then."

"It's Mykonos?" Lora Cyone, who'd taken command of the 1st MLI a few weeks ago, asked. Lora and I went way back. There was even a time when we were more than just professional colleagues. But both of us had traveled a lot of light years since then and talked little about what we'd endured together.

"It is indeed. Give the lieutenant colonel with the funny hat badge an extra sticky bun. What I'm about to say is classified top secret special access codename Rubicon. You will repeat nothing I say outside of this room or discuss it among yourselves. Our Marines are used to going in without the full picture, and this is one of those times. As you'll understand in a few moments."

I gave them a condensed version of Grand Admiral Larsson's words and watched as their faces took on somber expressions.

"This could be the most important mission of our careers, folks, one where we succeed if nothing happens and where we might fail if we have to open fire. Before I touch on specifics, does anyone have questions? I'll answer the easy one right now — you're here because you and your commands are coming with me. Anyone not here right now isn't going to Mykonos."

I glanced at each in turn — Josh, Lora, Haru Ishida, who had the 2nd MLI, Harjit Gill, who had my aviation squadron, and Sergeant Major Paavola — but they shook their heads. I wasn't surprised. They were among the smartest, most experienced people in SOCOM and could figure things out themselves.

"Officially, we are forming the 1st SF Brigade to train the Mykonos Regiment in counter-insurgency techniques. The rest of the Regiment will continue the current deployment, training, and recovery cycle. The Mykonos Regiment will be responsible for our logistics, which means we're not bringing support elements beyond those organic to your units. Unofficially, Ghost Squadron, with help from Naval Intelligence, will find and neutralize threats while the two MLI battalions will provide visible security to the constitutional convention by training near where it'll be held. And since we might need to move fast, I'm bringing our own aviation assets rather than depending on those of the Mykonos Regiment. Now the only thing your people get to hear is the official story. If they figure out there's more going on, I hope they'll have the brains to stay quiet. And if they don't, I expect you to fix it."

I paused for a moment to let them absorb my words.

"Just to show you how seriously the information control measures will be, no one in the brigade HQ troop will know our unofficial mission, save for the NILO, who should report sometime today. She's a jump-qualified Marine captain whose normal duty station is Naval Intelligence's Political Analysis Directorate. The fact she and I have the same last name and share the same genetic lineage has nothing to do with her secondment to the brigade. Captain Saga Decker is the analyst who first figured out what the OutWorlds were planning secretly and has been following developments more closely than anyone." I allowed myself a little smile. "And be warned, she's a chip off the old block, a true Decker in every sense."

"That's excellent news," Josh said, grinning from ear to ear. "I can't think of anyone more suited for the NILO job on this deployment. And yes, she's your daughter all right, Colonel."

"I'm bringing the Regiment's S2, with whom Captain Decker will work, the S3, and the S4 with us. The S3 is busy crafting our deployment plan and orders — you'll see them tomorrow. But they are not aware of what I told you just now. If it becomes necessary, I have the authority to read them in. Yes, I know, the opposition will suspect the truth as soon as we land, but the goal is keeping just enough plausible deniability so everyone can save face. And, of course, the Grand Admiral's and my most fervent hope is that we will be a deterrent, so nothing happens. The Mykonos Regiment and us might even get some useful training out of it." I touched the tablet. "And you now have the official warning order in your queue, so consider this the start of our battle procedure. Questions?"

I'd barely settled behind my desk when Lora poked her head through the door. Tall, sharp-faced beneath silver hair, her features marked by a hard life, she had changed little since I last saw her on Marengo many years ago, except for deeper lines around the eyes and mouth. But she'd gone from command sergeant to lieutenant colonel in that time, a testament to her professionalism and drive. Mind you, Marengo was a long time after we briefly became lovers until our return to the Commonwealth from the Trans-Coalsack and my return to active duty.

"Got a moment?"

"Sure." I gestured at the chair across from me. "What's up?"

"Mere curiosity. I didn't know you had a daughter old enough to be a captain in the Corps. You never mentioned her."

"It's a long story. We were estranged for twenty years, not by choice, but because her mother divorced me and took Saga back to her home world when she was only four. My ex didn't grant me any parental rights. We met again during the attempted coup d'état against the Scandian government a while back. You might have heard of it."

Lora nodded. "Yep. That was you who saved the day, along with your wife, the spy, right?"

I cracked a grin. "Former spy. We now refer to her as 'The Admiral.' Anyway, a few things happened, and my daughter realized her mother had denied her a father for selfish reasons and could no longer look at her mother the same way. So, after earning her doctorate, she joined the Corps under the direct entry officer program in the Intelligence Branch and made captain after the minimum time in rank as a lieutenant."

At that moment, I saw movement by my open office door — a tall blonde woman with eyes the same color as mine, shiny new captain's pips on her uniform collar and the Intelligence Branch badge, a compass rose over diagonal red and green stripes surrounded by a wreath of stars. She stamped to attention at the threshold, and when I gestured at her to enter, Saga took one step forward and saluted.

"Captain Decker reporting to the colonel as ordered, sir."

I grinned at Lora. "And now you get to meet my daughter. At ease, Saga and take a seat. This is Lora Cyone, an old friend who I met before Hera. She recently took command of the 1st MLI. We were just talking about the fact I wasn't the only Decker in the Corps doing sneaky work since I mentioned your imminent arrival to the commanding officers going on the Mykonos deployment earlier."

"Please to meet you, Colonel." Saga extended her hand, and Decker watched them study each other intently as they shook.

"Likewise, Captain. I can definitely see the resemblance to your father. He never mentioned you when we first met, long ago. Nor during our brief reunion years later. Hence my curiosity. We were rather close at one time."

An amused smile lit up Saga's face, and I immediately knew what she was thinking. "I gather there's a story in there somewhere, one which my father or the admiral haven't told me."

"I can tell you the tale over a drink at the Pegasus tonight if you like." Lora grinned at me. "The censored version, of course. I wouldn't dream of embarrassing your father."

"Moving right on. How did you come up from Sanctum?"

"I took the train to Carrick and then a taxi. Since we're leaving shortly, I booked myself into the transient officers' quarters and dropped my luggage there."

I couldn't suppress a snort and glanced at Lora. "Captain Decker is bound and determined to be just another officer, and that means no staying with her father in the CO's residence. Hence, she quickly arranged for the alternative and occupied it before visiting me."

My daughter briefly smirked at me but remained silent.

"Don't be so hard on Captain Decker. She'll have enough on her plate fitting in with the rest of your staff without spending her off-duty hours over the next few weeks with Fort Arnhem's sole master after the Almighty."

"No worries. It's what I expected. I'd have been surprised if Saga had asked to stay with me. They teach the young ones well during basic officer training, contrary to what we old noncoms commissioned from the ranks might believe. Now, was there anything else either of you wanted to discuss? If not, I'll take Saga around and introduce her to the staff and the commanding officers." I glanced at Saga's beret. "And get her a winged dagger badge, so she doesn't stand out."

# — Six —

When I walked into the Pegasus Club's dining room a few hours later, I saw Saga deep in conversation with my S2, Corinne Renaud, over a plate of the daily special. Corinne was a mustang who came up the noncom ranks, like me. But her military occupational specialty was intelligence, so Saga probably had more in common with her, professionally speaking, than with me.

No, I wasn't checking up on my daughter. I took my midday and evening meals in the main dining room almost every day because, even though I was a pretty good cook, I didn't enjoy whipping up elaborate meals for one. And by elaborate, I meant programming an autochef. Besides, eating alone surrounded by people deliberately ignoring me so they could give me some privacy beat eating alone with nothing more than my reflection in the residence kitchen window. Breakfast, on the other hand, wasn't an issue. The autochef popped out my favorites — bacon, sausages, eggs, beans, home fries, and toast — reliably every morning at the same time as my coffee machine filled a jug, black, no sweetener. That only varied when I was home. Hera wasn't a fan of the whole Marine meal deal.

I made my way through the serving line, then carried my tray to the corner table set aside for the CO of the 1st SFR and Fort Arnhem. It was a six-seater, but I usually ate alone. The CO of the Pathfinder School, my equal in rank, and the commanding officers of the various units under my remit either took their evening meals at home or in Carrick, where many of my officers and senior noncoms lived. I didn't mind. My home was with Hera in Sanctum.

When I finished, Corinne and Saga were still deep in conversation, and I walked across the Fort to the residential section under a canopy of stars without visiting the bar. I only ever drank there on special occasions or the rare Friday I wasn't going to Sanctum. A good CO stayed away from the Pegasus most of the time so his troopers could unwind and blow off antimatter.

My colleague who had the school did the same. Besides, he lived in Carrick and sped through the Fort's main gate at one minute after sixteen hundred most days. That's not a criticism, by the way. He and I agreed. When a day's work was done, it was done. No point in hanging around and making our subordinates wonder whether they could afford to head home before the old man left.

Over the following three weeks, while my staff and the unit commanders prepared, I saw Saga in passing daily since she worked in the S2 office down the hall from mine, but she never once joined me in the club or at my residence. And from what Sergeant Major Paavola told me in confidence, folks around Fort Arnhem were noticing with approval. As usual, I spent my weekends with Hera in Sanctum. Meanwhile, Saga stayed back to hike or just relax with the friends she'd made among the officers and command noncoms, not just in my regiment but the School and the MLI battalions.

The evening before our departure, Hera, Jimmy, and Kal came up from Sanctum aboard an aircar from the motor pool. Surprising me none, Kal wasn't bringing any staffers with him. He didn't even have an aide. Whatever staff support he needed would come from my tactical headquarters, and something told me he'd not want much from us since his role was mainly political. Based on the last flurry of instructions, it had become clear doing the dirty fieldwork would be my job entirely. The rules of engagement Kal developed and gotten approved by the Grand Admiral left me about as much latitude as if this were a straight-up combat operation, meaning no calling Kal for approval if I considered it was time to go weapons-free.

The four of us dined in my residence, the meal delivered by the Pegasus Club and the booze hauled out of my wine cellar. Then, right after the meal, Kal and Jimmy headed off to the transient officers' quarters to give Hera and me a night together before I left. Both were old romantics at heart — Jimmy had married long ago, and though Kal never seemed to stay in a relationship for long, he swept every new prospect off her feet. Look up the definition of serial monogamy, and I'm sure he'll be mentioned as the perfect practitioner. And with his rugged good looks, charm, and charisma, he should make a lot of new conquests on Mykonos.

But with our friends gone, we did as we had for many years and gave each other a charge that would hopefully last for my deployment.

Afterward, I turned to Hera and asked, "Do you think this could be one of those inflection points where the course of history is irrevocably changed?"

She met my eyes, and her reply, though not unexpected, made me wonder whether my own sense of incoming trouble wasn't a tad optimistic.

"I don't know, Zack. My crystal ball has never been so cloudy. The psychohistorians' theories turn to mush whenever small but powerful groups of humans are involved in momentous events. You'd have more luck predicting the draw of the next card at a blackjack table."

I reached out with my index finger and ran it along her jawline as tenderly as I could. Over the years, I'd come to understand that Hera had a great void inside her. Perhaps she didn't have a soul, at least not how most understood it. She certainly killed without compunction, but only if necessary.

I was the only one for whom she could feel human emotions, though she faked it well with my daughter. Yet she was always a reliable oracle about anything related to her job and mine. Hera may not have emotions like normal humans, but she understood them and their motivations better than anyone else. Those vanishingly few times she drew a blank meant an ancient curse was about to descend on us, the one that goes 'may we live in interesting times.'

When I voiced those words, she touched me with her fingertips as well. "Isn't that what keeps us alive?"

"Some days, I don't know. Sitting on the terrace of the seashore place, watching a tropical storm head straight at us while sipping Shrehari Ale, and timing when I need to shutter everything before the first gusts hit us is just about enough excitement. Watching the Commonwealth unravel in real time might be more than an old Pathfinder like me wants to handle."

A sardonic smile twisted her lips.

"Would you rather be close enough to the action so you could help make sure whatever comes next is best for the survival of our species, or wait and see what the idiots left in charge unsupervised come up with? Because those are the options. We'll sip our poison on that terrace, waiting for a Middle Sea storm once we've survived the typhoon about to engulf our species."

"Has anyone ever mentioned your optimism would cause the most cheerful human to consider suicide?"

"Good thing you're a grumpy old man."

***

The following day, bright and early, Hera and I shared a full breakfast. Then she drove me, clad in my combat armor — it was easier to transport that way — and my gear to the aviation squadron's landing strip. From there, Kal and I would ride up to the tactical transport *Ragnarok,* along with Ghost Squadron, aboard the regiment's dropships. Meanwhile, shuttles from the Commonwealth Fleet Auxiliary ships *Carentan* and *Normandie* would lift the 1st and 2nd MLI from Fort Arnhem's parade square turned spaceport for the occasion. Jimmy would see them off from there.

Because of the rules, Kal, Josh Bayliss, and I took different dropships. And as was my habit, I sat in the jump seats behind the pilot rather than in the passenger compartment, where personal and collective gear, ammunition, and supplies took up most of the space.

The transport's skipper, Commander Jake Marquez, met Kal and me on his ship's hangar deck once the space doors were closed. We both knew him in passing since *Ragnarok* was almost exclusively used by SOCOM units.

"General Ryent, Colonel Decker, welcome aboard." He snapped off a crisp salute that Kal returned with equal precision.

Kal nodded once. "Thank you, Captain."

"We'll break out of orbit when *Carentan* and *Normandie* report ready. We're the lead ship in the convoy, with the Fleet Auxiliary captains responsive to my sailing orders." Marquez gestured at a line of spacers waiting by the inner airlock. "My bosun's mates will guide your people to the barracks. Messing will be with my crew — wardroom, chiefs' and petty officers' mess, and junior ranks' mess. Your aviation crews will be allowed on the hanger deck daily for maintenance, but your folks should take what they need for the trip with them. My bosun will explain it to your people once they finish disembarking and have formed up. I can take you to your quarters now if you like."

I glanced at where my brigade staff officers were clustered, Saga included, waiting for instructions. Will Chosiak, my S3, was an old hand at moves aboard tactical transports and knew the score. He'd make sure the others didn't wander off. Since this wasn't the time for Kal and me to hang around, watching the squadron commanders and their sergeant majors sort things out, Kal indicated the inner airlock and picked up his bags.

"Why don't we do that now, Captain?"

"Follow me."

As we passed the staff, a bosun's mate approached them to issue instructions and guide them off the hangar deck as well. I knew from extensive experience the crew would have both squadrons off the deck and in the barracks in under thirty minutes. This is what they did for a living, and they did it well. Based on what Curtis Delgado had told me about *Carentan*, who'd ferried his company to Tyrell Station last year, the Fleet Auxiliary civilian crews were no slouches, either.

My cabin wasn't more than a glorified closet with a single bunk and a small desk, but it had private heads and enough storage space for my armor, gear, and weapons. Kal's, next door, was the same, as were the cabins for the squadron commanders, field grade officers, and sergeants major. Ranks from command sergeant to captain doubled up in larger compartments while the rest got quads. Although we ate with our Navy counterparts, there was a separate, all-ranks passenger lounge and a gym with enough entertainment amenities to keep embarked troops amused during the trip. Both would be crowded, but we'd reach Mykonos before mischief-causing boredom set in. Besides, my troopers were veterans and knew how to occupy themselves productively while their ship was traveling FTL.

Less than forty-five minutes after we landed on the hangar deck, the public address system called *Ragnarok*'s crew to departure stations, and we were off. This was my first time away from Caledonia since before I took command of the regiment, and I hadn't realized how much I missed traveling after Hera's and my long years crisscrossing the Commonwealth on undercover assignments were over.

# — Seven —

"That's your recommendation?" Secretary General of the Commonwealth Brodrick Brüggemann, who'd been standing by the tall windows overlooking Lake Geneva, turned back toward Andreas Bauchan, Director General of the Sécurité Spéciale. The latter was sitting in one of the uncomfortable chairs fronting the SecGen's desk, seeming perfectly at ease, elbows on the chair's arms, fingertips pressing together. "We do nothing?"

Brüggemann's tone, though conversational, held a querulous edge revealing irritation at Bauchan's advice.

"Indeed, sir. Ignoring the so-called convention is better than acknowledging it and thereby granting it some form of legitimacy."

"How can we grant it any form of licitness if it's unlawful, to begin with?"

"Strictly speaking, several star systems getting together to discuss their grievances is perfectly legal."

"You're splitting hairs, Andreas."

A faint smile twisted Bauchan's lips. "I'm not, sir. Yes, a constitutional convention with less than two-thirds of the sovereign star systems and two-thirds of the Senate approving that call isn't valid, but it isn't illegal. Trying to enforce constitutional amendments that aren't approved by the dual two-thirds majority is, but we're not there yet. Let them have their convention and present their demands. Have those demands examined by a Senate committee which will take its sweet time doing so. Meanwhile, we keep going ahead with the centralization of power on Earth."

"And when they realize their demands will never be accepted?" Brüggemann retook his chair and studied Bauchan through narrowed eyes.

"We'll have gained time to head off the sovereignists, and time, as you know, sir is the most precious commodity in politics." Butter wouldn't have melted in Bauchan's mouth.

Brüggemann gave him a stern look. "I'm not sure I enjoy remaining silent while the OutWorlds plot to rearrange the Commonwealth. But fine. We'll do it your way for now. There are the colonies, however. Both federal and star system. Their governments cannot take part in this farce. Surely these colonial citizen's assemblies who deputized delegates are overstepping the bounds of legality."

Bauchan grimaced. "True. Technically, the citizen's assemblies and their delegates could be considered guilty of advocating sedition. However, I still think we shouldn't intervene. At least not yet."

"Why?"

"Because the OutWorlds will see it as a provocation, and it's best if we avoid those altogether."

"For now."

Bauchan heard the steel in Brüggemann's voice and inclined his head. "For now."

"Your people will keep the convention under surveillance. I want to know everything that's happening."

"Of course, sir."

"And what of the Fleet? I understand a brigade from SOCOM is heading for Mykonos."

Bauchan's faint smile returned. "It is. And I'm sure its leadership will strictly observe the letter of your orders that no Armed Forces units or personnel get involved in offering the convention military protection."

Brüggemann let out a soft snort. "But it won't observe the spirit, is that it?"

"Doubtful. A man by the rank and name of Colonel Zachary Decker is in command of the Special Forces brigade. We — my agency — have had many interactions with Decker over the years. He's not the sort to idly stand by if he's needed. Nor is his superior, Major General Kal Ryent, who's a bit of a dark horse where we're concerned, but apparently a rising star in the Marine Corps."

"Is there anything we can do to ensure their hands are tied?"

"No, sir. But it shouldn't matter if we're ignoring the convention altogether."

Just then, Brüggemann's executive assistant appeared in the doorway, and the SecGen said, "Emilie is telling me my next appointment is here. We'll play it your way, for now, Andreas."

"Sir." Bauchan stood, inclined his head, then turned on his heels and left.

He returned to his own office — at least the one he used in the Palace of the Stars; he had another at Sécurité Spéciale HQ in another part of town — and found Britta Trulson waiting for him.

Trulson, the Deep Space Foundation's liaison on Earth, and he had become rather close over the last two years, and he enjoyed seeing her eyes light up whenever she saw him. Such as now. Bauchan didn't know that Britta Trulson was actually Chief Warrant Officer Miko Steiger of Naval Intelligence's Special Operations Division and the Deep Space Foundation, for all intents and purposes, an arm, albeit unwitting, of that same organization.

"Britta, my dear." She stood as he entered, and they embraced. "How are you this morning?"

Steiger smiled back at him. "Still feeling the afterglow of last night, darling. How did your meeting with the SecGen go?"

Bauchan sat behind his desk while Steiger took a chair across from him and made a face.

"He wants to intervene, to kill this convention before it starts. I suppose it's a natural reaction to a wide swath of Commonwealth worlds effectively telling Earth the relationship is no longer good enough. But I convinced him it was best to simply let the convention run its course and then sit on the demands by having a Senate committee examine them."

"Good." Steiger was pleased Bauchan had taken her recommendations on the matter to the SecGen, a recommendation which originated with Hera Talyn. "It wouldn't do to antagonize the OutWorlds. Once the current fervor for constitutional reform dies down, probably by the next election cycle, things will return to normal. And in the meantime, we continue to strengthen Earth."

"Have I ever told you your beauty is only surpassed by your intelligence?"

"Often, darling. But I can listen to you say it over and over."

# — Eight —

Mixed feelings bubbled up as I studied Mykonos' shimmering orb on the passenger lounge primary display after an uneventful trip spent reading, studying, and exercising in the space and with the equipment available. Curtis Delgado, mindful of his ambitions, had organized seminars patterned on those held at the War College to help him and any one else who wanted to join in preparation for the distance learning exams. Kal and I separately and jointly had presided over those seminars to help guide the discussions, and I was struck once more by how Kal approached profound and complex questions. If he wasn't the smartest of us, I didn't know who that might be.

"Going to visit your family?" Kal asked, breaking through my idle thoughts.

I grimaced. "No idea just yet. Chances are good my parents will turn me away at the door when I show up."

"Really? Even after this long?"

"I enlisted the day I turned eighteen, against the express wishes of my parents, and rode straight up to the starbase where I joined a large group of recruits — Navy, Corps, Constabulary — waiting for transport to the basic schools. No tearful farewells, promises to write, or any of that nonsense. I packed my belongings and told my dad I was leaving. His last words to me as I left the house were never come back, you ungrateful drongo."

Kal gave me a curious glance. "Who or what is a drongo?"

"Mykonos slang for dumbass. Don't ask me where it comes from. No one on Mykonos has the slightest idea. Anyway, at first, I sent subspace messages to let them know I was doing alright, especially after passing basic. There wasn't a prouder Decker alive that day. Never got a reply. Never heard from anyone in the family. After I graduated, the Corps assigned me to the 9th Marines when it was still here, thinking they'd do me a favor. But every attempt I made to contact my family was rejected. The regiment moving to Celeste was a relief because I wouldn't live surrounded by bad memories. I've only been back briefly once since then, during my time aboard a civilian freighter while I was in the reserves. Never even stepped ashore. This is my first homecoming in a long time, except my home is now on Caledonia, with my wife and my daughter. It's where I'll retire and be the annoying old Marine no one wants at parties."

Kal let out a soft chuckle. "Annoying? Sometimes, but I doubt you'll ever stop being the life of the party. There's not another Special Forces officer who can tell tall tales like you. So, no family visits? Understood."

"Well… I suppose I could always see if Uncle Attar is still among the living. I call him uncle, but he's a first cousin of my Grandfather Thomas, a famous hotelier at the turn of the century. We're a big family, even by Mykonos norms, and you could drive a genealogist mad trying to map out the relationships. Attar is on the Khanjan side and served under Admiral Dunmoore after the Shrehari War. Mind you, he must be over a hundred and twenty by now. But both the Khanjans and the Deckers are long-lived lineages. Uncle Attar was the only one who encouraged my dreams of becoming a Marine back then. He'd enjoyed his career in the Navy, and three of his kids joined up years before I was born."

"Did your paths ever cross?"

I shook my head. "No. Unlike Uncle Attar, who graduated from the Academy, they went into the Navy as ordinary spacers. They might not have done more than a hitch or two before returning home or entering civilian spacefaring. I never checked to see if there's still a Khanjan from Mykonos in the Armed Forces. Certainly, those three cousins should be retired by now if they served a full career."

"Is their mother still around?"

"No. She passed away when I was still a toddler."

Kal nudged me with his elbow. "Do yourself and Uncle Attar a favor and look him up. Or maybe your Grandfather Thomas. If they're still alive, one of them might be pleased to find out your made good and could tell you if your parents have mellowed to the point of allowing the ungrateful — what was that word again? Drongo? Back into their lives once they see you're a highly respected senior officer on the verge of becoming a general."

I cocked an amused eyebrow at him. "Am I? On the verge of becoming a general? Or are you just yanking my ripcord?"

"Wait and see, Zack."

"Well, it won't be Grandpa Thomas. He was just as furious at my enlisting as my parents. I was supposed to enter the family conglomerate after completing university studies in some related field like law or accounting and eventually take over one of its business lines. Grandpa was hoping for the hospitality division and dad for the agricultural division. I chose the Marine Division."

"Sounds like your family owns a zaibatsu."

"A tiny one, restricted to Mykonos. The Deckers of grandpa's generation built it with their own hands while the Khanjans swanned around the galaxy. All the business lines are, or at least were interconnected, unlike the big interstellar zaibatsus who have their tentacles in many disparate industries."

"I see, and you rejecting the Decker heritage to act like a Khanjan is what caused the rift."

"Got it in one. And I've known since I was a little boy that my dad and grandpa hold grudges like no one else. In their eyes, I betrayed the entire clan by throwing away my life and becoming a mercenary of the Commonwealth government instead of dedicating myself to building up the business and, thereby, the planet. And yes, mercenary is the word my dad used."

"Does that mean he'll be supportive of the constitutional convention?"

I let out a bark of laughter. "Dad and Grandpa will be supportive of outright secession. They hate Earth and its institutions like few I've ever met. That's why they disowned me when I enlisted. And no, I couldn't tell you why. It goes back to before my birth, and neither would ever discuss the matter with an angry, overgrown adolescent like me."

Before Kal could toss a barb at me for that last sentence, the public address system came on.

"Now hear this. Marine dropships will launch in one hour, and the hangar deck will open in fifteen minutes. That is all."

"I guess Fort Monash finally cleared us to land."

My tone must have been a little sharp because Kal said, "Be fair, Zack. Even though they knew we were coming and had to make room for a brigade's worth of troops and a squadron of aircraft, it takes a bit of time to make the last checks before letting us land."

Fort Monash, a sprawling installation in the rolling hills some fifty kilometers north of Petras, the star system capital, was home to the Mykonos Regiment. It had previously housed my old regiment, the 9th Marines, as well, which meant there was plenty of room for the 1st SF Brigade. The unused facilities were preserved, so should the need arise, an entire Marine regiment could move back in quickly.

Besides the main base, there were also satellite bases dotting the settlement areas on both major continents, mainly to support the Mykonos Regiment's reserve units. If the latter were fully activated, the regiment would be closer to an all-arms pocket division than anything else. Which was why the 9th left long ago for a part of the Commonwealth with more unrest. There just weren't many threats in this corner of the Commonwealth. At least not from non-human species or the various types of marauders. An oversized Army regiment, a minor starbase, other defensive orbitals, and a Navy squadron — not even an entire battle group — sufficed.

Funnily enough, the current CO of the Mykonos Regiment was a former Marine who'd transferred to the Army so he could finish his career on his home planet, and if I had the dates right, he would have been in my draft, though not in my basic training company.

"It's not like they needed to do much more than air out the buildings that once housed the 9th Marines and clear the accumulated junk from the unused section of the spaceport tarmac."

Kal gave me an exasperated look. "And get the unused dining facility back into operation, hire staff, buy food and other consumables, etcetera. My, but you're not a happy man at seeing your birth planet again, are you? Maybe we should have made Josh an acting colonel and given him the brigade instead."

"And missed out on having a brigade commander who knows so many people down there?"

"It might have been worthwhile."

"Yes, sir, General, sir. And you know what you can do with that observation, sir."

An announcement that all Marines were to don their armor, grab their kit, and line up in the passageway to prepare for embarkation aboard the dropships, saved Kal from a reply.

***

Fort Monash looked little different from what I remembered. The main base was built along the usual design of the Roman castra, with the Mykonos Regiment's lines in one quadrant, the former 9th Marines lines, now temporarily ours, in another, the spaceport and aviation unit lines in the third, and the joint support facilities in the fourth. The residential section lay to one side, while the ranges and training areas sprawled northwards for a hundred kilometers or more.

Army personnel in rifle green battledress stood at regular intervals along the flight line, ready to marshal my dropships, while more stood further away, waiting for the shuttles with the two MLI battalions. A row of trucks sat just beyond the flight line, ready to carry us and our gear. Not all at once, of course, but in several waves.

That's the one problem with being a Special Forces formation — we travel light because we have to move fast.

Sure, we have our own airlift, but little to no deployable ground transport, and we would borrow vehicles from the locally preserved wartime stocks as necessary. And once we left, the Mykonos folks would be stuck preparing them for storage again. I felt they might not universally welcome our arrival, even though we provided a distraction from the same old, same old every Army regiment faced.

Once the Marines in the dropship I rode disembarked, I swung my backpack over my shoulders, grabbed my duffel and helmet visor up, I headed for a central spot between the flight line and the rows of ground carriers. Within minutes, my brigade staff and Kal joined me while the command noncoms sorted out their troopers by companies. Behind them, the shuttles from *Carentan* and *Normandie* were landing in a precise sequence, and soon, they disgorged MLI battalions dressed and equipped like the 1st SFR Marines. A casual observer wouldn't have been able to tell the difference.

Once most troopers were formed in ranks, those designated to do so dropped their personal bags and climbed back aboard the shuttles to offload the collective and spare gear stowed inside matte green containers. It was as quick and efficient as I could have hoped, especially since this was the largest SOF deployment in years.

"Look sharp," Sergeant Major Paavola whispered from behind me as I quietly spoke with Kal. "Colonel Foster just showed up."

Both of us swiveled around to see a lanky, gray-haired man in Army green with colonel's oak leaves and diamonds on the collar and the Mykonos Regiment's badge on his beret — crossed rifles over a rising sun — climb out of a staff car alongside the first row of trucks. A van behind him disgorged a dozen command noncoms and company-grade officers. They split up and immediately headed for the squadron and battalion commanders waiting in front of their units.

"Cut it a little close," I muttered to Kal while putting on a friendly face.

As Foster approached, tailed by a dark-complexioned man wearing a regimental sergeant major's rank insignia, I studied his craggy face, large, aquiline nose, and deep-set brown eyes, trying to place him, but without success. We'd never met, or it was so brief I couldn't remember. Foster and his RSM stopped three paces in front of Kal and raised their hands to their brow.

"General Ryent, welcome to Mykonos and Camp Monash."

Kal returned the salute, then offered his hand. "Thank you, Colonel."

They shook, then Foster turned to me. "Colonel Decker, welcome. We'll have your brigade in barracks without delay."

We shook as well. Then he pointed at his RSM. "This is Jim Kemarre, my top kick."

"And mine, Teppo Paavola."

Both sergeants major sized each other up as they shook hands. Though they were a study in contrasts — Kemarre was dark where Paavola was pale — the former could have been the latter's brother from another mother based on their similar bearing and had clearly served in the Corps.

"May I suggest we take you to your quarters so you can strip off the tin suits and unpack, then meet in your office, General?" Foster asked. "We have the visiting unit HQ building set up for you. It's austere, but you'll have everything you need, including signage. My people will sort your brigade out and see everyone settled in by midmorning. I don't know if you remember the layout from your time in the 9th, Colonel Decker, but it hasn't changed."

"Good. I do, and call me Zack, okay, Dennis? I'm sure we met before when you and I enlisted and were shipped off to Caledonia for basic. I checked the dates."

"Can't say I remember offhand — that was a large draft of recruits — but if you say so." He gestured at the van. "Please go ahead. I'll see you in thirty minutes."

***

Foster wasn't kidding when he called it austere, but my quarters had a sitting room, a bedroom, and a bathroom, all spotlessly clean and equipped with the sort of indestructible furniture used in barracks, prisons, and mining camps. Not that I cared. A cot and a roof over the head beat sleeping outside during one of Mykonos' famous monsoon storms.

Unpacking took little time. The closets were equipped to take combat armor and had a lockup for weapons that I keyed to my biometrics. Standard stuff found on every military installation across the Commonwealth. Once down to my battledress uniform and beret, I headed across the parade square, at the heart of what was now our quarter, to the HQ building. As Foster said, it had a large sign announcing the 1st Special Forces Brigade, done up in SF colors and with a winged dagger insignia to one side, and the flagpoles flew the standard set — Commonwealth, Fleet, Marine Corps, and 1st SFR.

I entered the empty lobby and looked for the sign directing me to the CO's office. My memory told me the high-ceilinged space once held display cabinets full of regimental mementos and a tall case with the regimental colors. But they were long gone.

Once in the corridor with the offices of the regimental command team, I found the old CO's office door now bearing a sign that said MGen K. Ryent. The entrance to its left bore a similar sign that said Col Z. Decker, CO 1st SFB, and the door to its right, Bde SM T. Paavola. They'd really gone out to get us set up nicely. I made a mental note that we should present Foster with a winged dagger sculpture as thanks when we leave. Paavola had brought a few of them in case.

I opened my office door to find what I expected — more of the indestructible furniture in silver and black — a desk, a small conference table, a dozen chairs, two sideboards — and generic reproductions of battle scenes on the walls. When I sat behind the desk, a virtual terminal materialized, and within moments, I was connected to the Fort Monash network, where they'd kindly set aside a top secret node just for us. Not that we'd be leaving anything that highly classified lying around for the Mykonos Regiment's information analysts to find. Sad as that may sound, we Special Forces units carrying out Naval Intelligence's most highly classified missions trust no one outside our small community because we've experienced the level of treason within our very own ranks.

I heard the click of heels on the polished stone floor in the corridor behind me, and when I turned, Kal Ryent poked his head into my office.

"Dennis Foster seems to have done us well."

"No luxuries, General, but a solid roof, three squares, and all the amenities to run the mission will do us just fine."

"You and I know what real austerity feels like, don't we, Zack?"

"Aye. The Mykonos Regiment did us right." Movement outside my office window caught my eye. "And there's Dennis Foster coming up right on time."

"Then let's check out my office."

I followed Kal next door, and it wasn't much different — the same sort of furniture and wall art — but there was a stand of flags behind his desk, including a red one with two silver stars on it.

"Nice touch."

We heard footsteps in the hallway and turned.

"Finding everything okay, General? Zack?"

"Absolutely. This is great," Kal replied. "Thanks."

"Make nothing of it. Hospitality is an important thing around here. Besides, we don't get visited by such a large Special Forces contingent often. And if small contingents visited since I came back, we never noticed them. Do you mind?" Foster pointed at the office door. When Kal nodded, Foster shut it. "Let me get this out of the way first. You're here because of the constitutional convention and not for some last-minute joint training, right?"

Kal indicated the conference table. "How about we grab a seat?"

Once we'd settled in, Kal said, "You've no doubt seen the orders from Earth. The SecGen has called this convention illegitimate and is adamant that no Commonwealth government organization supports it in any way, shape, or fashion. The SecDef has warned the Grand Admiral that the Armed Forces stay away. Security will be the sole responsibility of the Mykonos government. And since Mykonos doesn't have a national guard, that means the police."

Foster inclined his head. "Yes, sir. I've read those orders."

"Then you know we're not here because of the constitutional convention. That being said, if, during our joint training exercises, we detect threats against representatives of the sovereign star system, I will decide whether the situation is one in which the Armed Forces are duty-bound to act for the greater good or to save lives." Kal tapped his stars. "That's why they made me an acting major general. As far as the SecDef and the SecGen are concerned, I'm the Armed Forces in the Mykonos System, and if I need to intervene, I cannot wait for permission from Caledonia or Earth. But let's hope nothing happens."

Foster, eyes narrowed in thought, didn't immediately reply. Then, he slowly nodded. "Understood, sir."

"Good. Just so that we can be ready, I'll need to have Zack's people recce the convention site — discreetly, it goes without saying, so they can do their contingency planning. But we will engage in the joint training exercises as previously announced. Your soldiers will find the MLI battalions interesting opposition forces."

Foster cocked an eyebrow at Kal. "And Ghost Squadron?"

I chuckled. "You'd have to find it first. But it'll be here, there, and everywhere. Seriously, though, once my S3 settles in, he'll sit with your S3 to hammer out the details. I'm thinking this afternoon."

"Can do. As you may have noticed, we've been expecting you. My S3 is keen on devising challenging problems that'll break us from our normal routine."

# — Nine —

Battalion and squadron commanding officers didn't like their brigade commander swanning about the training area while they were preparing, let alone breathing down their necks. My orders issued, I stepped back to give them space.

Josh sent his companies out in civilian clothes to reconnoiter the convention site, a high-end hotel and spa complex in the verdant hill country north of the Celadon River, approximately halfway between Petras and the port city of Tiryns. The Mykonos police were already setting up a security perimeter, which made the recon a little more complicated. Still, my SF operators could get into pretty much any site deemed secure by ordinary mortals. Meanwhile, the MLI battalions were setting up to put the Mykonos Regiment's infantry through their paces at the platoon and company levels. Eventually, they, too, would conduct reconnaissance patrols around the convention site since they were Ghost Squadron's backup.

Kal, proving once more that he was developing quite the political acumen, was meeting with President Van Kirten and various high-level star system officials, including the police chief, to make sure they understood that we wouldn't stand by idly if things went sideways. Or were about to. Or that we might just make sure no sideways motion ever started. But not in so many words, of course. And wise man that he was, Kal didn't take me along with him, just in case my old buddy Eugene the president, took exception to my ugly mug. We hadn't reconnected when I was back here after basic until the 9th departed.

All of which left me with little to do. Dennis Foster still had the day-to-day running of the regiment, and after making the rounds of his staff and units, I had no choice but to step back lest I annoy them. Which left me with that metaphorical elephant in the room — my family.

And after checking publicly available records, it seemed my Uncle Attar was still among the living, though instead of an apartment in a generation house alongside younger Khanjan and Decker families, as tradition had it on Mykonos, he lived in an assisted facility in Tiryns. Was that a hint Uncle Attar had cut links with the family or simply wanted a quiet life away from the epicenter of the extended family's miniature zaibatsu? Away from the seaport, Tiryns boasted scenic coastal neighborhoods and suburbs strung out along the shores of the Boetian Sea, many of them nicer than what Petras could offer.

Once I got beyond the do I or don't I, my next question was whether I should call Uncle Attar beforehand or simply show up after a few decades without contact. The last time we spoke — and it was shortly before I left Mykonos for good when the 9th Marines were transferred — he was cordial and a little sad at my departure. But that was then.

I finally decided a surprise might be the best. If he wanted nothing to do with me, he could always point at the door and tell me to leave, but at least I'd have seen him. Calling beforehand, well, he might decide ignorance is bliss and never even answer. And I was curious about my family. Since arriving the other day, I'd spent some time after work looking them up, seeing how the conglomerate was doing. And it seemed prosperous, much more so than the hardscrabble set of businesses I remember from my youth.

And so, on our first Saturday here, I signed out an unmarked staff car, put on my service dress blacks, and headed down the highway to Tiryns. Passing through Petras and the countryside along the Celadon River, I was thrown back to my childhood and early twenties. Nothing much had changed over the thirty-odd years since my departure. Clearly, whatever growth in population and industry Mykonos had experienced since then occurred elsewhere. Mind you, the people around here always had been stodgy and set in their ways. Maybe the other inhabited continent, Karinth, was blossoming.

Therefore, I was unsurprised to see the port of Tiryns unchanged, albeit from a distance, since the way to Uncle Attar's residential complex didn't need me to enter the city proper. I skirted it to the north, riding along the crest of hills surrounding the bay. As days on the west coast went, it wasn't too bad. Low clouds coming in from the sea, as usual, but at least it wasn't raining, and the occasional splash of sun made it through, giving the rippling waters a slight shimmer.

When I finally pulled into the parking lot, I had to admit Uncle Attar's old age digs looked pretty fancy from the outside, more than his Navy pension could cover. Nestled among tall trees and overlooking Horsehead Bay, it seemed more like a top-notch hotel for bored socialites than a retreat for hundred- and twenty-year-old veterans of the Shrehari War, or whatever Uncle Attar's actual age was.

A dozen two-story buildings clad in pink stone and capped by red, peaked roofs surrounded a central park filled with gazebos, bandstands, arbors, and trees of all kinds, native and imported from Earth. I knew from reading about it that the structures were connected via underground moving walkways so the residents could visit the restaurant, pool, gym, and other amenities even during the worst downpour and not get wet. Apartments were equipped with autochef kitchens and the most modern conveniences, and service droids did the cleaning twice a week.

I found signs for the reception center — it was the only way in for non-residents since it was a gated community — and walked up a smooth path bordered by a riot of flowers. An actual human sat behind the granite-topped reception counter rather than an AI's three-dimensional projection, a young man with thick brown hair atop a narrow face.

"Good morning, Colonel," he said, dipping his head once. I had to give him props for recognizing the rank insignia on my shoulder straps. "My name is Gio. How may I help you?"

"Good morning. My name is Zachary Decker, and I'm a relative of Attar Khanjan, who lives here. I would like to visit him."

"Is Mister Khanjan expecting you?"

"No. I arrived a few days ago on Armed Forces business and haven't had time to contact the family yet. Could you see if he's able to receive me?"

"One moment please." Gio touched something beneath the counter, and after a few seconds, I saw his lips move but heard no sound. He'd activated a privacy screen. A brief exchange of words ensued. Then he looked up at me again. "If you would please take a seat, sir, Mister Khanjan is on his way. It shouldn't take long. He is amazingly spry for a man of his years."

I didn't bother asking why Uncle Attar was coming here rather than me going to his apartment. Gio probably wouldn't have answered. Instead of sitting, I wandered over to a bank of windows and gazed at the complex.

A minute or two later, I heard a door open behind me, and a querulous, though surprisingly strong voice said, "He's big enough to be a Decker, that's for sure."

I turned and stared at a scowling Uncle Attar, who seemed thinner and more wrinkled than I remembered, though just as tall, with wispy white hair over a tanned scalp. His eyes, though, as blue as mine, were clear and hinted at the sharp intelligence behind them.

"And he's ugly enough to be a Decker." Then the scowl vanished, replaced by a smile that lit up the reception area. He came toward me, arms outstretched, and I could see he was still steady on his legs. "Zack, my boy! A Special Forces colonel and wearing ribbons for medals I thought they only awarded in wartime. Why am I not surprised?"

"Uncle Attar." We embraced — he with all the power his ancient muscles could muster, me careful of my strength so I didn't hurt him. "You're looking good."

When I released him, he gripped my arms and stepped back, eyes searching my face. "And you look like a recruiting poster — the perfect Marine officer."

Uncle Attar let go of me and turned to Gio. "Please log Zack in and put him on my permanent guest list."

"Yes, Commodore."

"How long are you here for, Zack?"

"I have the day, and I'm on Mykonos for a few weeks."

"At Fort Monash?"

"Yes."

He turned toward the door he'd come through moments earlier. "Come on, Colonel Decker. Let's get you a cup of coffee."

We left the reception area and headed along a smooth path lined with flowering bushes to the nearest apartment building.

"What brings you to Mykonos after all these years? It's been what? Almost three decades since I last saw you."

"I brought a brigade from the 1st Special Forces Division to train with the Mykonos Regiment."

Attar gave me a skeptical sideways smile. "Oh, so it has nothing to do with this constitutional convention nonsense."

I winked at him. "Nothing."

"You ever get back together with that wife of yours, Ingrid?"

"No. But I remarried. She's a Naval Intelligence rear admiral — Hera Talyn. You'd like her. And my daughter Saga is now a Marine Corps captain in the Intelligence Branch as well. She took the Decker name and joined up after receiving her doctorate. And she's my NILO on this deployment."

Attar stopped to face me. "Then you must bring her with you on your next visit. My lord. Your daughter is a Marine officer. Won't that make your parents spit with anger?"

"Will do." We resumed walking. "They're still sore at me, I gather."

"Oh, aye. The entire Decker clan has never forgiven you. They're deeply involved with this convention business just so you know."

Attar ushered me into the apartment building lobby and led me down a quiet, clean, well-lit corridor lined with doors bearing brass numbers. We stopped in front of number 10 and, at a gesture from Attar, the door slid aside quietly.

"Home, sweet home. And no Deckers or Khanjans to try my patience with their twin obsessions of politics and business."

I followed him into a spacious combination living and dining room whose high-end furnishings appeared handmade rather than mass-produced.

"Is that why you're not living in one of the family's generation houses?" I took off my beret and placed it on a sideboard while Attar headed for the kitchen and presumably his coffee maker.

"Yep. They drove me insane. Mind you, I'm another they never forgave for joining the Armed Forces."

I couldn't repress a chuckle. "That was decades before my birth, when both families barely eked out an existence, let alone ran a zaibatsu."

"The Deckers can hold a grudge until the heat death of the universe. You should know that. And if anything, their disgust with the Commonwealth has grown exponentially."

Attar reappeared carrying two mugs bearing the insignia of a winged woman with a flaming sword, the name *Iolanthe,* and a hull number. He placed them on the dining table, a slab of honey-colored wood bearing the patina of many years.

"Sit."

I obeyed and took one of the mugs, but I studied the insignia instead of taking a sip. "Are these off the original *Iolanthe,* the biggest, meanest, and most famous Q ship in the Navy's history?"

He nodded. "Yep. I served on Admiral Dunmoore's staff when she had the 101st Battle Group, and *Iolanthe* was her flagship. Is she still among the living?"

"As far as I know, she stopped making guest lectures at the Academy and the War College or appearing at ceremonies. Word is she rarely leaves her secluded property in the tropics nowadays."

"Well, we are all getting along in years." Attar raised his mug. "Your health, Zack. And welcome. I've often wondered how you were doing in the big, bad galaxy."

# —Ten—

Attar drained his mug and carefully placed it on the table, one antique atop another. I'd emptied my second serving long ago while he talked to me of his life and his children, who'd not joined the family firm after retiring from the Navy and had produced kids of their own, who, in turn, had given Attar great-grandchildren.

When I finished telling him about the last few decades of my life, Attar said, "You've had a heck of a career, Zack. And your wife sounds like a formidable woman."

"She's killed more bad guys with her own hands than I have."

He glanced at the old clock hanging above the living room sideboard. "Can you believe it? Almost noon already. You must be getting hungry after all that talking. Shall I have the restaurant send up a pair of bento boxes? They really do it well here."

"Sure." I could feel my stomach make soft but unmistakable noises. "So now that you're up on everything that happened to me since we last saw each other, how are mom and dad and the rest of the clan?"

Attar gave me the wait-a-moment signal and said, "Jeeves, order two bento boxes, menu of the day, from the restaurant."

"Yes, Commodore," a disembodied, androgynous voice replied. "Right away."

He turned his attention back to me and grimaced. "You sure you want to hear about the family?"

"I figured that since I'm on Mykonos for a bit, I might as well see if we can patch things up."

"You've been here now for how long?"

"Four days. We landed Tuesday."

"In that case, your Grandfather Thomas knows you're here. He's one of the drivers behind Mykonos' push for the constitutional convention and can call up the president whenever he wants. If General Ryent met with Van Kirten and other officials, Thomas and the rest of the Deckers are well aware of your presence. And yet, none of them have reached out. Or bothered to tell me, for that matter."

"You think?"

"I know. Nothing of any consequence happens in this star system without Thomas being aware of it. Deckhan Enterprises have an in-house intelligence service that can rival those of any interstellar zaibatsus. By Tuesday supper time, the entire clan knew Jack Decker's wayward son had returned. And as a highly decorated full colonel of Special Forces, thereby making a mockery of Jack's public pronouncement that his good-for-nothing son would never amount to anything. Why do you think you were shunned by everyone you knew when you came back after basic to serve in the 9th?"

"Sure. But that was then. This is now. I figure I should try. Hell, mom and dad have a granddaughter they've never met."

"And they have grandchildren who've not left Mykonos, let alone served the Commonwealth — your nieces. I can't see them caring about the outcast's daughter who followed in her father's footsteps." Attar paused and stared at his mug. "I'll tell you what, though. If you make the social rounds with your general, you're bound to meet relatives. The Deckers and Khanjans attend every major event hosted by the government or other notables, and it's no secret Thomas is one of Van Kirten's principal supporters and fundraisers. How about you let chance decide? There will be a Decker or two at the very heart of the convention."

"If you're trying to protect me from rejection, don't worry. My hide has become as thick as a starship's hull. A stint as janissary for alien megalomaniacs on the other side of the Coalsack nebula toughens you like nothing else."

"You won't be able to set foot on any property owned by the clan. They'll have their security make sure of that. The thought one of the Corps' finest senior officers might be treated as a criminal trespasser because of Jack's intransigence makes my stomach churn. But he wouldn't dare do more than simply snub you at a social occasion, and you wouldn't be the first. Let the Fates do as they wish."

I couldn't help but laugh at Attar's last sentence. "What?"

"Each company in the 1st Special Forces Regiment has a name taken from mythology. I commanded Ghost Squadron before my promotion, and one of its companies is named after the Moirae, which is Greek for the Fates. When they do as they wish, nothing much survives the encounter."

"What are the other names?"

I quickly ran through the squadrons, then told him the MLI battalions had jokingly proposed their companies take on the names of infamous penal institutions throughout history.

"They didn't."

"Oh, yes, they did. Having spent time in the MLI, I can tell you their sense of humor is rather peculiar and mostly morbid. Jimmy Martinson — our divisional commander — immediately shot the idea down."

"You must have fit in nicely."

"Oh, they're good people once they've had the nasties pounded out of them by MLI basic training. I thought I was tough going in, but I learned I needed a bit more toughening. Okay. I'll let the Fates decide rather than have corporate security escort me off the premises. Although there's nothing they can do if I enter a Deckhan Enterprises property in the course of my duties. Not that the family zaibatsu's rent-a-cops would dare try."

Attar made a face. "Deckhan Security is the star system's biggest and most sought-after. Thomas Decker may not like the Commonwealth, but he has no problems hiring former cops, spacers, soldiers, and Marines, hypocrite that he is. They wouldn't bat an eye at expelling a Marine colonel in full fighting order from a Deckhan property if the President and CEO ordered them to do so. And you can be sure Deckhan will work alongside the police to protect the convention. Knowing Thomas' ways, they'll probably be temporarily sworn in as auxiliary police officers so they have arrest and detention powers and can carry weapons openly."

"As I said, I'd like to see them try."

Attar was saved from a reply by the arrival of a service droid bringing our lunch boxes, and while we ate, the conversation turned to interstellar politics. There was nothing wrong with Attar's ability to see things clearly, which was why he opposed the convention, calling it a provocation that could lead to a permanent rift.

"Did I mention Thomas and your parents are secessionists?"

"No." I popped the last bit of sashimi into my mouth and savored the fish's buttery soft texture. "And what does that mean? They want Mykonos to go it alone?"

"Not just Mykonos. Every single OutWorld. Let Earth and the core star systems rot away on their own while the OutWorlds resume human progress and expansion."

"And thereby create a fractured humanity facing a united Shrehari Empire. You were in the war, Attar. With all due respect to Admiral Dunmoore and her spectacular raid, you know that we beat them through attrition in the end.

What'll keep the Shrehari from looking at a broken Commonwealth and wondering about a rematch?"

"I know the answer to that, kiddo. And so do you. We're the only ones in our clan who do, apart from my three offspring, and I'm not even sure about them since they never experienced the two-way shooting gallery. Does it matter? I couldn't begin to say. But you and I swore an oath. That alone sets us apart."

I chewed on Uncle Attar's words while the service droid reappeared, gathered our empty bento boxes, and vanished again.

"How do the local secessionists see it happen?"

Attar let out a bark of laughter. "With the greatest of ease. They believe most of the Fleet will side with them when the time comes — every unit, formation, starbase, division, and ship stationed in one of the OutWorld systems — and figure it'll be enough to discourage adventurism from hostile species. Fools."

I gave him a searching look.

"A lot has changed in the Fleet since you retired. Back then, in the wake of Grand Admiral Kowalski's reforms, the Commonwealth's future seemed a lot brighter, with the disputes between Centralists and sovereignists held in check by a politically neutral military. But it was an illusion. What Kathryn Kowalski, Admiral Dunmoore, and their friends pulled off merely papered over the fractures and bought us time. And during that time, most of the Fleet has become anti-Centralist. Why? For many of us, it's watching Earth, and the core worlds try to erase star system sovereignty through increasingly foul means.

"For others, it's simply out of loyalty to their planets of origin, and those don't include Earth and the Home Worlds. If the OutWorlds secede as a single entity, they will own most of the Armed Forces." I gave Attar a helpless shrug. "The only thing those of us who swore the oath can do is ensure the Commonwealth dies peacefully instead of descending into a Third Migration War."

Attar didn't immediately respond. Instead, he stared out the window for several heartbeats. "Is it really that dire?"

"We've actually been in a state of undeclared cold civil war for years. Undercover and deniable, of course. I've been on the front lines from the moment Hera recruited me. I, and many of the smartest people I know, my daughter included, figure the constitutional convention has a good chance of being the fuse that turns the cold war unendurably hot. And we can't let that happen."

"Which is why you're here — because you believe the time Grand Admiral Kowalski supposedly bought us has almost run out. Did she know her solution was only temporary? Because she certainly didn't behave that way."

I nodded. "An officer of her intelligence and accomplishment? Most assuredly."

"And where do you stand, Zack? Do you favor keeping the Commonwealth together at any cost, or do you support letting the OutWorlds decide their fate?"

"I can tell you where I'm not standing. And that's right in the path of history's rising tide. Those who try to fight it always get swept away and spat out on the other side."

We spoke about a few other matters after that, but I could see Uncle Attar tiring fast, and shortly after fourteen hundred, I said my goodbyes and promised I'd return with Saga the following Saturday.

Upon returning to Fort Monash, I found my daughter compiling the latest open-source intelligence concerning Mykonos and the convention in the S2 office. Since we'd only just arrived, most of my command were working. I entered the office and dropped into a seat across from her.

"Got a moment, Saga?"

"For my commanding officer? Always." She wore her usual poker face when dealing with me in public.

"This is NILO stuff. I just returned from visiting Uncle Attar, whom I mentioned on our trip here."

She nodded. "Yes, I recall. The only member of the family who acknowledged your existence after you enlisted."

I recounted my conversation with Attar about Mykonos and Commonwealth politics, my family, and the secessionist sentiment in this star system. As I did so, Saga took copious notes on her tablet, nodding now and then when I hit an item or issue she'd already come across.

"And you're coming with me the next time I visit Uncle Attar. He's curious about how I had a daughter with a doctorate and whose Marine Corps career is much better than mine."

"And yet you went from private to colonel in the most intense branch of the Corps' sharp end."

I scowled at her. "Flattery will get you nowhere."

My daughter, the captain, had the effrontery to smirk at me.

"Sure. I'd be happy to meet Uncle Attar. He sounds like quite a character, and anyone who served under Admiral Dunmoore has tales I want to hear. And thanks for the intel. That was valuable in filling in the gaps I've found. So the Deckers are hardcore secessionists. I wonder how we can exploit that."

# — Eleven —

"Zack." Kal Ryent intercepted me as I entered the messing facility set aside for the 1st SF Brigade that evening. "Let's grab our grub and talk about a few things."

"As you command, Oh Great General."

Kal gave me a mock exasperated look before heading toward the chow line. One of the many things I liked about him was his habit of not exercising the power of his stars and simply lining up with everyone else when no one would have bitched at a major general cutting in. Or a full colonel, for that matter. But we would only do so if we were in a legitimate hurry.

We took advantage of the opportunity to chat with a few troopers as we picked up trays and utensils and shuffled past the evening meal offerings displayed on a long serving table. So far, the food had been simple and to proper Armed Forces standards, but more than good, with definite hints of Mykonos' unique cuisine. There, too, our local Army colleagues had done us proud.

Surprising no one, an out-of-the-way table had unofficially become mine, Kal's, and Sergeant Major Paavola's, with another for the squadron and battalion commanders and their sergeants major nearby.

"So," Kal said as he split a warm dinner roll once we sat across from each other. "How's Uncle Attar?"

"For a veteran of the Shrehari War, he's surprisingly lucid, spry, and aware of local and interstellar politics." I gave Kal a thumbnail sketch of the more comprehensive rundown I'd given Saga earlier between bites of chicken marsala.

"Interesting," he said when I concluded. "In my talks with President Van Kirten and senior officials, there hasn't been a hint of secessionist sentiment, let alone anyone uttering the dreaded s-word. You having family here is turning out to be a valuable intelligence catch."

"I gave Saga the details of our conversation so she can work them into the political picture she's building. And I'm bringing her with me when I visit Attar next Saturday. He'll be glad to answer whatever questions crop up between now and then."

"He knows she's an intelligence analyst?"

I nodded. "Only a fool would keep things from Attar. Remember, he once worked for Admiral Dunmoore, and she saw to it he retired as a commodore. Now, what's on your mind other than enjoying a scintillating dinner conversation with me?"

"Hang on for a moment. Does that mean you told him why we were here — the real reason?"

"Didn't have to. He never asked because he figured it out the moment he saw me. I get the feeling our cover story is about a micron thick and fading."

Kal gave me a crooked grin. "Plausible deniability, Zack. That's all. No one needs to believe the official version, and I have yet to find someone in the Mykonos government who genuinely does — although I'm going on gut feeling. But it doesn't matter so long as people accept our story as an alternative to something infinitely worse for all parties. And most will."

"It's the ones who don't care about making things worse that worry me. For example, the local Sécurité Spéciale office, whose station chief will have noted our arrival and reported to Earth." I gave Kal a knowing look. "Mind you, Josh is sizing them up for future disposal."

"Only on my orders."

"That is understood. So, what did you want to discuss?" I speared a chunk of chicken and popped it into my mouth.

"You brought good civilian clothes that would pass muster among the local upper crust?"

I nodded while chewing.

"Good. You and I are guests for the midday meal at the Petras Town and Country Club tomorrow, courtesy of Mykonos' Interstellar Affairs Secretary Gudrun Liang, with whom I met earlier today. Do you know her?"

A shake of the head.

"Even better after hearing about your family's attitude toward you."

I swallowed and chased the mouthful with a sip of water.

"Hey, not everyone around here hates my ugly mug. You told me Eugene Van Kirten said hi when you came back from meeting him yesterday."

"And so I did. By the way, he seemed rather amused that you're still a Marine while he's the president of Mykonos. It's not been formally announced yet, but the star systems sending representatives have agreed that Liang chair the convention, seeing as how she'll represent the host government. That makes her our number-one contact."

I knew about the Town and Country, Mykonos' snootiest private club. The Deckers had been members since before I enlisted, and Grandpa Thomas probably did a few stints as president. My father as well, no doubt.

"Why will you and I be seen breaking bread publicly with Madame Secretary? Doesn't that defeat the purpose of our vague excuse for being here? And why am I even going in the first place?"

"Why are you coming with me? Simple. Madame Liang wants to meet you informally after I told her you were not only a native of Mykonos but a scion of the Decker family and the one who'd make sure nothing interrupted the convention. As to our being seen with her, consider it a tactical move that might make the opposition think twice without our actually breaking cover. With whom else but the Interstellar Affairs Secretary would a Commonwealth Armed Forces major general meet to informally discuss the affairs of the galaxy?" He gave me a wry grin. "Wearing stars means being a diplomat as much as a Marine, and I am the representative of the Fleet and Caledonia on this world."

"Let me guess — Larsson gave you secret orders I don't even know about."

"You may well think so, but I certainly couldn't comment."

One of Kal's favorite quotes, that. It was old before humanity left Earth. But who was I to talk?

"Fine, so you go ahead and schmooze while I make sure no one poisons the canapés or steals the bubbly."

"Oh, you'll be schmoozing right along with me, Zack. You're a native son of Mykonos and a scion of a family whose massive political and social influence around here I'm only beginning to glimpse. Now that you've given your squadron and battalion commanders their orders, you don't have that much to do. Besides, Josh can handle the black ops side without your supervision."

I scoffed, but that only made his sardonic grin widen.

"Did you ever visit the club before you enlisted?"

"Yep. And mightily bored I was. On the bright side, my behavior there, other than sullen, remained within the acceptable range, so they won't boot me out because of a lifetime ban."

"Oh, what joyous news. I'll have the staff car pick us up at eleven hundred."

We polished off the rest of the meal in silence. When Paavola appeared, tray in hand, he saw us almost ready to leave, so after a quick nod, he wandered off to find an empty chair with a group of command sergeants who were just starting to eat. I figured he'd rather be with his buddies than a major general and a colonel anyhow. I know I would have in his place, although I never got to experience the joys of being a first sergeant or sergeant major. No. It was command sergeant to chief warrant officer to major for me.

The combined mess set aside for us had a bar area, also all ranks but with dividers separating it in three. The smallest section was reserved for officers and warrant officers, the second largest for sergeants and sergeants major, and the largest for enlisted and junior noncoms. But everyone helped themselves at the same automated dispenser lineup, and that's where Kal and I headed for a drink and a bit of relaxation.

I never worried about my troopers and booze, not even those in the MLI battalions. Heavy drinkers were a liability in special ops, and if they showed a lack of control, off they went to a line regiment. No one wanted to be labeled as rejected by Special Forces for behavioral reasons. It meant the Fort Monash morale and welfare fund wouldn't rake in as much profit as some might have hoped with the influx of an entire brigade.

Sunday came bright and early, and I joined Ghost Squadron for the morning run, dressed just like any other trooper in a maroon tee shirt with the winged dagger badge on the front and black shorts. Since it was Sunday, we wore running shoes instead of combat boots, the sole concession for a day of lighter duties.

After breakfast, I sat with Saga and Captain Renaud in the S2 office to go over the latest intelligence reports, what

Renaud called the overnighters, then checked in with Josh to confirm the recon plan was still on track. That done, I was at loose ends, so I returned to my room, changed into civvies, and read a book until eleven hundred.

Was I enthused about lunching at the Petras Town and Country Club with the Mykonos Secretary for Interstellar Affairs? Not in the slightest. Oh, it wasn't Gudrun Liang, but the thought of re-entering that damned enclave for the rich and obnoxious I'd hated as a kid. My older brother Richard had loved the place. Even at seventeen, he was so good at aping the grownups that he passed for an adult in his late twenties.

He, of course, had never disappointed our parents or grandparents. At least not in ways they cared.

A few minutes before eleven, I put my book away, gave myself a last check in the mirror, and liked what I saw — fawn-colored slacks, a lightweight jacket, a white silk shirt, and tan oxfords. Precisely what a club member would wear to a Sunday luncheon.

I stepped out into the late morning sunshine shortly afterward and waited for Kal and our ride, an unmarked Mykonos Regiment staff car put at Kal's disposal for the duration.

Kal appeared first, and if I was dressed appropriately for a club guest, his sartorial splendor would impress the club's executive committee. His dark silk suit, impeccably hand-tailored, would have set most people back by quite a bit, as would the shirt, which was a delicate shade of salmon, and the subtly patterned casual cravat.

I let out a low wolf whistle. "You'll have the peasants kissing your Academy ring looking like that, *mon général.*"

"So long as the Mykonos upper crust approves, I'm good. No ring kissing needed." We both caught movement out of the corner of our eyes. "There's the car, right on time."

The Town and Country Club was on the other side of Petras from Fort Monash, close to the resort where the convention would take place, and it took us a good thirty minutes using the ring road. When we turned off the highway and headed down the long, tree-lined drive to the clubhouse — the term doesn't do the splendor of the complex justice — I felt that familiar sense of dread I experienced as a teen when I was forced to attend functions.

We emerged from the drive and into the parking area for guests, where a droid waved us into what was probably our reserved spot. After climbing out of the car, I studied the clubhouse, comparing it with the images in my memory. The principal, single-story building easily occupied an entire hectare, more if you counted the ten-meter wide veranda wrapped around its blindingly white walls.

The veranda's roof, slightly slanted and held up by Doric columns, was a brilliant red, just like the flat roof over the building itself. Here and there, chairs and settees were grouped around low tables while on either side of the open French doors, tables with four or six places allowed dining alfresco.

A full gym, with an indoor swimming pool, a dozen tennis courts, and the Almighty knew what else stood on one side, connected to the clubhouse by a covered walkway, while the stables — in this case, horses and various riding implements such as bicycles — were on the other.

It had been the most opulent privately owned property on the planet back in my youth, and that probably hadn't changed. At least the food was superb. I hoped that hadn't changed either.

"Mykonos to Colonel Decker." Kal's voice snapped me out of my contemplation. "Madame Secretary awaits."

"Right." But as I stepped off to follow Kal, I glimpsed a figure heading for one of the veranda's dining tables, a tall, powerfully built man a year or two older than me accompanied by three women, one his age, the others my daughter's age. He wore short sandy hair, and if we were any closer, I'd see he had the same deep blue eyes as Saga and me.

Richard.

# — Twelve —

The club's concierge, a dried-up stick of a man older than dirt wearing a morning suit, of all things, greeted us as we entered the main lobby.

"General Ryent and Colonel Decker." He bowed his head. "I'm Ames. On behalf of the Petras Town and Country Club, welcome. Secretary Liang is waiting for you in the main salon. And if I may, Colonel Decker, the house is pleased you're back after such a long absence."

As we headed off, Kal silently mouthed, *the house is pleased you're back?*

"What can I say?" I murmured back. "Ames was probably on the staff back then — he looks old enough — and considering my family's standing...." I hesitated for a moment. "My brother Richard is seated at one of the outdoor dining tables. I thought you might like to know."

"Noted. Try to keep the family reunion under control."

"I'm not the problem, Kal. The rest of them are."

"Is that like saying you're the only one in the formation marching in step?" He asked in an amused, albeit almost inaudible tone.

"Get stuffed, General, sir," I replied in the same manner.

We entered the main salon, a spacious area paneled in rich, honey-colored wood with a marble floor and dark furniture. A long, granite-topped bar backed by shelves groaning under the weight of expensive booze and staffed by humans covered most of one wall.

Kal made a beeline for a table by the window. There, a slender woman with an elfin face framed by long raven black tresses was waving at us and smiling. Madame Secretary Gudrun Liang. She looked a lot younger than her age and had the reputation of having not only a sharp mind but a sharp tongue, especially for criticizing policies from Earth that ate away at star system sovereignty. As the convention chair, Liang could fan the flames of OutWorld discontent at will.

She stood as we came near and held out her hand.

"General Ryent. Nice to see you again so soon. Thank you for accepting my invitation." They shook, then she turned to me and offered her hand again. "And you, Colonel Decker. General Ryent mentioned you're Thomas Decker's grandson and Jack Decker's son. How delightful to see you back on your home world. I understand you're an illustrious Marine Corps hero, or so the general says."

As we shook, I gave her my patented Decker smile. "You shouldn't believe everything he says. Like most Marines, he's an incorrigible teller of tall tales."

"And yet, sometimes reality outstrips the story by a wide margin. Shall we sit and enjoy a drink before lunch?"

"Certainly."

Liang took her chair again, and we sat across from her. Moments later, one of the serving staff materialized by our table with a tray holding two glasses of wine — one red and one white — and a foaming mug of Shrehari Ale. The man carefully placed the glass of red in front of Liang, the white in front of Kal, and then the mug in front of me. Obviously, someone had done their homework and prepared in advance. I knew Kal enjoyed a crisp Riesling, though I doubted the ale was a widely appreciated tipple in this club. My father would no doubt call it low brow, fit only for Marine Corps enlisted personnel.

Liang raised her glass. "Once again, welcome and to your health."

We imitated her. "Your health."

After taking a sip, Liang turned toward me. "I spotted your brother Richard, his wife, and his two daughters shortly before you arrived."

"I saw them taking a table on the veranda as we walked up to the main entrance."

"Go say hi whenever you want, Colonel."

"Thank you, Madame Secretary. Perhaps later."

Or perhaps never.

Liang sat back, fingers toying with the stem of her glass. "General Ryent tells me you and your people are experts at rooting out hidden threats, Colonel. In a way that no one notices."

"It's something we do well, yes."

"He also tells me you have a Constabulary liaison officer on your establishment."

I nodded. "We do. Chief Warrant Officer Aleksa Kine. She's part of Lieutenant Colonel Josh Bayliss' squadron headquarters staff."

"This would be the mysterious Ghost Squadron?"

"Yes." I glanced at Kal, wondering what he'd told her and what schemes they were developing. If I'd had any doubts before, they just vanished. He had received secret orders from the Grand Admiral dealing with the political aspects of the convention. Otherwise, he wouldn't be in cahoots with Liang.

"It might be useful if your liaison officer got in touch with the chief superintendent responsible for security at the convention site and learned about our dispositions. Purely on an informal basis, you understand. Then, the chief superintendent could point out his weak spots — there are always weak spots — so that you know how and where we could use someone's help."

I found it strange Kal brought me in on this conversation. He could have simply given me the order to deploy Kine as an informal liaison with the local police and left it at that. There was no need for me to break bread with the secretary. Wheels within wheels. Knowing Kal, he'd tell me why when he judged the time was right, so asking would be futile.

"That's easily arranged. Chief Warrant Officer Kine is used to working quietly with other law enforcement organizations on our behalf."

"Good. I'll warn the police and tell them to send you the meeting coordinates in the morning. It would be helpful if your liaison met with our people as soon as possible."

"She'll be ready to see your chief superintendent tomorrow, Madame Secretary."

"Good. In related news, the first delegations are arriving shortly, so we'll activate the security perimeter at the Celadon Resort and Spa in forty-eight hours."

A faint smile crossed Kal's lips. "How fortuitous. In just under forty-eight hours, Colonel Decker's two light infantry battalions are planning a training exercise in the Celadon Valley."

I kept my poker face, but thanks for telling me about this ahead of time, Kal.

"Fortuitous indeed." Liang glanced over my shoulder and nodded once. "Our table is ready. We can bring our glasses."

We stood and followed her across the bar to the open double doors where a maître d'hôtel waited, hands folded together at the waist.

As we neared, he bowed his head. "Madame Secretary, General, Colonel. If you'll please follow me."

He led us across the spacious, half-full dining room to a window table overlooking the back garden. It was situated well away from the door leading to the veranda where my brother and his family were sitting and away from other diners, so we couldn't be easily overheard.

But we ended up speaking of inconsequential matters while enjoying a delightful meal — the standards of the club's kitchen hadn't dropped. On the contrary.

About halfway through the main dish, I suddenly realized what this was about. Liang was meant to be seen dining with the two newly arrived senior Marine Corps officers by the notables of the star system capital now that someone had leaked her role as chair of the convention to the public. It was as much a warning to the opposition as a challenge to the federal administration's authority.

If I didn't already suspect Kal of blatantly, albeit secretly, violating the SecGen's orders at Grand Admiral Larsson's direction, I'd wonder why he was going along with this display. Why I was part of it still mystified me just a little. Everyone who knew anything about the Decker-Khanjan clan would know of my expulsion long ago by an irate grandfather and father whose ability to hold grudges was legendary.

"Coffee, Colonel?" The waiter, who'd snuck up on us unnoticed by me thanks to my deep thoughts, asked as he removed the empty plates.

I glanced up at him, aware he'd already taken Liang's and Kal's orders without me consciously noticing. "Sure. Thanks."

Kal gave me an amused look. "Woolgathering, Zack. Normally you're more alert than this."

"It's the surroundings, I suppose."

"Memories?"

"And questions."

Before Kal could ask what those were, Liang glanced across the room. "Your brother Richard and his family just came in from the dining veranda."

I kept my eyes on her instead of craning my neck to look. "Just so you know, Madame Secretary, my family disowned me when I was eighteen, and I returned the favor."

Liang let out a brief chuckle that pealed like tiny silver bells in my ears. "I doubt there's a political, financial, or industrial upper-class member who's unaware of this by now, Colonel. Your arrival on Mykonos revived a lot of old memories. But no worries, those memories are largely why you are here today."

"Why?"

She gave me a quick smile. "Local boy makes good after choosing his own way and comes back home to protect his people's right to decide their future. You're a symbol, Colonel. A powerful one, or at least you will be once we're done. You stand for grit, determination, and the strength to go it alone and thrive. You're a Decker from Mykonos who became one of humanity's most celebrated Special Forces commanders. Many folks around here, even friends of your family, truly respect what you've accomplished and what you can do."

I returned her politician's smile with a sardonic one of my own. "And all that in six days?"

"You'd be amazed at how quickly ideas propagate with the right push."

Another idea struck me, and I turned a gimlet eye on Kal, who was watching Liang and me with his usual faintly amused expression.

"Why do I think our arrival here was preceded by a few subspace messages from certain quarters, General?"

"Because you're getting better at figuring this non-kinetic stuff out." Kal glanced over my shoulder. "And speaking of non-kinetic, your brother finally decided on a course of action. He's making a beeline for our table, watched by his wife and daughters, who have wisely retreated into the foyer."

"Which means this will not be pleasant. Otherwise, he'd introduce me to them." I turned my chair to watch Richard, but his face, like mine, revealed nothing. He didn't even look at me but at Liang. And when he stopped by our table, he ignored Kal and me entirely.

"Madame Secretary." Richard bowed his head. "Always a pleasure to see you. Unfortunately, that pleasure doesn't extend to your company. As you might recall, I am on the club's executive committee, and my father and grandfather are its presidents emeritus. On behalf of the executive committee, this individual," he gestured at me without looking, "isn't welcome on the premises."

# — Thirteen —

"Colonel Decker is here as my guest, Richard. Surely as a club member, I have that privilege."

"You do indeed, except when it comes to people who've been barred from the club by decision of the executive committee, and my grandfather made sure Zachary Decker was on the banned list long ago."

I let out an indelicate snort. "Figures the Old Man would pull a stunt like that. He has two moods — greedy and splenetic."

Richard turned his eyes on me, and I saw emotion in them for the first time.

"Show respect for your betters, you disgrace to the family name."

"Glad to see you too, Brother."

"How about you don't embarrass yourself, Secretary Liang, and your general by leaving quietly? Your Marine Corps may have granted you the status of a senior officer, but you have no standing here. This is a private club, and its members are highly selective of who they'll let on the premises. You don't qualify."

"But you do? Funny how things work, especially in our family. Some of us stay home and inherit status; some go out into the galaxy and earn it. Yet it's the inheritors who qualify, not those who get their hands dirty." I climbed to my feet. "Madame Secretary, since my brother is still the same narrow-minded, intolerant asshole he was when we were teens, I will leave you and General Ryent to enjoy dessert and coffee."

I gave Richard a wintry smile that signified this wasn't over. He'd remember it from way back.

"Want to introduce me to your wife and daughters? I have a daughter as well. But you wouldn't like her. She's a Marine Corps captain who didn't inherit a damn thing either, except the Decker genes." I looked him up and down with a faint sneer. "Saga could probably kick your ass across the boxing ring without breaking a sweat."

By now, most of the closest diners were watching the scene surreptitiously, even though we'd been talking in low voices that didn't carry. No one could fail to notice the resemblance between Richard and me once I was standing or the tension enveloping us. I gave Kal a look that told him to cover my back, then, without warning, I headed across the room to the lobby, where my sister-in-law and nieces were waiting. It took Richard a second or two before he realized what I intended and come after me. How he'd manage my ambush without causing a scandal intrigued me.

All three were staring at me with curiosity rather than dismay or hostility, and I figured they didn't know who I was, though they could clearly see the family resemblance. I reached them a few steps ahead of Richard and stretched my hand out to his wife.

"Hi. We haven't met. I'm Zack, Richard's younger brother. I'm a colonel in the Commonwealth Marine Corps, and I've been away from Mykonos for a few decades. And you are?"

She looked at me with confusion writ large on her delicate features. "Brother?"

At that moment, Richard caught up with me. "Come on, Delia, girls. We're leaving."

He tried to usher them out, but Delia remained rooted to the spot. "Are you the one disowned by the Decker family for enlisting without permission?"

I gave her a big smile. "That would be me."

"But they said you were a ne'er-do-well, a worthless rogue who'd never amount to much, not a colonel. I have a cousin in the Corps, so I know how high up a colonel is and what sort of officer becomes one."

"Come on, Delia." Richard put his hand on her arm, but she shook him off. "This is not someone we can afford to be seen with."

"He's your brother, for heaven's sake."

"Zack has been no one's brother for a long time. Father will not be happy when he hears about him being in the club, let alone speaking with us."

The daughters were staring at all three of us, silent and unsure how they should react. That they carried Decker genes was evident in the blond hair and blue eyes, but they had their mother's fine features and svelte build and seemed to be in their early twenties.

"I'm not going anywhere, Richard. You and your parents clearly lied about your brother, considering he's a Marine colonel and was having lunch with Secretary Liang, the administration's third most important member. I'd like an explanation."

"Secretary Liang and Major General Kal Ryent, the most senior Commonwealth Armed Forces officer in the star system," I added, giving her a quick wink. "Pretty good for a roguish ne'er-do-well, isn't it, Delia?"

She smiled at me while Richard began fuming in a way that hadn't changed since I last saw him. "It is. These are our daughters, Annette and Martine. Girls, this is your uncle Zachary."

I bowed at the neck. "A pleasure to meet nieces I didn't know existed. I also have a daughter. Her name is Saga, and she's one of my officers, a captain, and a Marine Corps intelligence analyst. I'm sure she'd enjoy meeting you."

"And I would really like to meet Saga," Delia said in a determined tone.

"But it won't be here, alas. Richard came over to toss me out on my ear despite my being Madame Liang's guest. Apparently, I'm on the club executive's persona non grata watchlist, courtesy of Grandpa Thomas."

Delia turned a cold stare on my brother. "Really, Richard? Kicking your brother, the Marine colonel, out while dining with Gudrun Liang? Could you be any ruder?"

"Now is not the time for this discussion, Delia. Let's go home." He glared at me. "Finish your meal with Liang and then be gone."

"We will have this discussion when we get home. Count on it," she replied. "I'd like to know the actual story about Zachary being expelled from the family, not the bullshit your parents and grandparents have been spouting all these years."

For a moment, she sounded almost exactly like my wife, the judicious use of profanity included, though I didn't think Delia was an assassin in her younger days. But I was beginning to like her. I guess we Decker boys had a type.

I watched them leave, then quietly sauntered back to our table where my slice of pie and coffee cup waited and took my seat.

"Richard, under duress, granted me a stay of execution until after we're done, Madame Secretary."

"Whose duress?" Kal asked, smiling.

"That would be Delia, my sister-in-law, who just discovered the Decker family had been feeding her porkies about the prodigal son and wasn't thrilled about it." The pleased expressions on their smug faces gave me the ultimate piece of the puzzle. "You engineered this, didn't you? You hoped I'd accost Delia and, through her, find my way back into the clan for political purposes."

"It was one of many plans," Kal admitted. "Secretary Liang knew your brother and his family took their midday meal here most Sundays."

"And Delia Bisley is known for not suffering fools or foolishness gladly," Liang added. "It must make certain conversations around the table interesting when Thomas Decker convenes the entire family at various holidays and celebrations."

"Oh, they'll get even more interesting once she squeezes the true story out of my brother later this afternoon. Delia strikes me as someone with a touch of my wife's ruthlessness when she's irked. And Hera isn't someone you annoy twice."

Kal, seeming as amused as ever, nodded. "I can confirm that."

"Delia is a senior civil service official, and she has the reputation of being a bit of a terror when she's crossed. No doubt she gives your grandfather back as good as she gets, Colonel."

"Or perhaps the Old Man will have learned there's no profit in firing shots across her bow. Which is what you're counting on, right?"

"Finish your dessert, Zack."

***

Back at Fort Monash, once Kal dismissed the staff car, I asked, "Why are you and Liang so keen on getting me back in with my folks?"

"It's simple. Remember your Uncle Attar told you the Deckers were not only influential in government and business circles but also hardcore secessionists?"

"Yes. That was yesterday. Kind of hard to forget so quickly."

"Gudrun Liang told me the same thing, but she also said your family is among the leading secessionists. Liang and some of her cabinet colleagues are worried they might try to influence the constitutional convention. And though she didn't say it in so many words, she's afraid some of the hotter heads might try a false flag operation to convince the delegates that reconciliation with Earth was no longer possible."

"And you want me back in the family as the special ops prodigal who might help carry out a false flag? That won't work."

Kal ushered me into his sitting room next door to my suite.

"Let's not toss the idea out just yet, but that wasn't what we had in mind. You spent enough time as an intelligence operative to infiltrate just about anything. Since the Deckers are leading secessionists, we need to know what they think and what they plan around the convention, and who better to be our ears and eyes than you? Even the best undercover operative wouldn't stand a chance. Besides, the ones sent by Hera are busy looking for threats from the opposition."

"And if the Old Man stands pat with his orders to shoot me on sight if I show up on his doorstep?"

"It's worth a try, Zack. If it doesn't work, we have lost nothing, although I daresay Delia will ignore Thomas Decker's orders and take the initiative, provided your gut instinct about her is right and you have the best in the business. But if it works, we might gain invaluable intelligence that could help us stop the convention from lighting a fuse and collapsing the Commonwealth before we're ready."

"Fine. But I will report today's events to Saga word for word, including what you just said. Otherwise, she won't have the full picture."

"I wouldn't expect anything less." That smile returned. "After all, Hera made sure we appointed her as brigade NILO for a reason, and we remember what it costs to disappoint your wife."

# — Fourteen —

When I finished speaking, Saga shook her head. "Your family is so messed up they make the Lagmans appear sane, and considering mom, that's saying a lot. I can't believe your brother ordered you out of the club in front of Secretary Liang when you were her guest."

We were alone in my office, and I'd finished giving her the full rundown of yesterday's events — as her father more than as her CO.

"Believe it. Richard always let his arrogance outstrip his common sense, and he's about as slavishly devoted to our grandfather as possible since he aspires to become President and CEO of Deckhan Enterprises. Grandpa Thomas said Zachary Decker was to be shunned in polite society and kept away from places like the club or family properties, so Richard does his best to obey the Old Man's spiteful instructions."

"Because you didn't want to go to university after high school, get what they considered a useful degree, and enter the family zaibatsu once you graduated."

"Yep. Couldn't see myself as an accountant or a lawyer or some such thing. But the more the Old Man and my parents pushed, the harder I resisted when they could have compromised and let me find my own way into Deckhan Enterprises. I was just as stubborn as a teen as I am now — and I came by it honestly since grandpa, and my dad are as bad — but without the ability to get out of problems I developed later on."

Saga let out a peal of laughter. "From what Hera told me, it was much later on."

I pointed my finger at her and scowled. "Be more respectful of your father, young captain."

Merriment danced in her eyes. "Sir, yes, sir. You were telling me a story?"

"Right. So I did the worst thing I could do in the eyes of people who not only despised the Commonwealth but looked down on Armed Forces members as being low caste, with Marines the lowest of the low — I enlisted in the Corps. Never mind the Decker-Khanjans weren't much more than hardscrabble farmers and merchants back during the Shrehari War and never had an issue with Uncle Attar and his offspring serving in the Navy back in the day."

"You defied them and spat on the plans they nurtured for you, Dad. That sort of thing is enough to cause a permanent rift in many families." She studied me while shaking her head. "I shouldn't say this lest it encourages you, but I can see where I get most of my temperament from, and it isn't mom. And Kal wants you to infiltrate them? That's just as bizarre."

"They're your family too, Saga. Your cousins Annette and Martine are a few years younger than you are, but there's a distinct genetic resemblance."

"But I'd be as welcome on my Grandpa Jack's doorstep as you. Or on that of Great-Grandpa Thomas."

"Yep. But I must admit, Kal's scheme is twisted, and I like twisted schemes." I gave my daughter a wry grin. "You can blame Hera for me developing that sort of predilection."

"Heaven forbid I'd blame her for anything, Dad. She outranks both of us, and, in fairness, she's been good for you."

"Hera saved my life. And not just once. So, does knowing the Deckers are not only among the wealthiest industrialists around here but leading secessionists with connections at the highest levels of government add something to your assessment of the political situation?"

A dubious expression crossed her face.

"Not immediately, no. But it gives us a bit more focus on who might sponsor a false flag operation that could precipitate events. Do you think your sister-in-law Delia will create an opening for you? Because clearly, Kal and Liang, the latter knowing about your brother's character flaws, engineered the situation to provoke her. And she's a high-level official — an assistant deputy secretary — in the Off-World Mining and Natural Resources Department."

"Not a clue. I wish I could have overheard the discussion between her and my brother yesterday after they left the club. Or listened to my brother reporting the incident to our parents and the Old Man, which he will have as soon as Delia let him go."

Saga smirked in a most insubordinate manner. "So, beneath that veneer of indifference, you are curious about their reaction to your arrival on Mykonos. Interesting."

"Another data point for your intelligence preparation of the battlespace?"

"No. A sign my father suffers from conflicted feelings concerning his family."

"My family and yours, kiddo."

Just then, my communicator chimed. I pulled it out of my battledress tunic pocket and glanced at the display.

"My sister-in-law Delia Bisley calling from an official node — her full title is staring up at me."

"Better and better."

I placed the communicator on my desk and activated the holographic mode.

"Good morning, Delia. And how are you?"

Her disembodied head appeared in midair above the small device.

"Zachary, thanks for taking my call. I am well, and you?"

"Outstanding as always. I have Captain Saga Decker, my daughter, with me."

Delia's holographic head turned. "Good morning, Saga. A pleasure to meet you, even if it's virtually. Your father briefly mentioned you were a Marine officer yesterday. I'm impressed."

Saga smiled at her. "Don't be. I'm not a fighting machine like dad. Merely an intelligence analyst."

"Yet you're a captain, and you don't look much older than my two girls, who still haven't decided what they wanted in life and are slumming around Petras University, collecting degrees."

Since Saga had a doctorate herself, on top of undergraduate and graduate degrees, I quickly brought the conversation around before anyone said anything that might derail Delia.

"And to what do we owe your call?"

"Oh, I wanted to apologize for yesterday. Richard can be impossible sometimes, as you no doubt remember well."

"Stubbornness is written in the Decker genes. Besides, in fairness, he was only carrying out the Old Man's orders."

Delia made a face.

"Yes, and I wish he'd stand up for himself sometimes. Of course, I'm not afraid of your grandfather's vindictive streak like everyone else. It comes with being his equal in what passes for Petras society. He knows better than to use his intimidation tactics on me. But Richard came clean once we got home and admitted you were given a raw deal for standing up to Thomas and Jack and making your wishes clear. Once we were done, Richard went off to tell your grandfather and parents about the incident at the club. I've not heard from any of them yet. However, Gudrun Liang called earlier today, and we had a brief chat, secretary to assistant deputy secretary if you get my meaning. She informed me you were an honored guest of the Mykonos Government, and I could do it a favor by helping smooth over the estrangement between you and your family. On a strictly informal basis, you understand."

I glanced at my daughter, who wore a slight frown.

"Interesting," I replied. "I didn't know your government considered me as such."

Delia smiled briefly. "I'm sure we can come up with a good explanation. In any case, I thought it best I mentioned Madame Liang's call because I'd like to be as open as possible with you, Zachary."

"Zack, please. No one calls me Zachary."

Another smile. "Zack, then. Before she called, I'd already decided to invite you and Saga out for the evening meal tonight. After what Richard said and my ferreting around, I definitely want to become better acquainted with a Decker who isn't another corporate big shot with eyes on the bottom line."

"Will Richard come?"

"That's his decision. If you agree, I'll make reservations for the four of us at *Chez Stavros*, a small, intimate place that serves the best Mykonosian dishes in town. My treat. If Richard wants to climb off his high horse, stand up for himself, and apologize, he'll come with me. Otherwise, it'll just be us three. What do you say, brother-in-law? Does nineteen-hundred suit you and my niece?"

"It does."

"Good. I'll make sure your grandfather and parents know we're breaking bread. It might provoke interesting results."

Saga looked at me. "You're right, Dad. Aunt Delia has a few things in common with Hera."

"Hera?" Delia asked.

"My wife. Second wife, to be precise. She's not Saga's mother, from whom I've been estranged for a long time. Hera is a Navy rear admiral and one of the most respected officers in her field."

"You sound increasingly interesting with every word, Zack. I look forward to tonight."

"So do we."

"See you at nineteen-hundred." Her hologram faded out as she cut the link.

Saga and I exchanged a glance.

"Moving faster than you expected, Dad?"

"A lot more. Why do you ask?"

"Because I figured she'd call with an invitation sometime today, based on what you told me."

I studied my daughter for a few heartbeats. "Gut instinct?"

"Perhaps. I couldn't tell you why."

"Remind me to tell you about the times my gut instinct saved the day. You've obviously inherited the talent."

# — Fifteen —

I spent the rest of the day observing Lora Cyone and her battalion deploying into the field with a battle group from the Mykonos Regiment, then sat with Josh and Ghost Squadron's command group to review the results of their recon patrols around the convention site.

Shortly before eighteen-thirty, Saga pulled up in front of the senior officers' accommodation block behind the controls of an unmarked staff car borrowed from the Fort Monash motor pool. She wore simple yet elegant beige trousers, a white, long-sleeved blouse open at the neck, and flat-heeled shoes. Her long blond hair, usually bundled up at the nape, hung free, framing a youthful face that somehow mixed Ingrid's and my best features. Saga's eyes, though, held more wisdom and maturity than most officers her age and definitely more than those of her cousins.

I wore the same suit as the day before, albeit with a fresh shirt. If social engagements were going to be frequent, I'd be looking for a good, inexpensive clothing shop because I'd brought the bare minimum figuring Kal would be the

Fleet's public face. Mine wasn't exactly photogenic by comparison.

When the passenger side door opened, I jumped in. "You know where we're going?"

Saga tapped the side of her head with a long, slender index finger.

"Got the route memorized, Dad. What do you think I am? A second lieutenant who can't find the way to the heads without a sergeant holding her hand?"

"Some make it to captain without improving their ground navigation skills."

She snorted. "Yeah, but I'm your daughter, Dad. I was born with the ability to find my way around."

"Don't remind me. You were a handful as a toddler."

We found *Chez Stavros*, a small place with an unpretentious wood and stone facade at the heart of Petras' old town, with ten minutes to spare. After parking the car in a nearby space, we wandered around like tourists, studying the planet's oldest structures as they glowed in the setting sun.

At one minute to seven, we entered the restaurant. Its main room was a fraction of the one at the Town and Country Club but with ten times the charm. Cozy booths line the sides while a long bar of polished dark wood occupied most of the far wall. Wooden tables surrounded by rustic-looking chairs dotted the center. The restaurant oozed coziness with off-white walls boasting tasteful paintings and images, a floor covered in marquetry tiles of various shades, and a coffered ceiling. About half the booths and tables were occupied, but few voices carried, proof each table had its own sound dampener.

One of the staff, wearing black trousers and a black shirt, intercepted us within seconds.

"How may I assist you, Sir, Madame?"

"We're meeting Delia Bisley."

The man bowed his head.

"Ah, yes. Colonel Zack Decker and Captain Saga Decker. Madame Bisley hasn't arrived yet, but please let me take you to your booth."

Once we were seated side by side on a comfortably padded bench facing a polished tabletop, the man asked, "Can I bring you something from the bar while you're waiting?"

"Sure," I replied. "Do you have Shrehari Ale?"

"We certainly do, sir." He turned to Saga. "And you, madame?"

"A gin and tonic, please."

Her order didn't surprise me in the least. She'd picked up the habit from Hera, for whom it was the go-to pre-dinner drink.

Shortly after our glasses arrived, Delia Bisley hurried in — alone. She took the bench across from us, all smiles.

"Hello, hello. Thank you for coming. And it's a pleasure to meet a niece I never knew I had in the flesh."

"Thank you for inviting us, Delia. I guess Richard isn't joining us."

Delia's lips formed a moue of disdain.

"Your father used his usual threats to keep Richard in line. It's not as if your brother needs to work for Deckhan Enterprises. He can get another high-profile job elsewhere in a matter of hours. In fact, Thomas and your father need him more than he needs the aggravation they cause. He really is good at running Deckhan Hospitality. Better than anyone else in the Decker-Khanjan clan, and they're aware of it."

The waiter appeared with a glass of white wine and silently placed it in front of Delia. When she saw my curious look, she chuckled.

"Yes, I come here often enough that they know what I like as apéritif." She nodded at my mug. "Is that Shrehari Ale?"

"Yep. I got a taste for it when I was a sergeant."

"Don't let Thomas or your father know. They consider that sort of tipple lowbrow."

"I'm not surprised. Nor do I care." I raised the ale. "To our health."

"Our health."

We took a sip, then placed our glasses on the table as Delia studied Saga and me with her intelligent eyes.

"Where do I start with my questions? The only thing Richard could tell me about was the events leading to your expulsion from the family. Like the rest, he has no idea what you did afterward. And before you ask, I got the truth out of Richard, not the official story the Deckers have been peddling for thirty-odd years. We've been married long enough that he knows better than feeding me horse manure." She paused and gave me a rueful look. "Richard really is a good man. Yes, he has blind spots like most of us, and you're the biggest one, Zack. But that's on Thomas and your father. How about we order first? Then I want to hear everything about you two, the only warriors to come from the Decker bloodline and probably more steadfast than any of them."

By the time we pushed our empty dessert plates aside, I'd given Delia my life's story — at least the unclassified parts — including a bit about the other Delia I'd known long ago on a planet only a few light years from Mykonos. My sister-in-law was fascinated and appalled by her namesake's fate to live and die in exile on Desolation Island.

Our meal had been superb, and I enjoyed Mykonosian specialties I hadn't tasted since my early twenties. Saga's life story was much shorter than mine, but Delia had marveled over the circumstances of our reunion on Scandia during the coup attempt when I led a rescue team to retrieve her from the plotters.

"You've led such interesting lives. I'm quite in awe."

I shrugged. "That's why I don't carry a grudge against the Old Man. If I'd stayed on Mykonos, I would never have met Ingrid, and Saga would never have been born."

My daughter nudged me with her elbow.

"And the Marine Corps would have been poorer for not having you in its ranks, Dad." She winked at Delia. "I'd say more about his importance to the Fleet, but that would violate the Official Secrets Act."

"It's the impression I got from his modest portrayal of a career that sounds unique. I wish I could say it might impress your grandfather or great-grandfather enough that they'd welcome your father back into the family, but I know the old devils extremely well." Delia glanced at the time. "And as delightful as this evening was, I suggest we call it a day."

Since it was well past twenty-one hundred, I could only nod in agreement. When I tried to pick up the tab, Delia smiled mischievously. She said it had already been taken care of, although Richard wouldn't learn about his generosity until he glanced at the following month's expense statement.

Saga thought that was hilarious, and I realized she'd quickly warmed to her newfound aunt. Although I wondered how she would relate to her cousins, slumming at Petras University with little by way of goals in life. Still, I had a tough time figuring out how stodgy, stiff-necked Richard ended up marrying someone with such a broad intellect and a delightful sense of humor. Love was indeed blind. Which explained Hera and me as well.

# — Sixteen —

The delegates, two per star system, began trickling in the next day. Arriving first were those whose governments had splurged for a civilian aviso, a type of starship whose mass was mostly oversized hyperdrives mated to a tiny hull. They could reach the highest hyperspace bands and were the fastest vessels in known space, albeit short on creature comforts. And for those who were sensitive to such things, like me, pushing the outer envelope of hyperspace, where reality became blurry, traveling aboard one would often generate disturbing aviso dreams, some of which almost felt prescient.

The avisos, and over the following days, the small starships chartered by the respective governments, landed at the Petras spaceport, where a police escort met the delegates and whisked them to the Celadon Resort and Spa. By the end of the week, representatives from every OutWorld and colony had arrived. While their governments had officially mandated the former, those sent by the latter were in a more nebulous position since none of the colonial administrations had received authorization to take part. The colonies were still firmly under Earth's control, or in a few remaining cases, that of Home Worlds. Yet all of them had also sent delegates representing the various movements seeking to declare independence and attain sovereign star system status.

We kept our distance, of course. That my troopers were training in the general area of the Celadon Resort was unimportant, as far as the locals were concerned. My Constabulary liaison officer speaking with the police superintendent charged with the resort's security came under the heading of informal talks. Not that anyone noticed Chief Warrant Officer Kine since she wore civilian clothes, just like many of the police officers assigned to the operation.

By the time our second Saturday on Mykonos rolled around, all the delegates had arrived and played tourists before the opening session on Monday. I took Saga to meet Uncle Attar on Sunday, though I left the uniform behind this time, as did she. Attar was visibly delighted and emotional at meeting my daughter, and they got along as well as I'd hoped.

Monday morning at oh-eight-hundred, President Van Kirten opened the convention to great fanfare, an event broadcast around Mykonos and through the subspace news network. He made an impassioned plea for the delegates to decide on constitutional amendments that would reset the relationship between the sovereign star systems and Earth and give the Commonwealth a renewed lease on life. The alternatives, he said, were unthinkable.

And if that wasn't a warning for the federal government to pay attention rather than dismiss the whole thing, I didn't know what it was. And yet, it came too late.

"The SecGen sent a message to President Van Kirten and asked that it be played in front of all delegates before he opens the convention."

Kal, who'd just come back from meeting with various Mykonos officials, including the president, dropped into the chair across from my desk. As always, when playing on the political side, he wore an elegant business suit that made him look like anything but a Marine.

"Missed his timing on that. Did Eugene show it to you?" I sat back in my chair and studied him. Something about his tone and choice of words told me Brüggemann's missive might be incendiary.

"Oh yes. Gudrun and I sat with him as he played it."

"And?"

"Van Kirten doesn't want the delegates to see it, and Gudrun is hesitant."

"It's that bad?"

"I don't know who advised Brüggemann to make the speech, let alone who wrote it, but if I were his chief of staff, I'd fire everyone involved. Frankly, the fact he made it gives me cause to wonder not only about his fitness for office but his sanity." Kal grimaced. "To call the SecGen's words inflammatory isn't doing them justice by any stretch. That speech alone could push the delegates into abandoning a moderate approach."

I cocked an eyebrow. "Will you let me watch it? Or leave me to wonder. And what's your opinion about letting the delegates hear Brüggemann's inflammatory inanities?"

A crooked smile appeared. "Nice alliteration, Zack. I'd rather hear your opinion first."

He pulled a data wafer from his jacket's inner pocket and tossed it on my desk. "Since your daughter is our political intelligence analyst, she should see it, too."

"Hang on." I picked up the wafer and placed it on my desktop reader, which talked to a segregated network separate from that of Fort Monash and any unit outside my brigade. Then I pinged Saga and asked her to come over. She showed up less than ninety seconds later.

"Sirs. What's up?"

Kal repeated his earlier summary for her benefit, and I could see Saga's eyes widen, albeit minutely, as she listened.

When he was done, he nodded at me. "Go ahead and play the thing, Zack."

I tapped a control, and the office's primary display to my right lit up. We all turned and settled in while the Commonwealth government's coat of arms appeared. Broderick Brüggemann standing at a lectern, quickly replaced it with the massed flags of the sovereign star systems arrayed behind him, flanking the Commonwealth's blue and silver banner. He looked older and more bloated than I remembered. But as he spoke, his voice held the same strength as before.

"The remarks I will shortly make are addressed to the delegates attending the so-called constitutional convention on Mykonos and through them to their respective governments." He paused, eyes staring intently at the video pickup. "First, let me remind you that the constitution of our Commonwealth has a mechanism to address change, and triggering it requires two-thirds of the Senate voting in favor of opening said constitution up for discussion. Second, the senators themselves are appointed delegates of the sovereign star systems to discuss amendments. Third, two-thirds of the sovereign star systems must assent to any amendment before it comes into force. Those three elements are at the heart of our system. Your assembly on Mykonos violates not only the spirit of what the framers of our constitution intended but the very words that govern the Commonwealth."

Another pause.

"Should you proceed as intended, you will be in breach of the highest law of humanity across the stars, and your actions will almost certainly be considered treason by the Supreme Court of the Commonwealth, should I seize it with this matter. Nothing is more important than the unity of our species in a hostile universe, and your attempt to circumvent the constitutional rules for crass partisan goals jeopardizes our unity. That cannot happen. And I will not allow it to happen. As a result, should this convention go ahead, the Department of Justice will lay charges against all participants, and the governments involved will be sanctioned. We will arrest those who pretend to stand for colonies upon their return home.

"Make no mistake. I will not even give any proposals from this unlawful assembly a moment's consideration. And I can already tell you that any motion put before the Senate to open the constitution for debate per the law will fail."

The screen faded to black, and I let out a low whistle.

"Could Brodrick Brüggemann be slightly miffed?"

But when I glanced at my daughter to gauge her reaction, she wore a thoughtful expression.

# — Seventeen —

"Did anyone check the message for the proper origin and routing tags, General?" Saga asked.

"Yes. The Mykonos president's communications bureau. They do it with every incoming transmission for the government that originates outside this star system. If they found anomalies, they'd have said so. Why do you ask?"

"Because while it's convincing and looks like Brüggemann based on the latest images I saw of him, which weren't more than a few weeks old, I simply can't believe he would utter threats in such a manner. It's completely uncharacteristic, and yes, people do change, but not this drastically. Brüggemann always used soft speech and a swift, hidden dagger. Outright hostility and public attempts at intimidation just aren't in the man's nature. His words, his intonations, and his gestures, even the staging behind him, belong to a pre-diaspora autocrat, not the head of a twenty-sixth-century republican government, no matter how much he wishes to centralize power in his office."

"So, you figure it's an artificial creation, then, a false flag?"

"That's what my gut instinct is screaming at me right now, General. Faking the origin and routing tags, even government encryption, isn't that difficult. Dad and Hera spent years doing it to bamboozle the opposition."

"Assuming you're right, once word gets back to Earth, the SecGen's office will deny the message and supply proof. Then what?" I asked.

"Once the delegates see this, it won't matter whether the speech is genuine or a complete fabrication. The damage will have been done because it's what they expect from the Commonwealth government. How about the S2 section analyzing the transmission to find clues about its true origin? If I'm wrong, then so be it. But if I'm right, we have more problems on our hands than we reckoned."

I nodded as my gut spoke to me the way it usually does when trouble was coming.

"I agree with Saga. The more I think about it, the more I figure there's something off. You saw Van Kirten and Liang's reactions, Kal. Imagine a hall full of delegates feeling the same outrage and feeding off each other's emotions. If this is a false flag, it's designed to push the secessionist agenda."

My daughter smiled at me. "Precisely. The speech is intended to enrage the delegates, and such anger entails a loss of critical thinking. In other words, it could be a carefully crafted psychological operation that doesn't support any agenda Earth might be following. Or at least, I can't think of a good reason they'd do this."

"Okay. I'll speak with Van Kirten and Liang when we're done here and ask them to sit on it until the S2 section completes its analysis. Both might be secessionists in their heart of hearts, but I doubt this is the way they'd want to go about it. Forging a new future based on a lie makes for dangerously shaky foundations, and both are intelligent enough to understand that."

"Are you sure you're reading them clearly, Kal?"

"Clearly enough. You'll just have to trust my judgment on this."

"As we say on Mykonos, fair dinkum."

Saga stood and reached for the data wafer. "Can I take this and put it to the question?"

I gestured at it. "Go."

She grabbed the tiny storage device, slipped it into her tunic breast pocket, then drew herself to attention. "With your permission?"

Since it was my office and not Kal's, I nodded. "Dismissed, Captain."

Once she was gone, Kal gave me his usual stare. "What do you really think, Zack? False flag or not?"

"No idea. But I can tell you that releasing the speech to the delegates without warning them beforehand will not end well for anyone."

***

Just as I was about to call it a day, Saga pinged me with a request to report on the matter of the speech. Kal had gone back into town for another round of schmoozing with the high and mighty — I did not know how an honest Special Forces officer could stomach that much — and so I called her over.

Saga, for those who knew her well, seemed a tad excited when she entered my office. Anyone who didn't know her would have thought she was coming to report on the weather. But she was a Decker, and I knew my own flesh and blood.

"So?" I asked as she dropped into a chair across from me.

"Fake, through and through. We found enough markers to prove the routing tags were forged and that the Brüggemann in the video sequence was an AI avatar put together with bits of real speech videos. The Mykonos communications security folks would have figured it out if they'd kept analyzing. Unfortunately, they passed it up the line too early, and who enjoys admitting they screwed up?" Saga's smile said volumes about how the intelligence analyst in her viewed the foibles of mere humans. "But for a fake, it's high quality and was professionally done. It would certainly have achieved the desired effect if it had been released before we could authenticate the origin."

"Excellent work."

I pulled out my communicator and, not knowing what Kal was doing at that moment, sent a quick message saying Saga was right — the flag was false. Hopefully, he could convince Eugene and Gudrun Liang they were being played and quarantine the damned thing before it leaked.

"Any thoughts on who's behind this?"

"The natural conclusion would be secessionists, whether from Mykonos or another OutWorld. They all have an increasingly vocal faction clamoring for separation from the Commonwealth. We're trying to trace the message's actual routing, but I doubt we'll pinpoint the origin."

"Why does your use of the term 'natural conclusion' make me wonder?"

A faint smile danced on her lips.

"Because you spent enough time in intelligence to trust nothing at first glance."

"So enlighten me. What other possibilities do you see?"

"A trick by the opposition to discredit the secessionists by making everyone assume they were carrying out a false flag operation aimed at stampeding the delegates into abandoning the idea of constitutional reform. The Sécurité Spéciale would have known we'd figure out the message was a fake quickly enough."

"In that case, they're playing with badly contained antimatter. What if the speech had gotten out and pushed the delegates into the secessionists' arms by creating a furor against Earth? Hoping we'd intercept the message and debunk its supposed origins seems pretty reckless."

Saga nodded.

"Without question. But you may have noticed Earth and the government agencies, including the Sécurité Spéciale, aren't even trying to mitigate the disruptive second and third-order effects of policies and actions aimed at taking power away from sovereign star system legislatures and centralizing it in Geneva."

"It's been going on since before you joined the Corps. Okay. I'll buy the possibility the opposition is being overly cute with its schemes. They've done it often enough before."

"Of course, there's another possibility, and it involves one or more third-party actors attempting to manipulate the conflict between the star systems and Earth for their own gain."

I grimaced.

"You mean the interstellar zaibatsus? Definitely a possibility. I wouldn't put it past ComCorp and its ilk. They have the in-house intelligence services to do so. ComCorp drove the last attempt to weaken the OutWorlds until I put their Coalition out of business. If the federal and star system governments are quarreling, they're not paying attention to what the zaibatsus are doing in the colonies, on the outposts, and on the frontiers."

"Exactly what I'm thinking, Dad."

Before I could reply, my communicator chirped. It was Kal. I placed the device on my desk and activated it.

"*Mon général*, I'm with Saga going over her findings and discussing potential culprits. We've come up with three possibilities so far."

"Excellent. We can discuss it in person shortly, so you and Saga get cleaned up and put on your best civilian clothes. We're having supper with President Van Kirten and Secretary Liang in the president's private residence at eighteen hundred. The guard post will expect you aboard an unmarked Mykonos Regiment staff car."

"*À vos ordres, mon général.*" I sketched a salute even though we were on audio only, and my daughter grinned.

"Until then. Ryent, out."

"You heard the man. Get a hold of our loaner and pick me up in front of the senior officers' quarters at seventeen-thirty. And before you do that, send the recording and your analysis results off to Hera. She'll see the right people work on it."

She stood, came to attention, and sketched the same salute I had since she was bareheaded. "*¡A sus órdenes, mi Coronel!*

I gave Saga a sharp look because though her Spanish was flawless, I knew her intent was to tease me for using French with Kal. Well, two could play that game.

"*¡Rompan filas, Capitán!*"

At least she had the grace to execute a perfect about-turn and march out of my office, leaving me to smile at her receding back. A chip off the old blockhead indeed, my daughter. And proficient in more human languages than I was.

Supper with the president. It should be interesting. I hadn't met my old schoolmate yet, and even though Kal said he held no grudges against me, meeting face-to-face might stir up some old memories.

# — Eighteen —

We pulled up to the residence's side gate — the main entrance was for state visitors only — at two minutes to six. It was a massive, ornate thing made to imitate wrought iron, though I suspected the alloy used had more in common with a starship's hull. Anything short of a heavily armored vehicle wouldn't have so much as dented it.

A guard wearing the Mykonos Police Service uniform beneath body armor emerged from the guardhouse to one side with a battlefield sensor in hand. He wore a large bore blaster at the hip, and I didn't need to see the telltales to know it was powered and loaded.

Saga and I held up our credentials, which he scanned from a distance before approaching the staff car.

"Colonel Zachary Decker and Captain Saga Decker, at the invitation of the president," my daughter said once the driver's side window was down.

The guard studied us for a few seconds while glancing at his sensor several times. Then, he nodded once, straightened to attention, and saluted, which I knew was the signal to his mate in the guardhouse and the officers in the security operations room we were the right people at the right time. The gate slid aside soundlessly.

"Please follow the arrows to the visitor's parking space. An attendant will greet you there and take you to your destination."

"Thank you," Saga replied with a smile.

We drove through the gate and followed lit arrows, taking us to what I realized was a secluded parking lot far from prying eyes. The private residence, less than three kilometers away from Government House, where the president and his staff worked, was a single-story building with more wings than a Narakan hexadragon. Topped by a red metal roof, the white-walled structure was mostly surrounded by a covered veranda broad enough to land combat dropships. Trees, bushes, and flowers grew in profusion everywhere, turning the estate into something that resembled the tropical resorts further south more than the home of the star system's head of government.

When we slipped into our assigned parking, I noted another unmarked Mykonos Regiment staff car and a sleek, sporty red speeder that precisely matched Gudrun Liang's personality as I perceived it, which meant she and Kal had already arrived.

By the time I climbed out, a staff member in a high-collared white jacket and black trousers had materialized at the edge of the lot. When he met my eyes, he bowed his head.

"Colonel Decker, Captain Decker, if you'll please follow me. President Van Kirten is expecting you in the small reception room. General Ryent and Secretary Liang have already arrived."

I felt like telling him I'd noticed, but why? The guy was only doing his job. He didn't need smart ass Marine colonels discussing the merits of ignoring the obvious.

"Thank you."

We walked along a flower-lined path behind the attendant to the side door — as with the main gate, only state visitors entered the front door — which opened onto a spacious lobby. It had a sand-colored tile floor, white walls bearing paintings of Mykonos nature scenes, and a few polished wooden benches beneath them. Since we had no overcoats to shed, the man led us into a wide corridor with open doors dotting one side and floor-to-ceiling blast-proof windows on the other. We turned left at the first intersection, toward the residence's rear, and stopped at the next open door.

The man stepped through and announced, "Colonel Decker and Captain Decker, Mister President." Then he ushered us in. Eugenius Van Kirten, Gudrun Liang, and my boss were standing, glasses in hand, by a pair of French doors giving out on a secluded patio.

Eugene — no one at school called him Eugenius, though he drew the line at the even shorter Gene — was a tall drink of water with thick dark hair, a handsomely craggy face, and a politician's smile. He placed his glass on the nearest flat surface and advanced toward us, hand outstretched.

"Zack. How great to see you again after so long. And with a daughter who's also a Marine officer." His voice, always smooth, deep, and mellow, had taken on a further tinge of charm if that was even possible.

"Mister President." We shook like old friends and not the wary opponents we were during our last year in high school. "You look like you're prospering beyond your wildest dreams."

"Oh, I am. And based on what Kal told me, you're prospering beyond anything you dreamed of." He turned to my offspring and shook her hand. "Saga, it's an immense pleasure to meet you. Your father must be so proud. I can't believe my trouble-making classmate raised such a talented daughter."

"A pleasure to meet you as well, Mister President. Dad told me about you and him during your teenage years."

"Only good things, I hope." Eugene's smile couldn't have been more dazzling.

Saga returned the smile, measure for measure. "Dad speaks his mind, sir."

Eugene let out a bark of laughter. "He hasn't changed, then. Can I offer you an apéritif? Gin and tonic, Saga? And a Shrehari Ale for Zack? Or has my intelligence service got it wrong?"

"No, sir. It's spot on."

We joined Kal and Liang by the French doors while Eugene picked up his glass and nodded our hellos. The same attendant who guided us appeared moments later with a tray holding our beverages. We barely had time for toasts when the door opened, and a tall, auburn-haired woman of approximately my age walked into the room with an energetic stride. Piercing blue eyes framed a narrow nose, both set in a lean face showing worry lines around the nose and mouth. I recognized her from the S2 briefings — Ellie Pierce, the Director General of the Mykonos Security Intelligence Service. I knew without asking that Kal had overridden the compartmentalization principle with which we began our mission. We were now all in with openly, if not yet publicly, ensuring the convention's security.

"My apologies for being late, Mister President." Pierce had a low alto that was ideal for projecting menace during interrogations.

"It is a last-minute get-together, Ellie. No apologies are necessary. A drink?"

"I could murder for a gin and tonic, sir." Pierce turned toward us. "And you must be the Marine Corps Deckers. A pleasure to finally meet you."

As we shook, our eyes met, and I immediately knew she was no pushover, let alone a mere senior bureaucrat. I'd seen her type before and made a mental note to take extra care with anything I said or did in her presence.

"Likewise, Madame Pierce."

"Ellie, please. Since your boss and mine seem to have decided we would now gloss over the pretense and work together, we might as well skip formalities."

"Then it's Zack, please. Not Zachary. Only my parents and grandparents call me that."

"And you're still on the outs with them. Understood." She offered her hand to Saga. "I understand you're the mission Naval Intelligence Liaison Officer rather than an S2 staffer and have been attached to your father's command from Naval Intelligence HQ for this operation."

"Yes, ma'am."

"And your specialty is interstellar politics, correct?"

"Yes."

The attendant returned with a single glass, and once he was gone, Eugene said, "Saga is the reason we're having a quiet working supper, Ellie. She's the one who figured out Brüggemann's speech was a fake, and we need to figure out the next steps, fast, before it leaks and causes turmoil we can't afford. The convention has barely started as it is."

Pierce glanced at my daughter again. "You're sure of that?"

"As certain as any analyst can be, ma'am."

"My people are still dissecting it, but I understand Naval Intelligence has access to better tools and assets than we do. Not that it matters. Even if it weren't a fake, the damage that recording might do is incalculable, so we can't allow its release. But I'm eager to hear what you found."

"We all are," Eugene said. "So far, only Zack knows about the results of Saga's analysis. And before our Marines ask, this room, like most of the residence, is protected from listening devices and swept weekly by Ellie's countermeasures section."

"Thank you, sir," I replied, smiling, "but the enemy already knows about the recording. It's our side we need to keep in the dark. Do you want Saga to brief us now or when we're sitting?"

"Let's start now. We can discuss the next steps over the evening meal."

I nodded at Saga, who explained, in detail, what made the speech a fake. Some of her terminologies went right over Eugene and Liang's heads, so she had to backtrack and explain a few times, but when she was done, Pierce nodded.

"Well done, Captain. Would you mind sending me a copy of the report so my people can learn something from Naval Intelligence?"

"Certainly, ma'am."

"And now, how do we deal with this?" Eugene asked before draining his glass. "Let's go next door and sit around the dining table. I've ordered a selection of souvlaki skewers cooked over charcoal for us. The presidential chef is an absolute treasure, so they'll be excellent."

We imitated Eugene, then his attendant opened the connecting door to the small dining room, and we filed through. As with the reception room we were in, it was cozy, with simple furnishings, wood floors and wainscoting, and paintings gifted to succeeding presidents over the decades. A small chandelier above a table capable of seating twenty gave everything a soft glow.

Eugene took his place at the head of the table with Saga and me on his left and Kal and Ellie Pierce on the right. No sooner were we seated that a pair of house staffers entered from another door carrying trays bearing soup bowls, our first course. They served, then one of them took an open wine bottle from a sideboard and filled our glasses. It was a Western Mykonos white with just a hint of natural fizz. Hera would have loved it.

"Please dig in, folks."

We exchanged small talk while eating the soup — it wasn't the sort of appetizer that allowed profound discussions — though the former intelligence operative in me noticed that Ellie Pierce's questions for my daughter and me were anything but trivial. She'd obviously read the dossiers her people prepared on Kal and us and was probing for more personal information like a good spymaster. Since I was married to one of the most fearsome in the business, I couldn't help but approve.

Once the main dish was served and the red wine poured, Eugene took a bite, declared the grilled chicken skewer to be perfection itself, and washed it down with a sip of wine.

"So. Who wants to start the discussion of what next with that recording? I think we agree Saga made a compelling argument for it being a false flag operation designed to roil the convention. The big unknown is by whom, but it doesn't matter in our discussion. I'll leave finding the culprit to Ellie's and your people, Kal. If Saga could figure out it was a fake, I'm sure her Naval Intelligence colleagues can trace it."

"Everything we know is off to HQ with the overnight military subspace packet," Saga said. "And if I may?"

Eugene gestured at her to go ahead.

"When you don't release the recording to the delegates, I think whoever's behind this will do so instead, which means you won't control the timing or the circumstances, sir."

Eugene nodded.

"That makes sense. You think we should release it after making clear to the delegates that it's a fake designed to influence them."

"Yes, sir."

"Opinions?" He glanced at the rest of us.

"She's right," Kal said. "And I'm a little embarrassed I didn't think of it."

"Agreed," Liang and Pierce both replied.

"Zack?"

"My daughter has yet to be wrong about anything concerning this mission. That's why Intelligence assigned her as my NILO. I'd say go with her suggestion. And do it tomorrow at the start of the day's proceedings. The opposition got inside our observe-orient-decide-act loop, what we Marines call the OODA loop. We need to correct that and get inside theirs."

"So be it. How about we sit together after our meal and craft a statement for Gudrun to issue in the morning before showing the fake speech?"

# — Nineteen —

Once the dessert plates had been removed and a second round of coffee served, Eugene led Liang, Kal, and Saga next door to compose the statement, leaving Ellie Pierce and me to contemplate each other across the now-empty dining table. Apparently, neither of us was deemed necessary, which suited me fine.

I was struck once more by how much of a predatory aura she gave off — it was something I found irresistible. There was a time when I would have tried a little of the old Decker charm on her, just for kicks, but it was one of the many habits I gave up years ago.

"Did you start in the Security Intelligence Service, or did you have a life before becoming a spook?"

She gave me a faint smile that didn't even come close to reaching her eyes. "I'm more of a spook chaser. And I'm surprised you don't know about my past. Didn't you read the dossier your people have on me?"

"Oh, I did. But it's sparse. You've kept your life story well hidden. Congratulations."

The smile turned into a very brief smirk — had I blinked, I'd have missed it. "Thank you. Coming from a former spook, that's quite a compliment."

"So, you've read my dossier."

"It's also a little sparse on details. But we know all about your childhood and the break with your family. Your career until you transferred to the reserve as a warrant officer is also documented, if not in detail. Whatever drove you to take a hiatus after making command sergeant so quickly? It seems a little out of character. And why did the Corps make you a warrant officer when you moved to the inactive list?"

My records had been amended to erase several unpleasant incidents courtesy of my now-wife after I returned to active duty with Naval Intelligence. As far as anyone who didn't witness those incidents was concerned, my record was spotless.

I gave her a knowing wink. "That would be telling."

Pierce's faint smile returned. "An undercover assignment, then. Now, here's the interesting part of your dossier. After returning to active duty as a chief warrant officer, you were posted to Fleet HQ in Sanctum but with no further mention of your assignments. However, you were eventually commissioned as a major. The next time your records were updated was your promotion to lieutenant colonel and posting to the 1st Special Forces Regiment. So there's a big blank in your life, which must be tied to Naval Intelligence field operations. After all, you married an intelligence rear admiral with whom you'd been in a relationship for some time."

"Nice and succinct." I raised my coffee cup in a silent toast, then drained it. "You know more about me than I about you. Care to even the score, Ellie?"

"Not particularly, but since we'll be working together now that your boss tossed aside the Fleet's plausible deniability blanket, I'll tell you a bit about myself." She finished her coffee as well. "Shall we take a stroll in the residence garden? It's delightful at this time of the evening, and we can't be overheard there either."

She was obviously a frequent visitor because she unerringly led me to a set of French doors giving onto a terrace bordered by lush vegetation. The scents of the night flowers, now open to their fullest, tickled my nostrils and brought back old memories — my mother enjoyed the same species and filled the old homestead's backyard with them. We headed side by side for a stone path disappearing between dense bushes.

"All right," Pierce finally said once we were beyond the light spilling from the residence windows. "You're obviously aware I was born on Mykonos, am single, and have no offspring. I have some family in Thera over on Karinth — parents, one brother, a few uncles, and aunts. I joined the Mykonos Police Service after graduating from university and spent four years as a patrol officer. The Security Intelligence Service recruited me — we target law enforcement members who show potential as investigators — and I've been an intelligence officer ever since. That's it."

"It seems we have matching blanks in our work histories."

"A good thing we have decent pensions, too. Getting hired in the civilian world with a spotty resume after years in intelligence isn't for the faint of heart."

"Unless you're looking for mercenary work." I gave her a sideways glance. "Or a job with the feds."

"Perish the thought on both ideas."

"Not keen on your federal counterpart, the Sécurité Spéciale?"

"The agency that doesn't officially exist?" She let out a brief snort. "Now, why would any OutWorlder want to join them? They live solely to expand the SecGen's and their own power over human-settled worlds. Would I be right in assuming you're familiar with their operations?"

"We've met frequently." I allowed myself a smile. "It never ended well for the Sécurité Spéciale."

"You realize they have agents on Mykonos."

"They have agents everywhere, even inside the Fleet and the star system law enforcement and security agencies, yours included. I imagine the local office is keeping a keen eye on the convention and plotting mischief to disrupt it."

"You imagine right, and yes, we're cognizant there are moles in the Service. How does the Fleet deal with its moles?"

"They become stars on the wall of honor at Sécurité Spéciale headquarters in Geneva. What is it you do?"

"We have caught none. But then, a small service like mine doesn't attract much attention."

"Until now."

Pierce nodded. "Probably. Not that we've had any new hires since they announced the convention."

"But you may have had sleepers who've now been activated."

She stopped to look at me. "Any tips on how we should deactivate them?"

I grinned at her. "Step one, identify the newly awakened moles."

"Ah, yes. Your dossier mentioned you had a propensity for being a smart ass from an early age. How does that work with your superiors and your spouse, the admiral?"

"It's one of my more endearing character flaws. I'm sure you have a few as well."

"Not that I'll ever tell." Her smile and throaty voice made her words sound more intriguing than they should have been. Or was I unconsciously using the old Decker charm, and she was responding? Never mind. Those days were long gone.

"So, what's the plan going forward? You'll assign a liaison officer to my HQ, or I to yours? My Constabulary liaison officer has been quietly working with the Police Service since before the first delegates arrived. I suppose we can make that an open collaboration now."

"Your daughter is perfect for the liaison job, Zack. She can be an intermediary between my Task Force Hancock and your brigade."

"Task Force Hancock? Is that your unit charged with protecting the convention?"

Pierce nodded. "And I have a liaison with the police as well. With you now stepping in openly, I guess that makes us part of a law enforcement *ménage à trois*."

And if that wasn't a double entendre, I didn't recognize what it was. Maybe I hadn't lost my touch.

"Okay. Saga will be our liaison to your task force. Just send me the contact over in your shop, and we'll put them together tomorrow morning." We resumed walking. "I'm glad Kal stopped screwing around with plausible deniability. It'll make our lives much easier."

"Will there be any blowback?"

"From the Fleet? No. Whatever Kal does is per his orders. From Earth? What would they do to him? Only the Grand Admiral can dismiss flag officers. The SecDef and the SecGen have no say in the matter."

"I was more thinking kinetic blowback from the SecGen's hired guns."

"They wouldn't dare target a major general. At least not the current Sécurité Spéciale director general. He knows an all-out war with the Fleet will end in his abject defeat. Although that didn't stop the last director general of the Sécurité Spéciale's predecessor agency from going all out. You never fully grasp what the sort of sociopaths who make it into high office will do once their options become limited. But I wouldn't worry about Kal."

The meandering path had brought us back to the terrace, and we re-entered to find Eugene, Gudrun Liang, Kal, and Saga still rearranging words to find the best way of telling delegates who distrusted Earth that the latter wasn't guilty of the latest outrage.

"Shall we raid the president's private brandy reserve?" Pierce asked, throwing me a mysterious glance when we realized we weren't wanted as a test audience just yet.

"You can do that?"

"He doesn't mind."

She led me down the corridor to a small library overlooking the garden. There, she headed straight for a liquor cabinet and pulled out what I quickly identified as a bottle of Issos Castle, 20-year-old XO, the most expensive on the planet.

"Nice. And Eugene lets his head spook partake at her leisure?"

She winked at me. "One of the perks of office. Had it before?"

"No. The Old Man kept a private stock, but Richard and I weren't allowed to touch it until he decided we were mature enough. I think he figured no one under twenty should drink something older than they were, and I left at eighteen."

"So, this will be your first time." Once we both had a snifter in hand, Pierce raised hers. "To our collaboration."

"Hear, hear."

But instead of immediately taking a sip, we both inhaled the rich aroma, then lifted the snifters to our lips.

"So?" She asked.

"If you want the truth? Sure, this is a smooth drink. But I've had brandy from all over the Commonwealth and can't see it being worth the price tag or the reputation compared to other vintages, like the high-end cognacs from Dordogne."

"It will crush the president to hear that."

"It wouldn't be the first time I disappoint Eugene."

"So I've read. But it seems he's forgiven you."

"A successful politician can't afford to keep minor grudges."

"Unlike a successful businessman?" She gave me that amused look again. "No need to answer, Zack. By now, everyone who's anyone has a betting pool over whether you'll be welcomed back as the prodigal scion and, if so, when."

I scoffed. "No doubt."

We wandered over to the tall windows looking out on the garden, and sipped the brandy in companionable silence, side by side. Ellie Pierce was almost as tall as me, and somehow, after watching her move all evening, I understood that under the severe business suit, she'd be as fit as any of my Marines, unlike so many senior bureaucrats, uniformed or civilian. Her faint scent was vaguely floral but in an understated, almost mysterious way, just as I prefer.

In fact, she reminded me very much of Miko Steiger, an old friend with whom I'd shared a few adventures and the odd private bunk during my field operative days. I briefly wondered how she was doing as the Naval Intelligence disinformation conduit to the Sécurité Spéciale on Earth. Last I'd heard, she was still wrapping that agency's director general around her little finger, just like she had done with me for a time.

"Lost in thought, Zack?"

"Thinking about old friends. Brandy has that effect." Sensing her eyes were on me, I glanced at her.

"Or is it I remind you of someone?"

"Vaguely. A colleague who saved my ass once or twice during hairy missions."

We heard footsteps behind us, and a voice said, "The president asks that you join him and the others in the small salon."

Pierce raised her glass again. "Here's to hairy missions." Then she slammed down the rest of her Issos Castle like it was a shot of cheap Tiryns rum.

The only thing I could do was imitate her. A shame for the brandy. I was getting to like it.

"Ah." Eugene waved us into the room. "Our audience has arrived. Did you enjoy the Issos Castle, Zack?"

"Absolutely, Mister President." How he knew we'd hit his expensive booze wasn't something I could ask, although maybe he was aware Pierce made a habit of raiding the stash in the private library and figured she'd lead me astray.

"Then you and Ellie should take a seat on the sofa. Gudrun will read the statement, and I'd like your unvarnished critique."

It was short, to the point, and with none of the obfuscating words politicians and bureaucrats loved to use, so one could never hold them responsible for anything. I saw Kal's hand in crafting the statement and perhaps even

Saga's. Either way, the delegates would recognize the Mykonos government didn't believe it was genuine but a ruse designed to sow dissension. Since Mykonos was an acknowledged leader in the OutWorld movement, it enjoyed more credibility than most.

"And when they inevitably ask who would send such a fake, what will you answer, Madame Secretary?"

She smiled at me. "That we cannot fathom the origin and the convention speculating at length about the matter could go far in achieving the aims of the people behind it, namely causing disruption."

I nodded. "Fine by me. Ellie?"

"I agree with Zack. And I think General Ryent, Zack, and I should attend in the morning as spectators to gauge the reactions." She glanced at Saga. "And Captain Decker, since she's now the Armed Forces liaison to the Service's task force watching over the convention."

I turned to Kal and my daughter. "You both good with that? It makes the most sense."

"Fine by me," Kal replied. He gave her his habitually amused look. "And since we're Saga's superior officers, I'm sure it'll be fine by her."

"Sir, yes, sir."

# — Twenty —

The following day at oh-seven-thirty, I gathered the brigade's command group and announced that as senior Commonwealth Armed Forces officer in the Mykonos star system, General Ryent had agreed to President Van Kirten's request for aid to the civilian power. In other words, the 1st Special Forces Brigade and the Mykonos Regiment would help his government in securing the constitutional convention, beginning with the execution of the deployment plan prepared by the S3 the previous week, so we'd be in place ahead of the day's session which began at ten.

As I finished speaking, Josh Bayliss and Lora Cyone glanced at each other. Then the former pulled out a credit chip and slid it over to the latter.

"By how many days did you miss it, Josh?"

"Two. Lora got it the closest of us."

"All of you?" I looked around the table at the squadron and battalion commanders, my sergeant major, and the principal staff officers.

"As senior among us, Josh was holding the bets," Lora replied for her colleagues while an amused smile danced on her thin lips.

"And you nailed it to the day."

She nodded once. "Luck, more than anything else. But I speak for everyone when I say it's a relief."

"Yep," Josh chimed in. "My people are just itching to wade in and beef up the police's close protection perimeter. They're trying hard, but if the opposition makes a concerted effort, they'll get through. The Mykonos cops have little experience dealing with the sort of people we usually face. So, what precipitated it?"

"Ah. You're going to enjoy this." I tapped the controls embedded in the conference table, and the primary display at the far end of the room lit up with the fake SecGen speech.

My people watched in stunned silence until the end, then they turned toward me.

"What the fuck was that, Colonel?" Josh finally asked.

"A good fake with rather badly masked fake routing tags. It landed in President Van Kirten's classified message queue yesterday. He immediately gave it to General Ryent, who turned it over to me. The S2 section gave it a thorough analysis and determined, with almost one hundred percent certainty, that it was a fake. Last night, we had a working supper with the president to decide the next steps. And one of those steps was him formally asking the general for Armed Forces support."

Josh nodded. "Because that fake is from someone who wants to screw up the convention, and who knows what step two will be once the delegates see the speech."

"Right. At ten this morning, Secretary Liang will show the recording to the delegates and tell them it's not real but something concocted by parties unknown to disrupt proceedings and sow dissension." I went on to lay out the possibilities we'd discussed the day before.

When I was done, Josh leaned forward.

"How about an added possibility? Could this fake speech have been, at least in part, to smoke us out and put the Fleet, or even just General Ryent and us, on the federal government's shit list for disobeying orders from the very top? Because if so, mission accomplished. We should hear from Earth within the next forty-eight hours."

"The Grand Admiral will hear from Earth. If anything comes directly to the general, I think he'll pass it up the chain and let the sender know he's done so per regulations. But your idea is plausible." I turned to Corinne Renaud. "Add it to the intelligence packet and let Saga know. I'll advise the general."

"Yes, sir."

"Two last points before we break, Chief Warrant Officer Kine's appointment as our liaison to the Mykonos Police Service is now official. That means she'll be reporting to me directly for the duration. As of this morning, Captain Decker is our official liaison with the Mykonos Security Intelligence Service's Task Force Hancock, which is charged with the security of the convention. If there are no more questions or comments, let's activate Operation Barrier and show the galaxy it's not just fun and games anymore."

I looked around the table but saw nothing more than silent nods acknowledging my orders.

"All right. Thank you. Operation Barrier is a go."

They stood as I rose, left the conference room, and headed for Kal's office. He'd be meeting with Secretary Liang at the resort before the opening of the day's proceedings, so we still had a bit of time to talk. His door was open, and I stuck my head inside.

"Got a moment, General?"

"Yep." Kal gestured at a chair across from him. "Everything sorted?"

"Operation Barrier is on. In a few minutes, Chief Warrant Officer Kine will receive instructions for the Mykonos Police Service chief superintendent in charge of the convention site security, letting him know we're now his backup force rather than just informal advisers. Ghost Squadron's command post within the joint control center will be active when we get there."

And it was. My brigade had used the time between our arrival and the convention's opening gainfully, preparing and practicing plans for the most likely eventualities with the tacit help of the Mykonos authorities.

Chief Superintendent Sheila Parker, who headed the security effort, greeted Kal and me with a broad smile when our staff car pulled up to the joint control center in one of the resort's outbuildings. Designed as the planet's premier convention site, with purpose-built and equipped halls surrounded by a half dozen three- and four-story hotel wings, restaurants, recreational facilities, and other amenities, it covered several hectares of groomed parkland. An unobtrusive fence equipped with a sensor network surrounded the entire complex and its grounds, one patrolled at all hours by the security detail, which now included both Marine Light Infantry Battalions. Along with the police's Special Branch, Ghost Squadron would provide close protection of the delegates and a rapid response force.

"Good morning, General Ryent, Colonel Decker." She held out her hand. Tall, fit, tanned, and wearing a police tactical uniform, Parker exuded confidence.

"Good morning, Chief Superintendent. Our people are integrating seamlessly, I hope?" Kal asked.

"Oh, no worries, General. They showed up an hour ago and immediately set to it. The power of preparation on planning, eh?" Her toothy smile reappeared. "Chief Warrant Officer Kine did a bang-up job of getting us to know each other over the last two weeks. If you'll follow me, Lieutenant Colonel Bayliss is in the control center, along with Lieutenant Colonel Cyone and Major Delgado."

Kal gestured at the open door to what had been the ground keeper's storage building. "Lead on."

The control center did not differ from any other command post I'd seen in my career — walls covered in displays, workstations beneath them, with the senior watchkeeper's chair in the middle. In fact, it resembled a warship's bridge in many ways. Neighboring rooms would host the joint intelligence cell, the communications cell, the logistics cell, and various offices.

We'd established a process by which the police would provide the senior watchkeeper — after all, we were giving aid to the civil power, not running a military operation — and we, the deputy, one of the brigade's majors. Since Ghost Squadron's Erinye Company was taking the first official shift on close protection duty, Curtis Delgado sat in the deputy's seat.

Once everything was running smoothly, Josh and Lora would return to Fort Monash to avoid being in the way. Their companies would relay each other every eight hours while the 2nd MLI stayed in reserve, ready to tackle the unexpected or to reinforce the units on site. But I expected both to show up at random times to check on things. Just as I would do from now until we stood down after the convention wrapped up and the delegates left.

"Everything is good, Curtis?" I clapped the younger man on the shoulder. He's what I should have become if I'd had my youthful temper under better control.

He grinned at me. "So far. But we're only an hour in. Ask me again in three days, Colonel."

"I'll be asking you sooner than that."

We did the grand tour of the dispositions, not to learn about them or check the deployment of our troopers — Kal and I had approved all the plans a week after our arrival — but to show the flag and let everyone know we were on the job. If any delegates were watching from their rooms or the hall, they couldn't miss the armed Marines in battle dress, tactical harnesses, and helmets patrolling the grounds alongside Mykonos police officers. And they'd soon find out why.

At five minutes to ten, Kal and I, clad simply in battledress and blue beret, without the tactical accouterments, let alone weapons, left the control center and headed for the convention hall's main entrance, guarded by a pair of police officers. They scanned us and confirmed our credentials, even though it wasn't our first visit, and then snapped to attention and saluted.

As the senior of us two, Kal returned the compliment and entered ahead of me. Once in the high-ceilinged lobby, we took the broad spiral staircase leading to the mezzanine immediately to the right of the entrance. More police stood at the inner door to prevent anyone not accredited as a delegate from entering.

Saga was already leaning on the balcony's railing, gazing down at the floor where the seats facing the rostrum and the giant display were rapidly filling with men and women representing every OutWorld and colony. She pulled herself up when she sensed our approach and came to attention.

"Good morning, sir."

"Good morning, Saga," Kal replied. "All is well?"

"Yes, General. I met with the head of Task Force Hancock first thing and got the lines of communication established. He showed me around their setup, and I can't say I found anything that needed immediate improvement. They may not face huge security threats in this star system, but they're up to speed on the usual TTPs. As far as I could tell, Ellie Pierce hadn't shared the fake speech with them when we met, and they have nothing on their threat board. I'll be back with them after lunch to discuss intelligence sharing and contingency plans."

"Excellent, thanks."

I gave my daughter a quick wink. She'd rattled off her verbal summary like a pro. The change I saw in her from when we'd first reunited on Scandia until today still left me awe-struck.

The echoing sound of a gavel striking wood cut off any further words we might have had, and our attention turned to the rostrum below, where Secretary Liang was calling the assembly to order.

"Good morning," she said once the noise of individual conversations died away and all eyes were on her. "I trust you had a good night and are ready to face a day of deliberations. Before we start, I have a matter of the utmost importance to share. President Van Kirten received a message the day before yesterday purporting to come from Secretary General Brodrick Brüggemann. That message contained a speech by the SecGen addressed to us, the delegates, and was to be shown in this hall this morning. To call the words used in that speech inflammatory, derogatory, and downright libelous would be an understatement.

"However, as we do with such communications, especially when they appear abnormal — and no one who's watched Brodrick Brüggemann over his career would call the speech normal — we had it analyzed by the Mykonos Security Intelligence Service. Our people discovered the message and its contents didn't come from Earth, let alone the SecGen's office. The president asked General Ryent, the senior Commonwealth Armed Forces officer in the Mykonos system, for help in confirming our analysts' results, and he placed the resources of the 1st Special Forces Brigade at our disposal, including Naval Intelligence officers attached to the brigade's staff. They confirmed the Security Intelligence Service's findings."

I exchanged an amused glance with Saga. Turning the sequence of events around had been deliberate. The Mykonos Security Intelligence Service had more credibility in this assembly than anyone wearing a Commonwealth uniform.

"What this means is that parties unknown are trying to sabotage the constitutional convention via a false flag operation designed to increase the friction between our governments and Earth. It was only because an insightful analyst called the speech so uncharacteristic of Brodrick Brüggemann that it had to be a fake, as the in-depth analysis of the message finally proved. Who those parties might be still is in question. Our people and General Ryent's will continue working on the matter until we find the culprits. In the meantime, since this could be the first shot in a concerted campaign against the convention, which could easily escalate from disinformation to actual threats, President Van Kirten has asked that the Armed Forces aid our police under the federal aid to civil power legislation. As senior Armed Forces commander in the star system, General Ryent has agreed to the request, which is why you might have seen Marines patrolling with the Mykonos Police Service on the resort's grounds."

Liang glanced up at where we stood and nodded her thanks. As intended, this caused most delegates to turn and look at us. Kal almost seemed regal while returning her gesture with a nod of his own.

"I will now show you the recording. As you watch, remember that it's not Secretary General Brodrick Brüggemann on the display, that those are not his words, and that this does not reflect the federal government's policy. And, most importantly, that someone is trying to disrupt this convention. Once we've watched this fake, we will put it behind us and let the Security Intelligence folks do their thing. Then we'll get on with the day's agenda."

# — Twenty-One —

"Considering how they reacted, knowing Brüggemann's address to the delegates was a fake, I'm glad we figured it out beforehand. I can only imagine the chaos if they thought it was real."

Saga glanced at me as we took the stairs to the ground floor, leaving Kal on the mezzanine where he planned to stay for the day.

"And more than a few still acted as if there was a chance it could have been for real. That's how deep the distrust of Earth runs among the OutWorlds."

"I noticed."

We left the hall and headed for our car, intent on returning to Fort Monash. Once aboard, I asked, "Did you get any further insights on who might be responsible?"

She shrugged.

"I'm still thinking secessionists are our best bet. The problem is they're in every branch of the Mykonos government, even the Security Intelligence Service, which means there won't be much of a push among the locals to find out. And we don't have the resources or the access. I doubt the agents from Hera's division will do any better. But then, I figure it's not so much finding who hoisted this false flag. The deed is done, and the consequences will be what they are. I'm more concerned about what happens next now that the situation has evolved beyond what anyone expected."

"Especially Kal dropping the fig leaf without warning and getting us involved openly."

Saga nodded. "That will have surprised many people."

"But not my command team, apparently." She laughed uproariously when I told her about the bets while we drove through the outer perimeter gate.

"Figures. Who instigated it?"

"I didn't dare ask, but my money is on Josh. It's his style."

We ate an early lunch in the mess hall, then Saga returned to SIS headquarters for her afternoon meetings, and I got busy with the day's administrivia. That was the downside of this deployment. Kal got to enjoy the high-level stuff while everyone below me had a hand in carrying out the primary mission.

Yes, self-pity wasn't pretty, but this was one of the times when I wished I had a reason to loiter around the convention. However, Kal had made it clear he was the public face of the Armed Forces, and breathing down the necks of my company and unit commanding officers wasn't my style. I'd see action if there was trouble, but my job was to ensure nothing happened, leaving a tiny part of me conflicted.

But I needn't have worried about enforced idleness once I emptied my work queue and did my physical training for the day. I'd just signed off on the latest daily report for divisional HQ when the personal address on my communicator came to life with its soft chime. The only people on Mykonos I'd given it to was my sister-in-law and Uncle Attar, and it was neither of them. Otherwise, I'd see a name on the display. Everyone else called me at my official, meaning Fleet-issue address. The call was audio only, which suited me. I didn't enjoy an unknown, or perhaps too well-known face materializing in midair above my desk.

"Zack Decker."

"It's Richard."

Although I recognized my brother's voice, I couldn't help being a smart ass. He'd earned it by behaving as he did at the club.

"Sorry. Richard who? I'm not supposed to know anyone by that name on Mykonos."

"You haven't changed, have you? Don't make me regret doing this by being the same pain in the neck you were as a teenager."

"Doing what, Richard? Saying hello to your only brother long after he arrived on your patch? What happened? Did Delia finally get through your thick skull?"

I kept my tone light and amused. It would only aggravate him further. And no, I couldn't help myself. But I could picture him seething at the other end and clamping down on his temper before he spoke. Both of us had inherited the Old Man's short fuse, although it took me longer to learn self-control.

"If you promise to stop testing my patience, maybe I can explain why I'm calling."

"Alright. Let's start again. Hello, Richard. How nice to hear from you. To what do I owe the honor?"

A few heartbeats later, he replied, no doubt through clenched teeth. "Better. I understand you had supper with the president at his private residence last night. At least that's what grandfather says."

"Guilty. If it makes any difference, it was a working supper, and I was one of the lesser guests."

"Your daughter was there as well, correct?"

"Yes, and she was one of the more important guests. Don't let my higher rank fool you. She's the brains of the outfit."

"No doubt."

"So, what is this about? Does the Old Man object to Eugene breaking bread with me? Do you?"

"If by Old Man you mean Grandfather Thomas, then he's extremely curious why you were given the honor after he expelled you from the family long ago and made it known that those who refused to shun you would pay the price."

I let out a bark of laughter. "Let's see him take Eugene down a notch on the grounds of disobedience. That should go over well. So, what does he want? I assume you're calling me at his orders to act as his informant since he's too stubborn and mean-spirited to call me himself."

"Insulting grandfather won't help."

"Oh, right. He's either listening in on this call, or you're recording it for him. Hi there, you old bastard. I just want you to know I got the best revenge of all for your treating me as you did. I'm living well, surrounded by friends and colleagues I respect and trust with my life. I have a daughter who puts the rest of her generation in the extended clan to shame, and as an added bonus, I get to kill people. For that, I guess I owe you my thanks. My life as a zaibatsu drone wouldn't have been near as fulfilling."

"Are you done? And yes, he'll hear a recording of this conversation later."

"I'm done and thank you for that bit of honesty. Now, ask what the Old Man wants you to ask so we can move on."

"Why were you and your daughter dining with the president? Does it have something to do with the bombshell Secretary Liang released this morning and the president making a formal request to the Armed Forces for aid to the civil power?"

"Come on, Richard. You realize I can't discuss what happened in private conversation with the president and the others in attendance."

"So, I can take that as a yes?"

"You can take it any which way you want. I'm not allowed to comment."

"You were never shy about talking out of turn."

I let out a soft sigh.

"I'm not eighteen anymore, Richard. Colonels in the Marine Corps are expected to show impeccable discernment. Officers who can't, never get promoted that high. Sorry that your quest is a bust. But I would like us to sit together, break bread, and find a way back to being the brothers we were before the Old Man tore us apart. We're both grown men with successful careers, families, and the respect of our professional communities. To hell with our father and grandfather, Richard. We're brothers. We never were enemies before the Old Man threw me out. What do you say?"

"It will disappoint grandfather that you didn't see fit to share what happened at the president's private residence with your own family."

"I'm not part of your family, remember? Or is the Old Man an even bigger hypocrite than he was back then?"

"Goodbye, Zachary."

Richard cut the link, leaving me to shake my head at our grandfather's sheer gall. He knew I couldn't reveal what happened, sure, but invoking the sacred obligation to put family before president? Unbelievable. I shut my office, returned to my suite, and changed into exercise gear. A good long ten-kilometer run would sweat the annoyance out of me. It usually did. But thinking about the Old Man's anger when he heard the recording of the conversation with Richard would cheer me up even more.

That evening, I briefed Kal and my daughter, then promptly pushed the matter from my mind when the day's subspace packet arrived. Hera had sent me a private message. Finally. When I fell asleep that night, I believe it was with a smile.

The following days passed in a blur. Kal spent his time watching the deliberations from the hall's mezzanine. My troopers patrolled the site in shifts while Saga liaised with the SIS, Chief Warrant Officer Kine with the police, and no one with the undercover operatives my wife's division had sent in ahead of us. I made my daily appearance at the resort, chatted with Chief Superintendent Parker, said hello to whoever from the 1st Brigade sat in the deputy's chair, and walked the perimeter with the patrols. And I went in to sit with Kal and see if the delegates had progressed beyond voting on procedures. They hadn't. It seemed agreeing on the framework for debate was taking forever. Meanwhile, Earth would know about the false flag operation, as would the Sécurité Spéciale agents here and elsewhere.

Kal received daily encrypted missives from Fleet HQ, which he didn't share with us, and sent equally confidential reports to a coded address which I realized belonged to the Grand Admiral. He didn't share the content of those with me either.

Four days after I spoke with Richard, when the convention finally moved on to the first item on the list of constitutional amendments demanded by the OutWorlds, a formal invitation appeared in my message queue. It was addressed to Colonel Zachary Thomas Decker, Commonwealth Marine Corps, my name being followed by the post-nominals of my various decorations for valor. It commanded me and Captain Saga Decker, who hadn't yet earned post-nominals, to appear for dinner at Carnarvon Mansion, the Decker family homestead on the western outskirts of Petras, that very evening at eighteen-thirty. Yep. Commanded. It wasn't worded in such a way, but I understood an order when I saw one.

And it was signed Thomas Alban Decker. The Old Man himself.

# — Twenty-Two —

"Wonderful as usual, my dear Britta." Andreas Bauchan rolled over onto his side and contemplated Chief Warrant Officer Miko Steiger, who was now so used to her cover identity as Britta Trulson, she didn't have to think twice. In fact, she sometimes wondered whether she wasn't losing part of herself by being Trulson for such a long time, much longer than she or her superiors had expected.

"Yes, it was."

She turned onto her side as well, facing him, and ran an extended index finger along his jawline, smiling fondly. Bauchan was a sociopath, incapable of feeling empathy for others, but he faked it well with her, a testament to Steiger's seduction skills. She'd seen him in his official guise and had been frightened by the emptiness within him where ordinary people had a soul and the intensity with which he could focus.

"Something preoccupies you," Steiger said, placing her hand on his cheek. "I can always tell."

"Even when we make love?"

"Especially then."

"It's that blasted convention on Mykonos," he replied after a moment.

"Oh? What are those unpleasant people doing now?"

"That's what I'd like to know. Someone faked a speech by the SecGen addressed to the delegates and their governments. An inflammatory piece designed to drive a wedge between the delegates and the federal government. And it wasn't us. I don't know who's responsible for it."

"Do you have a copy of that speech?"

"Yes."

"I wouldn't mind watching it. Perhaps I can see something that might indicate its provenance."

"Sure. We can look at it later." Clearly, Bauchan was still basking in the afterglow and wasn't ready to get up yet.

"Is the SecGen aware of it?"

"Not yet. I intend to raise the matter tomorrow morning."

"Do you have any suspicions?"

Bauchan closed his eyes as she continued to caress him.

"As to who's responsible? My first suspicion is secessionists. They would gain by sowing dissension among the delegates."

He suddenly opened his eyes, sat up, and swung his legs over the side of the bed, then stood and retrieved his bathrobe from a nearby chair.

"Stay right where you are, my dear. I'll put on the fake speech, and you can tell me who you suspect."

Bauchan vanished for a few moments before reappearing just as the bedroom's primary display came to life. Steiger sat up and leaned against the headboard, heedless of the sheet falling away, while Brodrick Brüggemann appeared.

"The remarks I will shortly make are addressed to the delegates attending the so-called constitutional convention…."

When the brief speech was over, Steiger glanced at Bauchan, who'd taken the deep, comfortable chair by the side of the bed.

"Well, wasn't that special? It looked like the SecGen and sounded like him, but you're saying it's a fake?"

He nodded. "Yes. That was determined by the Mykonos folks in collaboration with the Fleet and confirmed by my people. It's an exceptionally good fake, though. Professionally done, with routing tags sufficiently masked to obscure its origin. If the intent was to enrage the delegates against the federal government, it failed. It was presented to them as a fake designed to interfere with the running of the convention and dismissed. But that someone went to the trouble of creating it worries me."

"And you're sure it wasn't anyone in or related to the government?"

Bauchan allowed himself a slight grimace. "No, I'm not. It could have been someone in the SecGen's office, just as it could have been one of the interstellar zaibatsus or the secessionists. But the latter are the ones with the most to gain."

"I agree, although the secessionist groups are tiny on any of the OutWorlds, some barely alive. We've been watching them for over a year now, and there's simply no appetite to leave the Commonwealth among most in the political classes, let alone the population."

Outright lying to Bauchan had also become second nature for Steiger, and she did so convincingly enough that she knew he believed her. After all, the Deep Space Foundation, an organization dedicated to promoting Centralist policies and happy to work with the Sécurité Spéciale, backed her.

"Strange. That's not what my people are saying."

"Oh? And what are they saying?"

"That while organized secessionist groups are small, the sentiment is growing both among politicians and the citizenry."

It wasn't the first time her reports didn't quite match what Sécurité Spéciale operatives told HQ, but she always successfully ascribed it to different ways of seeing things in the Rim Sector. She made a moue.

"And so it is, but the appeal of secession is still rather limited. That's why, the more I think about it, the more I'd ascribe the fake to secessionists."

Naval Intelligence would have a copy of the speech by now, but at least Steiger could report that it didn't originate on Earth, which was useful.

# — Twenty-Three —

"Are you sure he's not messing with us, Dad?"

"Not a hundred percent, no. But despite his many character flaws, the Old Man takes certain things seriously, and hospitality is one of them. He'd no more invite someone to humiliate them than I would mock the jump wings on your chest. And by commanding us to appear, he's acting as the patriarch of the Decker family, speaking to his progenies. Which means, for some reason, the Old Man has acknowledged our existence and our ties of blood."

I gave Saga a critical once-over as we spoke. We both wore silver-trimmed black service dress uniforms with rank insignia on shoulder boards, ribbons, and qualification badges on the left breast, and devices such as unit commendations on the right. Or at least I was. The only badge my daughter wore on her tunic other than the three pips of her rank were her jump wings. She hadn't been around long enough to get any medals or commendations. But the wings made a statement of their own, as did the winged dagger insignia on our berets and the miniature version thereof on either side of the opening in our tunics' high collars, backed by a square of maroon cloth, the color of Special Forces. Our trousers, bloused above calf-high, brilliantly polished boots, bore twin stripes of the same maroon on the outer seams.

My daughter had been inspecting me simultaneously, and obviously, I was presentable because she nodded once.

"Looking good, Dad. They're beyond hope if they're not impressed by your recruiting poster turnout, let alone the awards for valor at the top of your fruit salad."

"Well, the invitation had the abbreviations for them in the proper order of precedence after my name, so the Old Man will know what they are. He's a stickler for details and for protocol, a deadly combination when someone else makes a faux pas. Okay. You pass muster, kiddo. Let's go."

The staff car we'd ordered, marked as belonging to the Mykonos Regiment, was already waiting for us in front of my quarters, having come from the motor pool under AI control. As before, Saga climbed in on the driver's side, and I took the passenger seat.

After a leisurely thirty-five-minute drive, we turned off the side road and headed along the private lane leading to Carnarvon Mansion. Though the fence surrounding the main house was still a good kilometer away, hidden behind tall trees, we were already on land owned by Deckhan Enterprises. No one personally owned real estate in the extended clan. It was all property of the zaibatsu for obvious tax reasons and to keep black sheep such as me inheriting any and disposing of it out of sheer spite. Mind you, that is something I would have done so the Old Man's rules on real estate weren't so dumb.

Soon the high stone wall pierced by an ornate, wrought iron gate hove into view, and at our approach, the gate opened, which meant the security system had been told to expect us. Or someone entirely different who was scheduled to arrive at the same time. With the Old Man, who knew?

It didn't slam shut in our faces at the last minute, and we drove through manicured parkland toward the two-storied, u-shaped manor sitting at the center of the property, like a venomous arachnid of ancient fantasy stories. Clad in gray stone and topped by a peaked, verdigris copper roof, it seemed plucked from the estate of some nineteenth-century Northern European merchant with more money than aesthetic sense, which described the Old Man, who had it built to a tee.

The common rooms — reception, dining, kitchen, entertainment, etcetera — formed the center of the building, while the wings held the private suites of the inhabitants on one side and guests on the other. Behind it and hidden from our eyes were an indoor swimming pool, exercise facilities, and stables. Saga showed no reaction to the manor's gloomy magnificence, proving she'd scouted it moments after I relayed the Old Man's invitation.

I pointed at the row of expensive ground cars lined up on one side of the main doors in the spaces reserved for family members.

"Let's park this government issue clunker with all the showboats instead of the guest spots."

She gave me a sideways smile. "Making a gesture, Dad?"

"Always. Pay attention over the coming minutes, and if I don't give everyone a stroke right off, the next few hours. Gestures in the form of words, their meanings barely veiled, will be hurled at us fast and furious. Even now, many pairs of eyes are watching us on security monitors, judging, evaluating, dissecting, disparaging."

After stopping beside what I took to be Richard's car, we climbed out and adjusted our uniform tunics while glancing around, as Marines do when they arrive in an unfamiliar environment, even if the threats in this area of operations were social and not kinetic.

When we finally headed for the short flight of stairs and the entrance at a measured pace, the doors opened and a white-jacketed butler appeared in the foyer. He bowed his head when we crossed the threshold.

"Welcome home, Colonel Decker. And welcome to Carnarvon Manor, Captain Decker. My name is Bates.

"Thank you, Bates."

"You can leave your berets on the side table."

He pointed at one of the ornately carved pieces lining the foyer's walls. Like most common areas, it had a gray marble floor, blond wood wainscoting up to half height, and white walls dripping with artwork above. A glass chandelier hung from the high ceiling while a broad stone staircase wound its way up the far wall. The doors on either side of the staircase and those piercing the walls to our left and right stood open as well, but I couldn't tell where this tender family reunion was taking place. The Old Man had the embarrassment of choice.

Would it be the formal reception room where guests were entertained? Or would it be the smaller, cozier family-only living room? When Bates turned right, I knew it was the latter. Interesting.

"If you'll follow me."

The family room gave onto the back terrace; therefore, we walked down a short corridor before turning left and into another hall that cut through the width of the house and ended at yet another open door.

Bates passed through, stopped, and announced, "Colonel Zachary Decker and Captain Saga Decker, 1st Special Forces Brigade, Commonwealth Marine Corps."

He stepped aside to let us in, and after taking a deep breath, I entered. And there they were. My Grandfather, Thomas Decker, Grandmother Joanne Decker, my parents, Jack and Emily, and my brother Richard with his spouse, who was the only one smiling. I offered the Almighty a brief thanks for limiting the attendees to the bare minimum before stopping three paces in front of the Old Man and bowing my head at the neck. Saga, who stopped beside me a fraction of a second later, did the same.

"Zachary." The Old Man's voice had lost nothing of its strength and deep timbre over the years. But though he remained tall and big-boned, he seemed sunken in on himself, his hair white and sparse instead of sandy, his face a mess of lines and crags. Only his eyes held the same old spark I'd learned to hate. "You are welcome. And you, young Saga. One look, and I can see you carry Decker blood in your veins."

"Grandfather. Thank you for the invitation." I turned to Joanne, who'd aged more gracefully than the Old Man and stood as erect as ever, round-faced, with laugh lines around the mouth, but her hair was white as well, though thick and wavy. "And you, Grandmother."

When I met my father's eyes, I saw discomfort, confusion, and perhaps a wee bit of something I hadn't seen since before I announced my enlistment in the Corps. Grudging respect? No. That wasn't it. At least he didn't look as worn as I'd feared and still carried himself like a slightly older version of Richard and me, right down to the deep blue eyes.

"Father, Mother. I'm glad to see you again after so long and present your granddaughter Saga, a fine scholar, officer, and human being."

"Zachary." Mom, as tall as any Decker, though slender, with platinum hair framing a delicate face, turned light blue eyes that revealed nothing of her thoughts to my daughter. "A pleasure to meet you, Saga."

The discomfort in the room was so palpable I almost considered telling a ribald joke to either break the tension or get us thrown out. Instead, I winked at Richard and gave Delia a broad smile.

"So," I said, forcefully expelling the tension gripping every muscle in my body. "Now that we've made sure we remembered each other's names, Saga and I wouldn't be averse to something like what you're all holding in your hand."

The Old Man glanced at Bates, who'd been standing silently along the wall.

"A gin and tonic for my grandson and great-granddaughter."

No Shrehari Ale here, and that was no doubt on purpose. If his private intelligence service told him about Saga's favorite pre-dinner drink, they surely told him mine. The first gesture, then.

"Let's not be coy, Zachary. There's a lot of bad blood and unpleasant history between you and us — the people you betrayed."

"Good. I'm a Marine, Grandfather. I prefer directness. It avoids misunderstandings, and we've had plenty of those in the past."

"Yes. I can see you're a Marine and, by all accounts, one of the best combat officers in the Corps," he said grudgingly. "I understand those decorations for valor you earned aren't easy to come by."

"Each of them matched by one or more scars on my body."

"We'll not be asking to see those."

"I wasn't offering."

Bates handed us our drinks, and I raised mine.

"Thank you for inviting us."

After a moment of hesitation, they imitated me, and we took a sip.

"Now, why are Saga and I here, Grandfather? Shortly after our arrival on Mykonos, Richard made it clear that I was still on the persona non grata list, and because of me, so was Saga."

I saw them. I recognized them but realized I felt nothing for them at that moment. No kinship, not even the love a son should feel for his mother, who had at least tried to prevent my expulsion. She was the only one aside from Attar who understood my desire to experience something outside the family before settling. Still, in the end, my mother bowed to the Old Man and my father and went along with my expulsion.

The only person in the room for whom I could find any sort of feeling was Delia because she welcomed me without judging. The others, my brother included, were strangers, though my daughter and I bore physical resemblances to all of them. I'd made my peace with the shunning long ago and expected little of this less-than-tearful reunion after decades apart. What I didn't expect was to feel nothing. These were strangers who'd invited us to a cocktail party.

"People I respect made it clear to me they consider you a distinguished son of Mykonos, an honorable man, and a credit to this world, someone destined to become a famous general."

"How kind of them." I kept from sounding sarcastic. Barely. But I could guess Eugene was involved. Probably Kal as well. He seemed to have his finger in every pie around here.

"Indeed," the Old Man replied, but he couldn't quite keep a faint tinge of sarcasm from surfacing. Or maybe I was too sensitive. "And those same people believe continuing to shun you now that you've returned as a respected senior Marine Corps officer reflects badly on the Decker name."

And there we had it. This was about his reputation and that of his damned commercial empire, not about the prodigal grandson. I saw Delia shoot him a poisonous glance out of the corner of her eyes. Everyone else kept carefully neutral expressions.

# — Twenty-Four —

"So, I'm being welcomed back to protect the family's reputation among the high and mighty of Mykonos now that I've proved to be the opposite of the fuck-up you publicly disowned?" I asked in a conversational tone. "Not because you're forgiving me, let alone admitting you might have overreacted all those years ago. Thank you for your honesty, Grandfather."

I took a sip of my drink, eyes locked with the Old Man, daring him to let his temper show. Of course, I would not give him the satisfaction of walking out, be it in anger, disgust, or indifference. I'd see this evening through to the end. He was sorely deluded if he hoped I'd make myself the bad guy again. And if it made him and everyone else uncomfortable, tough. I'd had more than my share of discomfort in life.

"Please avoid swearing, Zachary. I realize Marines use foul language as punctuation marks, but this is Carnarvon Manor, and you're a colonel, not a private."

"Fair enough. My apologies. But I'll confess I'm amused it took your concern for the reputation of the zaibatsu to finally meet your great-granddaughter."

I had the satisfaction of seeing the Old Man's eyes narrow in irritation at my use of the term zaibatsu to describe the family conglomerate. He and many in the OutWorlds associated it with the interstellar mercantile empires exploiting humanity with Earth's tacit approval since the Second Migration War and using any means necessary to amass profits, even underwriting criminal enterprises.

"You will not use that cursed term to describe our family business, Zachary."

I allowed a faintly ironic smile to cross my lips.

"As you wish, Grandfather. Is one of those who told you a prodigal grandson plays better in your social circles than a rejected hero, my old school friend Eugene? The one who had Saga and me to supper the other day?"

"If you must know, yes, though I don't like your choice of words. And it's President Eugenius Van Kirten. Or do you reserve proper deference to a head of state for that fool Brüggemann on Earth?"

"I like Eugene and would never disparage him. I know he doesn't mind being called that because I never called him anything else when we were young. But yes, I called him Mister President. Secretary General Brüggemann, on the other hand, has all sorts of nasty nicknames in my social circles, Grandfather. Most of them aren't mentionable in Carnarvon Manor."

"You don't like him?"

"I don't know anyone in the Fleet who does."

"Humph." The Old Man took a sip of his gin. "Then perhaps you're not all fools."

"We generally keep fools occupied with useless administrative work in the far corners of headquarters' buildings and don't send them out on important missions. I understand that most big business conglomerates do the same, although, from my experience, a few sometimes rise to the top and ensure the business sinks to the bottom. From what I've read, you seem to keep your fools at bay so far, Grandfather. But that never lasts. Whenever we invent something idiot-proof, the universe, with its questionable sense of humor, comes up with a better idiot."

A big smile spread across Delia's face, though she didn't say a word. Richard suddenly seemed fascinated by the back and forth between the Old Man and me, as if he couldn't quite believe our grandfather would put up with my repartee.

"All right," Grandmother Joanne said in a sharp voice, finally breaking her silence. As she expected, we turned our attention on her, the Old Man included. "Zachary, your grandfather is trying hard, and whether he realizes it, admitting he might have been wrong is very difficult. So please stop being flippant. Thomas, our grandson is not the same man you tossed out. According to Delia, he experienced things that would have reduced every other Decker or Khanjan to tears, which means he's probably the toughest, most adaptable, and most capable of us. Stop treating him as if he were still an angry eighteen-year-old. He's a colonel and a future general."

The Old Man and I exchanged surprised looks. But I knew an order from a higher power when I heard one. Whether grandfather did, I couldn't tell.

"Yes, Grandmother." I bowed my head contritely. "My apologies for my unseemly behavior."

"Apology accepted, Zachary. And this time, I really mean it. Welcome home." She glanced at the Old Man. "Thomas?"

"Very well, dear." At that moment, a chime sounded, and his lips twisted in a wintry smile. "Saved by the proverbial bell. That means we should head for the dining room. Bring your drinks."

With the Old Man and grandmother in the lead, we headed through the connecting door and to the family dining room next door, where the table was set for eight, with little place cards by each setting. Per tradition, my grandparents sat at either end, with Saga on the Old Man's right and Delia on his left. Richard sat on Saga's right and I on Delia's left, then came father and mother, on either side of grandmother, with my mother to my left. Three guesses about who'd decided on the seating arrangement. And the first two don't count.

"Oh, Zachary," my mother said softly, patting my hand once we were seated. "What a mess we make of things."

I gave her a smile I hoped would pass as fond, though I still felt little for the people around me other than Saga and Delia.

"I'm the man I've become because of grandfather, and from where I sit, that's a good thing. So, I suppose I owe him a vote of thanks. Otherwise, I'd have never had Saga or met my wife Hera, let alone the good men and women I served with over the years." I patted her hand in return. "Don't worry. I'm okay with how my life unfolded.

"If you're sure, Zachary."

Was that excess moisture in the corner of her eyes? I couldn't quite tell in the dining room's lower light. But a glance to my right told me the Old Man was giving Saga the third degree, and I tuned in on what they were saying, just in case he was fishing for intelligence. But it concerned her early years, so I tried to engage my father in conversation by asking about the business, but he remained decidedly monosyllabic. Then, the appetizer arrived, the butler poured the wine, and we went silent while we ate.

I monitored Saga's wine consumption because the Old Man was known for being generous to loosen tongues in social settings but needn't have worried. Apparently, pretending to drink while remaining cold stone sober was one of the performance objectives on the basic intelligence officer course because she barely touched the white before one of the Old Man's favorite — and pricey — reds replaced it.

I'll say this about my family. They knew how to make small talk around a dinner table, awkward and stilted as it was, despite the best efforts of my grandmother. And the food was superb. You wouldn't find many restaurants in Petras that could serve anything better. Between them, my grandmother and mother slowly plucked away at the story of my life since leaving home while my father and brother listened without comment. However, I could see Richard's eyes widening when I told them about becoming a janissary, a slave soldier in the Trans-Coalsack. They widened even further when I recounted that one of my fellow janissaries, and at the time a close friend, was now one of my battalion commanders. The part about being tortured in the juluk pit recounted without the gory details made my father shake his head. At what? I couldn't tell and didn't ask.

"What an extraordinary life you've led, Zachary," my mother said when the empty main course plates vanished, replaced by a cheese platter and port. "And to think you survived these things. I would certainly like to meet your wife, Hera, someday. She sounds like an extraordinary person."

I grinned at her. "She is that."

"Here's to a life well lived." Mother raised her glass. "And to your return among us."

# — Twenty-Five —

Throughout the meal, I'd watched my father and brother's alcohol intake — a tendency to drink was another trait we shared — and it had been several times mine. I had learned the hard way where excess could lead, but tonight, I figured it also came from growing resentment at my life away from the family. Don't ask me how or why, but I knew the eruption that had been silently building since I walked into the living room was about to burst.

And as I expected, it came once my father had eaten his cheese and poured his second glass of port. I'd just finished describing Hera and my wedding when he gave me a sarcastic round of applause.

He sneered at me and said, "Here you are, the prodigal son. At least in the eyes of some. But I'm reminded of a passage from scripture that fits your character better. *Being filled with all unrighteousness, fornication, wickedness, covetousness, maliciousness; full of envy, murder, debate, deceit, malignity; whisperers. Backbiters, haters of God, despiteful, proud, boasters, inventors of evil things, disobedient to parents. Without understanding, covenant breakers, without natural affection, implacable, unmerciful. Who knowing the judgment of the Almighty, that they which commit such things are worthy of death, not only do the same but have pleasure in them that do them."*

Trust my father to remember that passage. I'd last heard it when he threw me out.

"Jack!" Mother scowled at him. "This is hardly the time nor the place. Thomas has invited Zachary as a gesture of reconciliation, not to suffer abuse."

The conversation stopped, and everyone looked at me and good old, sloshed dad, including the Old Man, who wore an even deeper scowl.

"Well, what?" Father asked in an irritated tone. He gestured at me. "Zachary qualifies on most counts. Just because he came back wearing a fine uniform with more decorations than is decent doesn't change that fact. Not even a daughter we never knew existed —" my granddaughter, who looks like a Decker through and through. And she's wearing the same damn uniform. Worse yet, that uniform is a symbol of the central government we despise, and my son and granddaughter are servants of that government by their own sworn oaths. And this family does what? Fawns over them as if nothing had happened? As if all is forgiven? Until he betrays us again, this time to his masters on Earth."

And just like that, I felt my temper flare up. But how could he know I despised the central government on Earth as much as he did? That I fought its agents for years and that even now, I was flagrantly disobeying the orders of the SecGen and the SecDef for the sake of Mykonos and the other OutWorlds and colonies. I glanced at Saga, whose eyes beseeched me to stay calm, take my father's abuse, and think of the mission first.

"I've betrayed no one, Father," I replied in a voice as calm, polite, and conversational as I could make it while I fought my urge to lash out. "Least of all Mykonos and this family. You need not believe me, and I won't explain myself to you or anyone else, but it's true."

"Enough." The Old Man's voice cracked across the table like a whip. "Zachary and Saga broke bread with President Van Kirten, who has nothing but good things to say about both of them. That's a sufficient endorsement. Besides, if what I've pieced together is correct, our two Marines are, at least in part, responsible for averting a crisis that might have plunged the convention into chaos."

He speared me with his gaze.

"Isn't that so, Zachary? Your dinner with the president was to discuss that fake recording of Brüggemann, a fake Saga detected, and you brought it to the attention of your general, correct?"

I raised my head and turned to look at him.

"You are remarkably well informed, Grandfather. And yes, we are here to ensure the constitutional convention goes ahead undisturbed by anyone, in case you still have doubts. The alternative, a convention disrupted by those inimical to its aims, cannot and will not be countenanced by the Armed Forces because we will not watch a Third Migration War unfold before our eyes."

Then I met my father's furious gaze.

"If that is betrayal in your book, Father, then I pity you for being unable to see anything beyond a narrow and sadly limited horizon."

He scoffed.

"You're a fine one to speak about narrow horizons. Imagine if that recording had fired up the delegates to do the only right thing and do it now instead of pleading for change and hoping Earth drops us a few crumbs. There's only one solution, which isn't reforming what we can never reform because the hour is much too late. Thirty years ago? Perhaps. But not now. By forestalling the inevitable, you've temporarily repelled unstoppable forces, and when they muster for the ultimate attack, things might turn out much worse than the sum of your fears. How's that for a military assessment, Marine?"

Everyone was looking at me for a reaction, and when I glanced at Saga, I saw my thoughts reflected in her eyes. What if father was right, unlikely as it may seem at first glance?

"And let a lie stand for the truth?"

"For a righteous cause!" He thumped his fist on the table. "Something you lackeys of Earth don't understand."

"The mother of lies cannot give birth to the true, the good, and the beautiful. Whatever future stems from it will not last the test of time. It may not even last a single day."

My father let out a derisive bark of laughter.

"My son, the philosopher, quoting Jackson Thorn. Well, his ideas don't hold any water with me."

If only he knew who Thorn had really been, my father would not have dismissed his words so lightly. But I wasn't about to enlighten him. Besides, my father would only mock me for being credulous.

"Be that as it may. Yet by our very oath to serve, we swore to uphold the truth and expose lies whenever possible because more humans have died in the name of falsehood over the last three thousand years than any reason other than natural causes."

This time, Delia clapped her hands in a slow round of applause, but it was approving rather than sarcastic.

"Hear, hear. A military man who understands his profession exists to prevent war. If only the secessionists could see the price of spurning the Commonwealth so clearly."

Father scowled at her.

"We know your opinion of the secessionist movement, Delia. But this family will no longer bend the knee to Earth, and the sooner we stand on our own two feet, the better. If it takes some propaganda and a bit of embellishment, then so be it."

And now I couldn't help but wonder whether my father or his associates were behind the fake, and annoyed we'd smoked them out so easily.

"I guess we'll stay at odds over this matter, Father. Some things aren't open to interpretation or compromise. In any case, I think Saga and I should return to Fort Monash. The morning run comes earlier every passing day at my age." I met the Old Man's eyes. "Sir, thank you for welcoming my daughter into the Decker family home. Whatever differences we had decades ago, they are not hers, and she is not guilty of anything. And thank you for inviting me back. I regret triggering my father's acrimony over matters on which we can never agree, and for that, you have my apologies."

I heard my father choke on his port, but I ignored it.

"How about we have a pleasant lunch together at the club on Sunday," Joanne proposed in the ensuing silence. "Now that we've overcome the awkwardness of the reunion. Even if we reserve one of the smaller rooms off the main dining hall, we'll be seen by those who matter. Richard and Delia's girls can meet Saga, and we can see whoever else in the Decker and Khanjan families wants to come. What do you say, Thomas?"

The Old Man considered his wife for a few seconds, then glanced at my father and me.

"Under one condition. There will be no talk of politics whatsoever. The last thing we need is another outburst like the one we just witnessed."

"Of course, sir," I replied. "And thank you for the invitation."

My father grudgingly chimed in a few moments later while my mother gave him a look that could freeze methane. Judging by his continuing hostility, even though the Old Man was making efforts to heal the breach, let alone my mother and grandmother visibly thawing by the minute, I was beginning to wonder whether Jack Decker wasn't the one who pushed the family into disowning his younger son. Dear dad never was one to brook resistance from his offspring on any subject. He drove me out and broke Richard's resistance. Maybe because he'd been raised by a stiff-necked, stubborn father himself.

As we said our goodbyes in the foyer, the Old Man surprised me by shaking my hand and embracing Saga in the traditional way, with a kiss on each cheek. Richard imitated him after a moment of hesitation, then my grandmother, mother, and sister-in-law embraced Saga and me with varying degrees of trepidation. My father was nowhere to be seen. I suspected he'd poured himself the cognac we skipped by leaving right away and was quietly fuming on the terrace.

Once strapped into our car seats with Carnarvon Manor fading behind us in the darkness, Saga sighed.

"Well, that was quite an experience. As I may have mentioned before, they make the Lagmans seem sane by comparison, and that's saying a lot."

Her mother's family had quirks of their own, not least Ingrid, who'd denied me the joy of watching my daughter grow from a small child to a post-graduate student.

"I won't argue the point. They are quite the personalities. But did something strike you as strange?"

# — Twenty-Six —

Saga didn't answer as we passed through the open gate, which slowly closed behind us. As was typical on Mykonos, we drove without lights, relying on the artificial intelligence managing the car and its night vision receptors to see better than our eyes. A projection of our surroundings filled the front and side windows, while a display in the control panel showed our rear.

"Your father — my grandfather — was surprisingly hostile toward you when I would have expected your grandfather to be the least agreeable to our presence."

"Yep. It makes me think my ejection from the family was because of my father, not the Old Man. Which, in hindsight, makes sense since I clashed with dear dad almost daily during my last year of school. He wouldn't listen when I said I needed a few years of doing something else, anything not related to the family business where I'd worked each summer, so I could make a more informed decision about my future career. Anything else?"

She nodded. "His opinion the president should have misled the delegates and accepted the fake recording as real to help precipitate secession. The moral and ethical dimensions of such a suggestion are staggering. Could he be involved in creating it?"

We turned off the private lane onto the main road under a canopy of stars. Lights from various human structures dotted the dark landscape in the distance, but according to the sensors, we were alone on this stretch, and the car sped up under Saga's control.

"Possibly. Mind you, I never thought he was the type who'd propose scamming something as momentous for our future as the constitutional convention. Which shows you how little I know about him and how much he might have changed over the decades. While we may have clashed when I was eighteen, I never had reason to think he was anything other than an honest, upstanding businessman. A stubborn, unbending bastard of a businessman, but with a strong moral backbone. I looked up to him at one time."

"Investing one's soul in a political movement or ideology will eventually destroy even the saintliest human being." She turned her head and gave me a sad smile. "A corollary to Lord Acton's dictum about power corrupting. Sorry, Dad. But your father is now on our list of suspects. I shall include tonight in my report to HQ."

"Oh, won't Hera enjoy reading about the Decker family's reunion? Don't worry about Jack Decker being a suspect in trying to create a false flag event. He became one in my mind tonight the moment I processed his words. The fool shouldn't have been drinking and brooding so much. He might have reflected before speaking and held his tongue. However, our family has a propensity for over-imbibing. I'm glad you didn't get that gene."

Another smile. "I have the gene, Dad. Fortunately, I also developed self-control when I realized I could easily mess up once I went to university and found myself surrounded by opportunities."

Something caught the corner of my eye, and I studied the rear-view display for a good minute.

"How long has that car been behind us, keeping just at the edge of our sensor range?"

Saga frowned. "No idea."

She touched the controls and called up the rear-view trip record from when we turned onto the public road.

"There. It comes over the rise beyond Carnarvon Manor Lane just as we reach maximum sensor range, and it's been keeping pace with us. Is your instinct telling you something, Dad?"

"Maybe. It's past twenty-one hundred hours on a weeknight, and this isn't a much-traveled stretch of road. But it's the keeping pace that caught my eye. Slow down by ten klicks and see if it narrows the gap. Gently, so they don't notice right away."

It quickly became apparent the car behind us was programmed to stay at the same distance when it slowed as well, then accelerated again when Saga increased our speed. Now it could just be that the car's occupants had a thing for staying at the outer limits of another vehicle's nighttime detection range.

"Are we hooked into the central traffic control system?"

"Yes."

"Cut the link."

"They won't like it and will report to the Mykonos Regiment's transport section."

I scoffed. The locals could report all they wanted. No one would send a warning to my commanding officer.

"Tough."

"Link cut."

"Okay." I called up a map of the area and tried to remember the lay of the land from both my younger days and the re-familiarization tours I had made since arriving.

"You think someone's tailing us, Dad?"

"Don't ask me how or why, but I sense trouble coming. I'm probably wrong, though."

"The Marines of Ghost Squadron swear by your instincts."

I chuckled. "They also swear at many other things, me included."

My daughter was quick to nod. "True."

"Let's play a game. Assuming the chumleys in the tail are tangos and not drunk Mykonos aristos heading home after a boozy meal with partners in crime and obsessive about vehicle separation, what's their aim?"

"To monitor us for others," she replied without hesitation. "They're not part of a kinetic action team because they're too far behind. At best, they might be a cut-off."

"Go on."

"If someone wishes to take aim at us, they'll be up ahead somewhere. In a place where we're hemmed in and out of sight from casual observers. Not that there will be any equipped with night vision gear anyhow."

"So how do we counter?"

She grinned. "We vanish."

"Easier said than done. Any proposals, Captain? Remember, you are responsible for the welfare of a Special Forces brigade commander."

"You're having fun with this, aren't you, Colonel, sir?"

"Yes. And your point would be?"

"How would you like to teach me by being our navigator? And retrieve our sidearms from the car's lockup?"

"Sure."

"First thing, find where, ahead of us, we'll be stuck in a funnel with no way to turn except a hundred and eighty degrees. That could be a potential ambush site."

I chuckled. "Someone taught you a few tricks."

"Blame the Pathfinder School. They wanted to turn me into the most famous NILO since Hera. Told 'em it wasn't going to happen."

"Well, something could happen soon. The only ways off this road before we hit the main highway are farm tracks on either side just before the upcoming wooded patch and a kilometer-long defile between the trees. You might remember it when we came up while it was still light enough to see unaided. Dense forest. Excellent ambush country. After that, we can take any of a dozen ways back to Fort Monash."

I reached for the hidden gun safe beneath the control panel in front of me, and it opened silently at my touch. Leaving the base unarmed was against my orders, and entering my family's manor armed would have triggered the security system, which wouldn't have made the Old Man better disposed at my arrival. Even less so my father. I handed Saga her weapon — a service-issue blaster — and placed my Shrehari hand cannon in my lap, its holster discarded at my feet. Even if there was no danger, this was a good training drill for us.

"Take the farm tracks?"

"They don't go anywhere but into the fields. What's the best course of action when you're aboard a vehicle and find yourself being ambushed?"

The answer came straight away. "Punch through as hard and as fast as you can with guns firing."

"Then stand by to hit it, Captain."

"Yes, sir." A pause. "You really think someone wants to stop us?"

"Aren't you entertained by preparing for battle?"

She slowly turned her head to look at me and cocked an eyebrow.

"This is why I don't have a significant other, Dad. Every prospect vanishes when they find out I'm Colonel Zack Decker's kid. They fear being drafted into a risky special operation."

"More like they're intimidated by a tall, fit, NILO qualified, Pathfinder wings-wearing intelligence officer with a doctorate from a major university."

"Sure, Dad."

Saga could do sarcasm like a champion.

We entered the dark defile that cut through dense forest, and the banter ceased while we watched the road ahead, which curved about halfway through, so we couldn't immediately see the other end, where it joined the highway.

"Shall I reduce speed?"

"No. Keep going."

Our car took the curve, and the rest of the road slowly came into sight all the way to the junction.

Nothing. No cars, no suspicious shapes, no obstacles. Without prompting, Saga increased our speed so that we covered the last kilometer in the space of a few heartbeats, then she braked when we were a few dozen meters from the edge of the forest, where it gave way to a wide-open swath with the ring highway surrounding Petras at its center.

Moments later, we turned left onto the northbound lanes unscathed. The sensors picked up other cars headed in both directions; however, I kept my eyes on the rear-view display, looking for our tail to appear. But it never showed by the time we passed out of detection range.

"Well, that was fun while it lasted." I slipped my weapon back into its holster but kept it in my lap. "Let's keep our eyes peeled for any more vehicles behaving suspiciously. When is the best time to ambush an enemy?"

"When they're almost home and no longer have that paranoid edge," Saga replied without hesitation. "Human nature being what it is."

"Well done." I studied the sensor readings, looking for a new tail and perhaps even one or more vehicles ahead of us. "What's the drill if multiple vehicles try to box us in and force us to stop?"

"Depends. Do they have police markings and beacons?"

"Does it matter?"

She considered the question for a few seconds.

"On Mykonos. Places like New Tasman, Hispaniola, or most of the Home Worlds? Not in the slightest. At least for us. Why? Do you see a pattern forming?"

"No. But it's either discuss tactics or the family. I've had about enough of the latter for one night."

Saga scowled at me.

"Did you really see a car tailing us on the side road?"

"Yes, I did. At least it was always keeping the same distance from us and staying at the edge of our sensor range. This would have been their sensor range since it wasn't a combat car with military-grade gear."

"So you—"

The rest of Saga's words were lost when a flash of light brighter than a thousand suns lit up the car's left side, and the Almighty's celestial sledgehammer smashed into the left rear quadrant, sending us spinning off the road like a demented, two-ton child's toy.

# — Twenty-Seven —

That spin turned into a series of barrel rolls as we came down the embankment. After six or seven times, we ended up in a pasture looking at the world from the wrong side. I did a quick inventory of my physical condition, and, thanks to the safety harness, I was stirred, shaken, and getting angry but unhurt.

"You okay, Saga?"

"My brain is still trying to catch up with my skull, but yeah, nothing broken, though I'll have bruises where the harness held me tight. We are upside down, right?"

"Yep." I fished my communicator out of my tunic pocket and activated the emergency channel. Within moments, a voice came on.

"Niner-niner, this is Zero. What is the nature of your emergency?"

"Someone or something attacked us on the ring road. No idea what it was, and our car is now lying on its roof at the bottom of an embankment. Whoever did this could still be around and looking to finish the job. Activate the quick reaction force and send them to the coordinates of my communicator. At this point, Captain Decker and I appear unhurt."

"Wilco, wait, out."

"Time we evacuate, kiddo."

I shoved my communicator back into my tunic and turned the harness buckle in the middle of my chest one-quarter to the left, and the strap brakes loosened enough to gently let me down. Once I braced myself, I turned it a further quarter, and the harness released me to scramble upright. I finally noticed that I'd kept a hold of my holstered blaster throughout. A good thing because if it had gone flying through the compartment, Saga or I, or both, could have been brained. I made a mental note to forbid loose weapons in vehicles from now on.

When I finally got my bearings, I saw my daughter, looking none the worse for wear, also freed from the restraints and crouching upright. Surprising me not a whit, the vehicle's sensor suite was dead, which left us in almost complete darkness against an attacker who would surely have the benefit of night vision gear.

"On three, we pull the emergency door release and roll as far as possible from the car. Then up and along the embankment for a hundred meters direction north, meaning the embankment to your left. Got it?"

Saga repeated the instructions back to me, then reached for the release on her side.

"One. Two. Three. Go—go—go!"

We rolled out into the darkness, and after a few spins in what I hoped didn't include cow patties, I climbed to my feet and stuffed my gun holster into my tunic. Then, Shrehari hand cannon at the ready, I ran at a steady pace, eyes on the ground, looking for anything that might send me flying. My ears picked up the soft thump of Saga's feet and her breathing a few meters to my right, but other than that, the night was silent.

After what I judged was a hundred meters, I came to a stop and crouched, facing back toward the wrecked car. Seconds later, Saga joined me and dropped as well, facing the other direction.

"Still okay?" I asked in a whisper.

My communicator chose that moment to vibrate on the emergency channel. Since I didn't want to make it overly easy on the tangos who attacked us, I ignored it, assuming it was Zero, the operations center, telling me the QRF had launched since the timing was about right. Ever since the convention began, I'd kept a platoon of the MLI and two dropships from my aviation squadron on standby at all times, ready to move at the slightest hint of trouble. A further two platoons and the QRF company headquarters with additional dropships could launch in under fifteen minutes.

"A slight headache, but everything is functioning within normal parameters." Though I couldn't see her face, I knew Saga was smiling. "And I guess your instincts were right. Someone was looking to do us mischief. Just not via ambush. What hit us?"

"Something with a lot of energy behind it. Large bore plasma, rocket, or missile. If it had enough velocity, it didn't even need to carry an explosive warhead, though I saw a flash of light a heartbeat before we went into that spin, so it wasn't that. But I'm going to guess the firing position was within two hundred meters on the other side of the highway. Probably at the wood line."

"Do you think they meant to send us off the road as a warning, or were they aiming at the passenger compartment and missed?"

"No idea. At this point, we should assume the latter and expect company before the QRF lead element lands."

The clouds, which were closing in while we were still on the side road, had now cut off the moon and starlight, and I could smell the moisture of an impending downpour. Excellent. Nothing like rain to further reduce the ability of a standard-issue human's senses against an adversary equipped with night vision gear and portable sensors.

My communicator began pulsing regularly, telling me a friendly sensor had locked onto its signal. "The QRF advance flight is within visual range, Saga."

"Good."

At that moment, the first fat drops plopped on us, and I knew we'd be soaked before help arrived. Well, I'd been privately bemoaning my status as a chairborne warrior while my troopers had all the fun. Still, crouching in an open pasture in the dark while wearing service dress uniform, with a typical Petras downpour starting, wasn't quite what I had in mind. And still no sign of whoever shot us off the highway.

The heavens suddenly opened with the force of a bursting dam, crowding out any sound, sight, and thought of staying dry. Or any other thought for the first few seconds, such was the onslaught, proving monsoon season had arrived. Yet, the low hum of approaching dropships flying nap of the earth reached my ears, and I looked up in time to see a dark shadow descend slowly — the drop ship carrying the immediate response platoon. The second ship should be circling above, hammering the area with its sensors, looking for tangos.

But I doubted they'd find any. Otherwise, we'd have seen some sort of follow-on from the shot that kicked us into a spin — another salvo of whatever hit or a team coming to check on our status. This made me suspicious that it was a one-and-done, no matter whether or not we walked away from the scene.

The dropship settled, and its aft ramp opened, disgorging armored Marine Light Infantry troopers who came toward us as they spread out in a protective circle. One of them homed directly in on our position — the platoon leader.

As he got closer, the command sergeant flipped up his helmet visor — Sigurd Berg, C Company, 2nd MLI.

"You and the captain okay, sir?"

"We're like a good martini, Berg. Wet, shaken, and ready to be served."

Berg chuckled. "I prefer mine dry. Sensors haven't picked up any tangos. Whoever fired on you is long gone. I suggest you and the captain get aboard our dropship, sir. Last I checked, it didn't leak. Zero says to tell you the local cops are on their way, along with spooks from the Mykonos Security Service. They're treating this as a major incident and will want to speak with you. Brigade HQ has a team of investigators from the S2 shop on the way to collect data on the event."

"And I'll be glad to speak with everyone, but after we get a dry uniform on the outside and a hot coffee on the inside. Let Zero know we'll meet with the investigators in my office at the Fort."

"Roger that, Colonel."

Berg had us aboard quickly, with his platoon embarking immediately after. Moments later, the dropship shot into the air and headed back to Fort Monash with its escort above and to starboard in the overwatch position.

As usual, I'd taken the jump seat behind the pilot and spotted the rest of C Company inbound to secure the wrecked staff car and comb the area, along with civilian first responders racing to the scene. Coordinating everything was going to be messy, especially since I'd decided the Armed Forces would claim primary jurisdiction. Of course, Kal could override me, but a naked attempt to kill the second-highest-ranking Commonwealth officer in the star system was beyond the local police and the Mykonos Security Intelligence Service. And there could be no doubt it was connected to the convention.

Our dropship landed on the parade square fronting my HQ building, and we hurried across it through the rain.

Dry clothes could wait until I was happy about how things were proceeding. The moment we were beyond the safety perimeter, the dropship lifted off again to join the rest of C Company at the site of the ambush.

I found Zero, the brigade command post, in full swing, with staff officers and noncoms talking to the local authorities and coordinating activities. Video feeds from the site, taken by pickups with night vision and infrared capabilities, showed a staff car that wouldn't return to service anytime soon, if ever. The entire rear was one gigantic piece of scrap, which meant the powerplant was effectively destroyed. Only the armor englobing the passenger compartment had saved us from death by shrapnel. If the tangos had struck a meter and a half further forward, Saga and I would have been slated for a military funeral with full honors in the Fort Arnhem cemetery back on Caledonia.

"We found the car's event recorder, Colonel," Major Chosiak, my S3, said the moment he spied me. "It'll be here shortly."

"How about local law enforcement? Are they giving us any trouble?"

"Not in the slightest. They're happily collecting data and making friends with the QRF company commander. I've sent Chief Warrant Officer Kine to the site, both as our lead investigator and liaison with the local cops."

"Okay. If we get any static from the police or the security service, route it straight to me. I'd like the S2 to take my and Captain Decker's statements for the official record."

"She's in her office, getting started on the intel collection. And the general would like to see both of you in his office the moment you can."

I glanced at Saga. "You okay if we see the general before making our statements?"

She knew I was asking the NILO, whose ultimate boss was the Chief of Naval Intelligence, not my daughter.

"It's fine, sir."

The door to Kal's office was open, and he was sitting behind his desk, though in a civilian suit rather than battledress like the rest of the duty staff.

"Colonel and Captain Decker reporting to the general as ordered, soggy, shaken, but otherwise unharmed, sir," I announced as we walked in.

"Grab a seat." Kal studied us intently as if wondering whether we were in a rougher shape than I let on. "And tell me what happened."

# — Twenty-Eight —

I gave him the story, starting with a thumbnail sketch of the family reunion because I figured there might be a link between it and the attempt on our lives.

"Any idea what hit you?"

"No, but after seeing the imagery of the wrecked staff car, I think it was probably a miniature missile with a high explosive warhead, the sort fired from launchers attached to plasma rifles, which raises a few additional questions. First, those missiles have a terminal guidance package. If it had been aimed at the passenger compartment, it would have hit the passenger compartment, not the powerplant. This tells me the attackers didn't intend to kill us, meaning they knew enough about the survivability of the staff car to fire a disabling shot. Secondly, that sort of missile and launcher aren't easily available, even through the ordnance black market. But Army units like the Mykonos Regiment would have hundreds of launchers and thousands of missiles in their armory."

"Meaning I should speak with Colonel Foster about doing an inventory check in the morning."

"If you would, General. Third, whoever set it up knew we were supping at Carnarvon Manor tonight. The Old Man keeps his personal guest lists confidential, so no one outside the immediate family and the house staff would have known ahead of time, and I'm not even sure that the staff was told until earlier today who the guests would be. Welcoming Saga and me back into the family would have been so intensely personal for the Old Man, he'd have imposed need-to-know rules, just in case it went sideways."

"Based on your father's reaction to our smoking out the false flag video of the SecGen, do you think he might be involved? We already suspect he's in deep with the Mykonos secessionists."

"Before tonight, I'd have said no. But after him quoting one of the harsher bits of scripture at me and excusing the use of false flags to speed up secession?" I shrugged. "And he did intimate I was worthy of death, although I couldn't say whether he truly meant it or was just lashing out at my coming home a success after he dismissed me publicly as a loser who'd never amount to anything."

"Will you discuss this with Ellie Pierce?"

I thought about it for a few seconds, then, for reasons I couldn't quite explain, I shook my head.

"No. And not because of the family relationship. Or at least not yet."

"Why?"

"Gut feeling. Let's see how they deal with tonight's missile attack on our car. This was a sophisticated attack for all its simplicity, not something a few secessionist malcontents can put together on the fly."

"And I would venture there's a good probability it was another false flag," Saga said. "Since we're now openly protecting the convention against express orders from Earth, an attack on the brigade commander can easily be interpreted as an attack on the delegates themselves, one sponsored by elements hostile to the aspirations of the OutWorlds."

I jerked my thumb at her.

"What the NILO said. Which means we downplay this as much as possible. Let's blame off-worlders who had a score to settle with me."

Kal gave me his habitual, slightly sardonic smile.

"You mean lie?"

"Sometimes, a little fib can save a lot of grief. There's a significant difference between using the big lie of the fake SecGen's speech to stir up secessionist sentiment and, in the absence of other suspects, putting the blame for the attack on anyone but federal operatives or their mercenaries to avoid stirring up said sentiments."

"But you must admit there's a hint of irony at work. Sometimes, the ends do justify the means. Our problem is deciding at which point we cross the line into unjustifiable. But fair enough. Until we uncover the identity of your attackers, we'll do what we can to avoid inflaming secessionist sentiment, which means limiting our discussions with local officials about the incident to the facts. No speculation with Ellie Pierce, the police, or even the president."

"Understood. I'll also ensure a full report, speculation included, goes to HQ once we make our official statements to the S2. In fact, I think our NILO will draft it, but tomorrow morning. It's already getting a tad late."

"I agree." Kal's communicator chirped, and he glanced at it. "Word that the Mykonos Regiment is short a staff car must finally have reached Dennis Foster. I'll deal with him. You go ahead and make sure the command post has things in hand, then get some rest. You might have walked away from a missile strike, but there's always the possibility of a delayed reaction."

"True. And we will visit the base infirmary if something requiring medical attention surfaces." I climbed to my feet with more weariness than expected. "Good night, General."

Kal waved us away as he opened the link with Foster.

"Good evening, Dennis. I gather you're calling about the attack on Zack Decker and his NILO?"

After making our statements for the official record — they'd be shared with the Mykonos Police Service, the Security Intelligence folks, and the Mykonos Regiment, of course — Saga and I brought Corinne Renaud up to speed on the items we didn't include, and our suspicions so she could dig in the right spots for answers. Then, after a last check with operations to confirm they'd received the events recorder, that the QRF had handed the scene over to the police and withdrawn, and that the Mykonos Regiment was sending a flatbed transporter to recover the car — it would receive complete forensic analysis in the morning — I invited Saga into my office for a dram.

After pouring a splash of Glen Arcturus from my private reserve into two tumblers, I raised mine.

"Here's to walking away from a hit, kiddo. May all such attempts fail."

"Sentiment seconded, even though I'm convinced it wasn't designed to kill us. Can I suggest you and I go with Kal to the opening of tomorrow's deliberations so we can be seen smiling and relaxed on the spectators' mezzanine?"

"Already ahead of you. That was going to be my next order. Besides, inspecting the security setup beforehand will ensure I'm seen up close by our troopers and the police. The rumors must be running wild by now."

My communicator chimed in what was to be the first of many calls over the next twelve hours. I fished it from my damp tunic pocket and glanced at the display.

"Ellie Pierce. Of course, she'd call."

I placed the device on my desk and accepted the link.

"Good evening, Ellie. And what can the 1st Special Forces Brigade do for our Mykonos Security colleagues? You're in luck. My Naval Intelligence Liaison Officer is with me at the moment."

"Good evening, Zack, Saga. I understand you had quite the adventure earlier."

"I'm not sure I'd call it an adventure, but we're unharmed though the staff car is a write-off."

"The police say you're claiming jurisdiction."

"That's correct. An Armed Forces vehicle with Armed Forces personnel aboard was struck with what I believe to be military ordnance, which makes it more than the police can handle. We've already retrieved the event recorder, and the wreckage will be taken to Fort Monash for examination once the forensics investigators — ours and the Police Service's — release the scene."

"Military ordnance? You're sure?"

"Considering whatever hit us destroyed the car's rear end, including the powerplant, it wasn't a hunter's fowling piece, Ellie. I'm guessing something like a miniature missile with a high explosive warhead launched from a plasma rifle attachment. Nasty little things carried by the infantry to punch holes through walls, doors, and unarmored vehicles, among others. Thankfully, whoever took aim was sloppy and set the thing to strike about a meter behind the passenger compartment. Otherwise, we wouldn't be speaking."

"I see. Any idea who might have carried out the attack?"

"Search me. Over the years, I made a long list of enemies, and they've tried many times. Apparently, I'm a hindrance to their business interests."

A pause, then, "Do you think it's related to the convention?"

"Not a clue. Though I can't see how killing my daughter and me might matter. We're replaceable, and other than my unit providing security for the site, we're uninvolved in proceedings. Like I said, I figure old enemies followed me to Mykonos, hoping I'd be more vulnerable here than on Caledonia or during any other deployment in recent times since this is aid to civil power rather than a combat operation."

"The Sécurité Spéciale, perhaps?"

"Not directly. They prefer something deniable since they know we'll hit back twice as hard. Mercenaries employed by the Sécurité Spéciale, or one of the great zaibatsus, would be more likely."

"I see," she repeated in a thoughtful tone. "Well, I daresay you'd know better about your enemies. Would you mind sharing everything you have on the attack? My agency must investigate this sort of thing, especially if it involves off-world interests."

"No problems. Saga will contact your office in the morning and pass along whatever we've uncovered."

"Thank you. May I suggest that, until further notice, you and your daughter travel in a more heavily armored vehicle or by air? I doubt the doers came to Mykonos with only one of those miniature missiles you mentioned and will certainly try again if they went to the trouble."

"I'd already planned on it."

"Good. We'll speak again tomorrow. Have a good night."

"Thanks, Ellie. You too."

"Pierce, out."

I glanced at Saga. "Do you think she bought it?"

"Not for a second. But she's playing along."

"If you're wondering whether this was another attempt at a false flag by the secessionists, then I have no choice but to consider Ellie Pierce and her people among the suspects. A Security Intelligence Service focused on the convention taken unawares by a military-style attempt on the senior Armed Forces officer responsible for said convention's security means its people are incompetent or in on it."

"I just wish I knew what Hera's people are doing and what, if anything, they've found," Saga said in a wistful tone.

"They're probably looking for whoever carried out the attack. Don't worry. If they uncover anything, they'll get it to us. Otherwise, it's just as well we stay blissfully ignorant, considering what Hera and I got up to as field agents."

"True."

"Okay, kiddo. Time to hit the rack." I drained my glass. "See you in the morning."

# — Twenty-Nine —

Early the next morning, Delia called on behalf of the family — the Old Man had deputized her as she freely admitted. I told the same story as I'd told Ellie Pierce about suspecting off-world hired guns contracted to assassinate me because of something I'd done to powerful and wealthy people on past missions.

Whether she believed it, I couldn't say, but if the story got back to my father, so much the better. The more I thought about the previous evening, the more I wondered about him and his motivations.

After breakfast, Saga and I headed for the convention center aboard one of the combat cars the MLI had borrowed from the Mykonos Regiment's warehoused inventory, driven by an MLI corporal. I would have invited Kal to travel with us, but he didn't show up at the mess hall, and when I checked on him, he was already making the rounds of senior government officials in Petras before the day's deliberations began.

We detoured to the scene of last night's attack and stopped where our staff car had gone off the road. The traces of its tumble down the embankment were clear, though the wreckage itself was gone and now sat in one of Fort Monash's hangars, waiting for the regiment's investigators. I stared across the four-lane highway at the woods beyond.

"What do you think, Saga? Two hundred and fifty meters? Pretty short range for a miniature missile. Whoever aimed it wouldn't have missed the car's center of mass. They deliberately targeted the aft section where the powerplant would absorb most of the warhead's explosive force."

She studied the area for a few seconds, then nodded.

"Even a sniper with a plasma rifle or railgun would have hit the car's passenger compartment. I agree. This was probably not an assassination attempt but either a warning or another false flag. I'm sure the police and Ellie Pierce's people will figure that out quickly if they haven't yet. Both organizations have specialists who know everything there is to know about weapons, miniature missiles included."

"Let's hope Hera's people figure it out." We climbed back aboard the combat car. "Off to the convention, Corporal."

"Yes, sir."

Shortly after he swung back into traffic, my communicator chimed. Another well-wisher? I retrieved it and glanced at the display. Unknown caller. Still, I accepted the link.

"Colonel Decker," a low man's voice asked before I could say a word.

"Yes? Who are you?"

"My name is Lyman. We've never met, but you know of my boss, Director General Bauchan."

Saga and I exchanged a surprised glance. Andreas Bauchan was the head of the Sécurité Spéciale, which meant this Lyman character was an operative of the opposition.

"I do. What do you want, Mister Lyman?"

"The attack on you and your daughter last night wasn't sponsored, let alone carried out by my agency. I wanted you to know that."

"You're the Mykonos station chief, I take it?"

"Yes, though Lyman isn't a name you'll find in the directory. Our orders from HQ are to observe the convention and the intervention of the Armed Forces and report back only. I'm not authorized to engage in any action. Besides, if you hadn't heard, there's a moratorium on treating our Fleet counterparts with, as you folks say, extreme prejudice. My boss doesn't want a ruinous inter-agency war, considering the political situation in the Commonwealth."

"A wise choice, Mister Lyman. Now, why did you break cover to tell me this?"

"Because certain people inside the Mykonos government, along with their allies in a particular political movement, and several off-world delegates, are playing a foolhardy game, one which could bring humanity to the brink of civil conflict. Since the Armed Forces and my agency are both sworn to defend the Commonwealth, even though we don't agree on anything beyond the color of our common flag, I thought you might want to look for those trying to rig the outcome."

"I see. And why should I believe you, Mister Lyman?"

He chuckled. "Because your spouse has informed Director General Bauchan that she will arrange for his untimely demise should anyone in his employ or contracted by the agency harm you or your daughter. And Mister Bauchan takes that extremely seriously."

"I'm curious. How do you know about that?"

Another chuckle. "I was well briefed about you, your relatives, and your friends before leaving HQ to come here once we heard the Fleet was deploying the infamous Colonel Decker and his crack commandos."

"So, you're not the regular station chief, then?"

"No. This is a temporary assignment. You might say I was deployed to Mykonos for the same general reasons as you and will leave once this convention is over and the delegates gone."

"If you're fishing for an alliance, or even an information-sharing arrangement, don't bother."

"Nothing of that sort, I can assure you. But on behalf of my agency, try to stay alive, Colonel. If ever I hear of another threat against you, I will call. And with that, I wish you a good day listening to the endless droning of people who don't understand the galaxy is a harsh and unforgiving place."

Lyman cut the link before I could reply, and I tucked my communicator away and gave my daughter an amused look.

"Hera will love hearing about this," she said.

"Oh, without a doubt. You'll take care of the report?"

"That's my job, Colonel, sir. Do you believe the guy?"

I grunted. "This is the first time a Sécurité Spéciale agent engages me in a non-lethal conversation, so I have no frame of reference. I killed so many of his sort I lost count, though his buddies will have kept an exact tally in stars on their wall of honor and know me for being their destructor. Was Lyman protesting too much? Maybe. But why try to convince me they didn't make an attempt on us?"

"Perhaps his aim was making you consider secessionists the perpetrators."

"Perhaps, but even if they were the guilty party, there's nothing we can do about it. Nor should we at this point. A crisis averted no longer holds sway over the mood of the convention."

We reached the resort and our combat car came to a stop at the outer perimeter guard post so we could go through the security checks.

I let Saga do her NILO rounds while I visited the command post and walked along the perimeter, speaking with every trooper and cop I met. A few asked about the attack, but most seemed glad to see me in fine fettle.

A few minutes before ten, I passed through the sentry post at the convention hall's main entrance and headed up the stairs to the mezzanine, where I found Kal and Saga discussing the call from Mister Lyman of the Sécurité Spéciale in a low voice.

As I leaned against the railing, Secretary Liang climbed onto the stage and looked up at me. Her expressionless eyes held mine for a few seconds, then she lowered them and scanned the assembly before raising her gavel, leaving me to wonder what that was about.

But even as she called the delegates to attention, more than a few impassive faces glanced at me before they gave Liang their full attention.

"Why are they looking at me as if they're displeased that I'm hale, hearty, and blaming old enemies from the other side of the universe for last night?" I asked in a soft voice. "Sorry, make that Saga and me."

"No worries," she replied in the same tone. "This is about you. I just happened to be there. You want a paranoid NILO analysis?"

"Shoot."

"Could it be some of them were hoping for an event that might help the secessionists by blaming Earth for attacking one of Mykonos' favorite sons?"

I gave my daughter an ironic look.

"Do tell, Captain. And their bomb turned out to be a fart in a hurricane. So now what?"

"Another incident, of course." She smirked back at me. "A faction on the floor, perhaps led by Madame Liang, though that's only a gut feeling, wants to turn the convention's demands for constitutional amendments to reform the Commonwealth into a declaration of independence by the OutWorlds and colonies."

"So, the delegates who gave me the fisheye just now are part of that faction."

Kal nodded.

"If Saga is right, that would be an explanation. You were supposed to breathe fire and brimstone against Centralist evildoers, not look like you had a pleasant evening with family and an uneventful drive back to the base."

"Is this convention one big secessionist conspiracy? Are we giving top cover to people who would fracture the Commonwealth and thereby crap on Kathryn Kowalski's legacy?"

Kal raised a hand.

"Stand easy, Colonel. Our job is ensuring the delegates do their thing without being interrupted, let alone harmed so that the Centralists don't accidentally trigger something we can't control. Nothing more. The Grand Admiral will decide anything beyond that."

I gave him a mock salute.

"Sir, yes, sir. I'll keep acting as a missile magnet. Mind you, I figure the answer from Earth to whatever the convention comes up with will be along the lines of go jump into a black hole."

Kal made a face. "I certainly hope it will be more nuanced and open the way to further negotiations, but I'm afraid the SecGen will reply with a brief rejection. He has no choice. Otherwise, his Home World allies in the Senate and the government will impeach him."

"Or worse," Saga said in a soft tone. "Growing signs that the Centralists are worried about the outcome of the convention have been mentioned in daily intelligence reports from HQ in the last two weeks. The most recent one I read before we headed out this morning, which I haven't yet had time to analyze, discusses the increasing pressure on Brüggemann to take a hard line. If he doesn't, he'll find himself surrounded by nothing but enemies and, shortly after that, out of office without the benefit of impeachment hearings."

I gave my daughter a searching glance. "A coup? That hasn't happened since early on during the Second Migration War."

She shrugged. "It would take a sixty percent majority vote in the Senate to impeach him anyhow, meaning the hardliners would need several OutWorld senators to vote in favor, and that simply won't happen. The Senate is rapidly heading for a permanent and irreconcilable split between the two factions. Which leaves the hardliners with no other choice."

"And then what?" I asked. "Are they expecting the Fleet to enforce a crackdown on dissenting OutWorlds and colonies merely by their replacement for Brüggemann issuing an edict? Good luck."

Saga, a wry expression on her face, nodded. "They are. The only part of the Armed Forces the politicians and bureaucrats on Earth see are the 1st Fleet, the 1st Marine Division, and the Terra Regiment, whose officers are almost all Centralist supporters. They can't fathom that well over half the Commonwealth's military and naval strength is composed of OutWorlders with little love for the federal government and its schemes to subvert the sovereign star system principle."

"Heck of a blind spot."

"But one deliberately created by successive Grand Admirals," Kal said. "Going back to Kathryn Kowalski. And it keeps the sort of officers who nearly led the Commonwealth to defeat during the opening moves of the Shrehari War where they do as little harm as possible. Although there are still plenty to go around the OutWorld-based fleets, unfortunately. But that's the nature of a peacetime military."

# — Thirty —

"The SecGen is getting pressure from all sides to do something about this so-called convention," Andreas Bauchan announced as he entered his office, where Miko Steiger was waiting for him. "And it's becoming harder and harder to dissuade him."

"What kind of pressure?"

Bauchan sat behind his desk and sighed.

"Home World senators want him to denounce the delegates publicly and take sanctions against sponsoring governments. Representatives of the great zaibatsus want him to simply arrest them. And members of the administration, including the cabinet, believe that something, anything, must be done to stop this nonsense. In other words, it's turning increasingly messy. And if we're not careful, Brüggemann might lash out in ways that'll be entirely counterproductive if he's feeling caught in the middle. Not that he has the authority to do anything against the delegates from sovereign star systems."

Steiger studied Bauchan, wondering whether now would be the right time to carry out her latest orders from Naval Intelligence and put the cat among the pigeons by suggesting a course of action that might contribute to increase the confusion surrounding the convention. Why she'd received those orders, Steiger couldn't say, but something told her Admiral Talyn was about to carry out one of her surprise moves.

"But he has authority over the colonies and their delegates."

"Yes." Bauchan returned her gaze with an impassive one of his own, clearly wondering where she was heading.

"Then why not act against the colonials? It might relieve some of the pressure Brüggemann feels while throwing the convention into a bit of disarray?"

Bauchan sat back, crossed one leg over the other, and rested his elbows on his chair's arms, hands joined at the fingertips.

"Act how, precisely?"

Steiger could tell he was interested because his whole manner had become casual.

"Ever heard of a little thing called sedition, you know, incitement of discontent against the government by acts or language breaching the public order? Isn't that what the convention is doing?" She allowed herself a sly smile. "Order the Constabulary to arrest the colonial delegates on charges of sedition. That'll help Brüggemann fend off those who want action while messing with the rest of the delegates."

Bauchan didn't immediately reply, though his gaze kept holding hers, and she knew he was parsing her suggestion for pitfalls.

"The federal judge for Mykonos will probably release them on their own recognizance the moment they appear before him."

"Sure. But he can forbid them from attending the convention as part of their bail conditions. Make sure the federal prosecutor for Mykonos demands it."

"Sedition, eh?" Bauchan tapped his fingertips against his chin. "Interesting idea. Quite interesting, in fact. I suppose it's worth a try." He reached out to tap his desk communicator. "Bauchan for the SecGen."

"Wait one," the anonymous voice of an aide replied a few seconds later.

A good half minute passed in silence before Brüggemann came on. "What is it, Andreas? I'm in the middle of a report from the SecAg."

"Sir, a partial solution occurred to me concerning the convention." Bauchan quickly explained the idea of charging the colonials with sedition.

"Do it. Get on to the SecJus and have her issue the order to the Constabulary in my name. Was there anything else?"

"No, sir."

"Brüggemann, out."

Bauchan glanced at Steiger again, this time with his usual smile, the one that never reached his eyes. "There you go, my dear. I trust you didn't mind that I appropriated your suggestion."

She smiled back. "Not at all, darling. I'm quite content to remain in the background, helping you and the Commonwealth government as best as the Deep Space Foundation and I can."

Inwardly, Steiger was jubilant. She didn't know whether it was the sort of intervention her superiors wanted, but it would surely shake up the convention.

# — Thirty-One —

The rest of the week passed quietly. Dennis Foster confirmed nothing was missing from the Mykonos Regiment's armory, meaning whoever fired at us probably brought their own weapon. On Sunday, Saga and I drove up to the Petras Town and Country Club at eleven-fifty-five for lunch with the extended family. We wore civilian clothes, this time, at Delia's suggestion.

The attendant ushered us into one of the private rooms, where we found three dozen Decker-Khanjans already clustered into small groups, glasses in hand, talking animatedly among themselves.

As soon as we appeared in the doorway, all conversation stopped, and two dozen pairs of eyes converged on us. The first to react was Delia, who gave us a big welcoming smile.

"Zack, Saga, how nice to see you again."

Before either of us could reply, the Old Man, trailed by Grandma Joanne, cut across the room and held out his hand.

"Zachary, welcome." He then turned to my daughter. "Saga, it's so very nice to see you again."

"And you, sir," she replied, inclining her head politely first to him, then to Joanne. "Good to see you again, ma'am."

I exchanged the usual kiss on the cheek with grandma, then my mother, and finally Delia, then shook hands with Richard. Of my father, there was no sign.

"Let me introduce you to the rest of the family, Saga," the Old Man said once we'd finished our greetings.

They began with Delia and Richard's daughters, Annette and Martine, who stared at Saga with undisguised curiosity — the aimless Deckers facing a cousin who was not only taller, fitter, and better looking but also had a successful career. The contrast between them was pretty noticeable.

"Where's dad?" I asked my mother in a whisper as I followed Saga around the room, greeting long-lost cousins, uncles, and aunts, many of whom seemed acutely uncomfortable shaking my hand and meeting my eyes.

"Off talking with some people. He'll join us momentarily."

I couldn't tell whether she was annoyed with my father for not being here, but she was undoubtedly irked about something. Along the way, I grabbed a mimosa and took a small sip. Top-notch champagne in the mix. But what else would one expect from the Old Man?

The rounds of the extended family done, I found myself face-to-face with my aunt Henrietta Khanjan, who studied me intently as she sipped her mimosa.

"So, Zachary Thomas Decker, back among the living, at least where this family is concerned." She was a tall beauty with shoulder-length platinum hair and deep blue eyes set in an ageless, slightly angular face that belied her seventy-odd years among the living. There had always been something fey about Henrietta, and that impression had, if anything, grown over the decades since I'd last seen her. Those eyes of hers gave nothing away but always seemed to know more than they could possibly see. "And a Commonwealth Marine Corps colonel with a daughter old enough to be a Marine Corps captain. My, things have changed for you, haven't they?"

I gave her my patented grin.

"And you haven't changed a bit, Henrietta. Still the most handsome woman around. What are you up to these days?"

Her lips twisted in a moue.

"I'm an adviser to the powerful and wealthy. I understand you were the target of an assassin's missile last Sunday. Who did you annoy?"

I shrugged, deciding to let her evasiveness pass. "The list is long. In my line of business, I've often cost the powerful and wealthy a lot of money and sometimes even their lives or the lives of their minions."

Amusement danced in her eyes as she took another sip of her mimosa.

"You don't really believe that, do you?"

"Oh?" I cocked an equally amused eyebrow at her. "And who do you think took a potshot at my daughter and me?"

"I wouldn't have the faintest idea, my dear. But perhaps you being the symbol of an increasingly disliked, if not outright hated, central government on a world hosting a constitutional convention to address the excesses of said central government might have something to do with it."

"So, you figure the secessionists are getting frisky."

"Perhaps." A mysterious smile briefly lit up her face. "You could always ask your father."

"He's a secessionist?"

"He just came into the room."

I turned to glance at him as he snapped up a mimosa glass, frowning, eyes on the far wall rather than on anyone. To say he seemed preoccupied might have been an understatement. He held the glass in his left hand, but his right hand hung at his side and twitched a few times. He finally met my gaze and gave me a tight nod, though his frown never wavered. I responded in kind, then turned my attention back to Henrietta.

"Didn't you know most of the Decker-Khanjan clan were secessionists?" She asked. "Other than a few outliers like Attar. That's why I'm doubly surprised you were let back into the family. Unless, of course, you're a secessionist as well."

"I'm a Marine officer and don't have political leanings either way."

She cocked her head to one side.

"Funny way of putting it. I'd have expected you to say you're a Commonwealth Marine Corps officer and take your orders from Earth."

"I take my orders from Caledonia. The Grand Admiral takes his orders from Earth."

"A not-so-subtle distinction." Henrietta took another sip. "And does your Grand Admiral sympathize with the OutWorlds? Or is he completely neutral? I mean, he is a Scandian by birth, isn't he?"

Interesting that Henrietta knew about Larsson's home planet.

"He is. But that doesn't affect how he carries out his duties. His job, and ours, is to protect human worlds."

Her mysterious smile returned, and she nodded knowingly. "The Fleet exists to serve humanity — OutWorlds, colonies, Home Worlds, even Earth."

"That's our ethos. We're not paid to mix it up in politics."

"And yet your General Ryent is acting more like a politician than a Marine officer."

I shrugged.

"He's under orders."

"As are you."

"Yep."

"What happens if the orders you receive go against those issued by Earth?"

Another shrug. "If the Grand Admiral goes against the orders he received, I'll presume he had a good reason to do so. Besides, that stuff is so far above my pay grade that I can't even imagine the decision-making process involved."

"Oh, I'm sure you know more than you're letting on, Zack. You always were shrewder than your brother, and he's no slouch in that area." She winked at me, then wandered away with her empty glass, looking for a place to put it down.

Delia and her daughters were in deep conversation with Saga, while Richard and our father were in a world of their own, discussing something of importance, judging by the expressions on their faces, though they glanced at me a few times. Since none of the cousins seemed inclined to chat with me, though they also gave me sideways glances, I decided to join dear papa and my brother out of sheer devilment more than anything else.

Both gave me frowns when it became clear my smiling face was headed for them, and I gave them an enthusiastic greeting.

"Father, Richard, how are you on this auspicious day?"

"Zachary." Dad met my gaze with an impassive stare as if his words the previous Sunday hadn't been spoken.

Richard nodded once. "If you'll excuse me." He headed off to where Delia stood.

"So, I understand you survived an assassination attempt," my father said.

"I don't know that it was an assassination attempt. The missile struck aft of the passenger compartment. If someone had wanted us dead, they'd have aimed a meter and a half or two meters further forward, which isn't hard to do at the range they fired." I took a sip of my mimosa, eyes locked with my father's. "Henrietta seems to think it was the secessionists expressing displeasure with a native son who wears the Commonwealth's uniform."

"Could be. What do you think?"

I made a face.

"No idea. I have plenty of enemies who'd love to take potshots at me. But like I said, I don't think whoever it was aimed to kill us. And since I've been away from Mykonos for so long, I can't see anyone wanting to warn me off. So maybe it was the secessionists, but not for the reason Henrietta suggested."

"How do you figure that?"

"A false flag, just like the fake SecGen speech. Something designed to make the Centralist cause look bad and push the delegates into actively considering independence from the Commonwealth."

My father scoffed. "And how would a botched attack on a Commonwealth officer do that?"

I allowed myself an amused air.

"While you're busy hating me, many people around Petras think I'm a native boy who did exceptionally well and who's now back home making sure the convention can proceed without external interference."

His return smile was about as cold as the top of Mykonos' ice caps.

"Oh, I don't hate you, boy. I just have a hard time seeing you as my son, now more than ever, since you're not only wearing a uniform that represents everything I despise, but you're a senior officer to boot."

"And what if I told you my views are in sympathy with the OutWorlds, not Earth, as are the views of many, maybe even most Marines?"

He gave me an appraising stare.

"Really? You Commonwealth minions are allowed to have opinions that go against the official party line?"

"Our job is not only to protect humanity from enemies foreign and domestic, but most of all, these days, it's preventing another Migration War. The way we see it, Earth and the Home Worlds are the ones pushing the Commonwealth in that direction."

I saw genuine surprise in my father's eyes for the first time.

"So, *Dad*, tell me something. The people who fired that missile at my staff car had to have known I was supping at the Casa Decker, and the Old Man isn't one to blab. But you're a secessionist through and through. If I'm right about it being another false flag, I have to ask — did you have anything to do with it?"

Before he could answer, a soft bell chimed, the signal to go next door and take our seats at the round tables. Still, he gave me a curious look before gesturing at the private dining room door.

"I think that's us."

Saga and I sat at the Old Man's table, along with Henrietta, Grandmother, and a few cousins. My parents were seated at the next one, and during the meal, I caught my father giving me calculating glances from time to time. And I was increasingly convinced he had something to do with the attack.

Once back in our car, after a long and somewhat painfully stilted luncheon, Saga and I gave each other commiserating looks.

"Survived the full blast of the Decker-Khanjan clan, kiddo?"

She gave me a rueful smile.

"Barely. I can understand why you wanted to get away from them the moment you came of age, Dad. I must say, though, that cousins Annette and Martine are nice but insipid. I can't believe they're Delia's daughters."

"You know what they say. The first generation builds, the second consolidates, the third coasts on the accumulated wealth, and the fourth loses everything. Your cousins are the fourth generation of the main Decker branch." I gave her a grin. "As are you, but you're not connected to the family wealth, so there's that. And speaking about the second generation, I think my father had something to do with the missile sniper."

Saga got our car moving along the private road headed for the highway and Fort Monash.

"I'm not surprised."

"Why?"

She turned her smiling face toward me.

"My intelligence analysis has been pointing at your — our — family as being among the culprits."

"And you were going to tell me this when?"

"Just about now, after watching the various potential culprits over lunch. The Decker-Khanjan clan is indeed deeply involved with the secessionists."

Before I could reply, my communicator chimed for attention. It was the operations center.

"Decker."

"Corinne Renaud, sir. I have the duty. The CO of the 55th Constabulary Group wants to speak with you. I gathered it was urgent."

"Patch me through."

"One moment, please, sir."

Seconds later, the face of Chief Superintendent Yolande Zakhar appeared on the display. We'd briefly met on our second day here, just by way of introduction. She was a compact fifty-something with short black hair and a dark complexion and hailed from Novaya Sibir.

"Colonel Decker. Thank you for getting back so quickly. I figured that I owed you an immediate call under the circumstances."

"What's up?"

"I've just received orders to arrest the colonies' representatives."

# — Thirty-Two —

"What?" I asked incredulously.

Zakhar's face was carved from stone as she stared back at me. "The various federally appointed colonial administrations have issued arrest warrants for their so-called representatives. I've received orders to enforce those warrants."

"On what grounds were they issued?"

"Sedition."

I couldn't help but scoff. "There haven't been charges of sedition laid in living memory. What sort of drugs are they taking?"

"And yet, I have received warrants issued by a dozen federal colonies. Valid warrants." Her tone was as flat as her expression. "Before you ask, they were staffed through Constabulary HQ, which approved my executing them."

I exchanged a glance with Saga, who was frowning as her agile mind parsed the manifold consequences of this new development.

"Anyway," Zakhar continued while our car turned onto the main road, "I intend to arrest the persons named in the warrants as soon as I finish negotiating my entry into the restricted area with the Mykonos Police Service. Which, I hope, will be later this afternoon."

"And what if the police won't allow you into the Celadon Resort?"

"That's where you come in."

"I beg your pardon?"

"You own the perimeter, even though the police are nominally in charge. If they don't let me in, then you will. I'm invoking the Inter-agency Assistance Regulations, which require Fleet personnel to help the Constabulary carry out its duties."

I glanced at Saga again; she now wore a thin-lipped air of annoyance, probably at Zakhar invoking the IARs. I also felt a touch irked.

"Understood, Chief Superintendent, but since the police are in charge, we have a subordinate role and cannot simply override them."

"You can if you want to, Colonel. And I'll be making sure you will. Zakhar, out."

"Ouch." Saga grimaced at me when Zakhar's image vanished from my communicator. "If it weren't because the orders came from Constabulary HQ, I'd call this another attempt by the secessionists to drive the delegates into voting for independence. But unfortunately, it fits with the increased signs of panic we're seeing from Earth."

"Kind of irrational to arrest innocent delegates from the federal colonies, though. And on charges of sedition? Talk about setting yourself up for an own goal."

"Historically, this sort of thing has happened with monotonous regularity, Dad — states acting against their best interests."

"I know. Overreach by Earth triggered both Migration Wars."

My gut was telling me whatever happened next could influence the entire future of humanity across the stars. And I was going to be in the middle of it.

"Time to let Kal know about this latest shit show." But when I pinged his communicator, it went straight to voice recording.

"Kal, this is Zack. We have a problem. The Constabulary has received orders to arrest the colonial representatives, and they want me to intervene under the Inter-agency Assistance Regulations if the Mykonos Police don't play ball. Talk to you soonest."

We spent the rest of the trip back to Fort Monash in silence, each lost in our thoughts. Once there, we headed straight for my office.

"Is this where it begins?" I dropped into my chair and looked at Saga, who took one across the desk from me. "And how it begins?"

"You mean, is it the beginning of the end for the Commonwealth?" She shrugged. "Possibly, but not likely."

"I got the feeling Zakhar would obey her orders no matter what happens. How about you?"

"She certainly sounded determined, but she shuttered her feelings tightly, making it hard to evaluate her true thoughts. What will you do?"

I gave my daughter a sly smile. "Pull our people out of the secure zone and keep patrols outside the perimeter only. That way, the cops are the only ones controlling access."

"You know Zakhar will see that as you evading the matter of assisting her in arresting the colonial representatives."

"Yep. And she can complain to my commanding officer and her superiors on Wyvern. By the time the latter sort things out at the Chief Constable to Grand Admiral level, the convention may well be over. And if it isn't, well?" I shrugged. "I'll deal with things when they happen."

"You going to run this by Kal beforehand?"

"Sure."

But with him being incommunicado and Zakhar pushing hard, I might have to act alone, good intentions notwithstanding. I glanced at the time — just before fifteen-hundred hours, which meant shift change in one hour. It would take Zakhar at least that long, if not longer, to hit a wall with the Mykonos Police since the latter would have to send the request to be let in so they could arrest the colonial representatives all the way up to the president's office.

"If I have time. And I don't think I have."

I called the operations center and issued orders that the Ghost Squadron company coming on duty at sixteen hundred stand down. Then, I called the police chief superintendent in charge of the security operation and told him I was withdrawing the troopers from inside the perimeter for the foreseeable future because of other pressing needs. The news surprised him, but after a few weeks of nothing happening, he took it philosophically. After all, the MLI troopers patrolling outside the perimeter fence would still be there.

Sixteen hundred hours rolled around without a word from Zakhar, and the Ghost Squadron company on duty inside the perimeter withdrew, leaving it entirely to the Mykonos Police Service. This meant Zakhar could invoke the Inter-agency Assistance Regulations, but I could no longer do a damn thing to countermand the cops if their orders were to keep the Constabulary out.

When he finally appeared from whatever meeting he was taking, Kal approved my move without hesitation.

It took until early the next afternoon before the Mykonos government responded by refusing to hand the colonial representatives over, and I got the expected call from Zakhar.

"What do you mean you can't?" She asked, her face like thunder after I told her I couldn't help with arraigning the representatives.

"I've withdrawn my troopers from the secure zone and handed full responsibility back to the police since they were clearly not needed for close protection. I'm sorry."

She didn't immediately reply, visibly chewing on her words as she processed my statement.

"You did this on purpose, didn't you, Decker?"

Aha. It was simply 'Decker' now, not 'Colonel' or 'Colonel Decker', although a Constabulary chief superintendent wore an oak leaf wreath with two diamonds to a full colonel's oak leaf wreath with three diamonds.

"I did what was necessary to further my mission and my orders, Zakhar. And I judged that the mission no longer needed troopers working alongside the police within the perimeter. You'll need to find another way of executing the arrest warrants. Now, was there something else?"

"You haven't heard the last of this. I'm sending a full report to HQ within the hour. Zakhar, out." Her image vanished abruptly.

"And a good day to you, too," I replied to a darkened display.

It had gone about as I'd expected, but if ever we needed Constabulary cooperation for anything from here on, it wouldn't be forthcoming.

Less than an hour later, the operations center called me to inform me of an incident unfolding at the main gate to the secure perimeter around the Celadon Resort and Spa. A hundred-strong Constabulary contingent led by Chief Superintendent Zakhar was trying to force its way in claiming federal jurisdiction and threatening to arrest anyone from the Mykonos Police Service who stood in the way.

With a sigh, I grabbed my beret and called for a troop from the quick reaction force and a pair of dropships to take me there. Since I had the biggest guns in town, I was stuck with keeping the peace, but Zakhar claiming federal jurisdiction didn't augur well.

When we landed on the cleared strip a hundred meters from the perimeter gate, I could see a good old-fashioned standoff in the making. I headed up the road accompanied by an armed and armored section from the QRF troop, although I was simply wearing battledress. But I had my Shrehari blaster on my hip.

The Constabulary members were also armed, wore police armor — gray to our black — and were deployed along the perimeter fence and gate, effectively blocking the main entrance. Facing them on the other side of the fence were bemused police officers who clearly did not know what was happening.

And observing both groups from a distance were my MLI troopers.

Zakhar, minus the armor and sidearm, was facing Chief Superintendent Parker, though they didn't appear to be speaking.

I wandered over to where the MLI company commander stood, eyes on the two police commanders.

"Fergie. How are they hanging?"

"In accordance with brigade standing orders, Colonel. Do you know what the hell is going on here? The Constab showed up twenty minutes ago and set up a roadblock."

"They have arrest warrants for the two dozen representatives from federal colonies, and the locals aren't letting them in."

Captain Ferguson let out a low whistle. "Ouch. What are the warrants for?"

"Sedition."

He turned his head to look at me in surprise. "How do they figure that?"

"No idea."

"So, what are we supposed to do, sir? I have received no fresh orders from ops."

"Just keep on doing your job and ignore the Constabulary folks. They're for the locals to deal with."

"Roger that, sir."

I gave him a wave and headed for where Chief Superintendents Zakhar and Parker were having their staring contest. They looked comical, standing at ease, hands joined in the small of the back, facing each other across the closed gate. Of a similar height, Zakhar was dark-haired and complexioned, whereas Parker was light-complexioned with blond hair. The one wore Constabulary gray with a sky-blue beret, the other Police Service dark blue with a black beret. They were as much of a contrast as possible, yet they seemed eerily similar.

I approached them from the side, or rather I approached Zakhar from the side, to try and make it clear I was a neutral party in their standoff.

"Chief Superintendent Parker, Chief Superintendent Zakhar. May I ask what's going on here? My troopers are puzzled."

"You know damn well what's going on, Colonel," Zakhar replied without looking at me. "The Mykonos government is refusing to cooperate with the Commonwealth Constabulary in the legitimate arrest warrants for several so-called colonial representatives."

"Is that a fact, Chief Superintendent Parker?" I asked, turning my head toward her.

"As much as I'd like to cooperate with the Constabulary, my orders are to keep federal personnel out of the secure perimeter. That includes you, sir."

"And what are your intentions, Chief Superintendent Zakhar?"

"I've asked the star system's chief federal judge to rule that the Mykonos government cannot prevent my carrying out the arrest warrants. In the meantime, I intend to keep the individuals targeted by those warrants from leaving the site." She glanced at me. "As well as anyone else currently inside the perimeter. And if they try by air, I have portable EMP generators that'll knock down any aircraft."

"Except mine. It sounds like you've declared war on the Mykonos government, Chief Superintendent."

"I'm claiming federal jurisdiction over the site and its surroundings, Colonel. Until I'm allowed to serve those arrest warrants."

# — Thirty-Three —

"Can she do that?" I asked my daughter over the secure radio link once I was beyond earshot of the closest Constabulary member, and I'd given her a rundown of the situation.

"It's a bit extreme, but yes. As senior Constabulary officer in the star system, she can temporarily declare federal jurisdiction over a discrete area or situation while a federal judge contemplates a request to force a star system government's cooperation."

"Who the hell thought up a law allowing that sort of thing?"

"It goes back to Kathryn Kowalski's day, meaning to the founding of the Constabulary. And it's not a bad law, really."

"How long does that judge have to contemplate?"

"Twenty-four hours tops."

"And what happens if the judge tells the Mykonos government to hand the colonial representatives over and the president refuses?"

I could see my daughter grimace in my mind's eye.

"Then, technically, Mykonos will be in a state of rebellion against the Commonwealth. But before that happens, the judge will likely order you — or Kal — to go in and seize the representatives on behalf of the Constabulary. Or at least neutralize the Mykonos Police Service while the Constabulary makes the arrests."

"And if Kal or I refuse?"

"Then it'll go straight to the Grand Admiral. If he says go in and help the Constabulary, and you refuse, you'll be relieved of command."

"Yeah, well, I won't refuse the big boss' orders. Hell, I won't even refuse Kal's."

"Glad to hear you say so."

"Okay. That was it for now. Thanks. Decker, out."

My daughter was an absolute marvel. She could dig up the most arcane bit of information at a moment's notice. If she stuck with a career in the Corps' Intelligence Branch, she'd make senior rank in no time.

I returned to where Zakhar and Parker were still staring at each other.

"So, anything from the federal judge yet?"

"No."

"Well, let me know when and if you get an answer."

With that, I wandered off to my dropship. I'd barely covered twenty meters when Zakhar's voice stopped me in my tracks.

"Colonel, I just received my answer from the chief judge. He enjoins the Mykonos government to let me arrest the so-called colonial representatives."

I returned to where she stood and addressed myself to Chief Superintendent Parker. "Will you admit the Constabulary?"

"No, sir. Not unless I get orders telling me to do so."

"The chief judge also enjoins federal authorities, Armed Forces included, to help apprehend the individuals named in the arrest warrants." Zakhar turned to give me a stern look. "I, therefore, ask for your help in allowing my people to enter this site."

"Not just yet, Chief Superintendent. Let's allow Chief Superintendent Parker's superiors time to digest the judge's injunction."

I walked away again to speak with Kal. If the Mykonos government disregarded the injunction, I needed his orders on whether we cooperate with the Constabulary. This time, he answered almost at once.

After I told him how things stood, he said, without hesitating, "If the Mykonosians persist in refusing the judge's orders, we have no choice but to step in, Zack."

"Good. That's what I wanted to hear."

"Is it, though?" He asked me in a curious tone. "Or is that the official Zack speaking, not the man behind the mask?"

"I'm all about being official, Kal. The various governments might play dangerous games, but I'm not participating. I'll stay true to my oath unless our government crosses the line. Arresting colonial representatives for sedition doesn't qualify. Especially not if the Constabulary thinks the warrants are valid."

"All right. You have your orders. If the Mykonosians don't want to play ball, you'll force the issue."

"Aye, aye, sir."

"Ryent, out."

I was a tad surprised Kal had sided with the Constabulary so quickly and easily. He'd been playing politics so much since we arrived I must have somehow thought he might prevaricate or even side with the locals. Which showed how much I knew about the man these days.

When I returned to the chief superintendent face-off, Parker was just informing Zakhar that the Mykonos government was disregarding the federal chief judge's injunction and wouldn't grant the Constabulary access. I let out a loud sigh, which attracted both women's attention.

"Since you can't play nice, here's what will happen. I will take my dropships and land inside the perimeter with a troop of my Marines and twenty Constabulary members. We will arrest the individuals named in the warrants and then leave. I trust you and your people are smart enough to not interfere, Chief Superintendent Parker." Before she could reply, I turned to Zakhar. "Designate the members carrying out the arrests and have them assemble by my dropships within the next five minutes."

I headed to the dropships myself and spoke with both pilots and the QRF troop leader, then with Captain

Ferguson, telling him that no one was to leave the secure perimeter until we were done. Ultimately, it took almost ten minutes before Zakhar and nineteen of her constables showed up. Parker had long since vanished, no doubt conferring with her superiors about my impending invasion. What I hoped she wasn't doing was preparing to resist. Or hide the colonial representatives.

We climbed aboard the dropships, which rose twenty meters into the air, their aft ramps staying open, flew over the physical perimeter, and landed on the lawn fronting the resort. Mykonos cops watched us closely as we exited and spread out to surround Zakhar and her constables, who headed straight for the convention hall, but they didn't intervene, let alone raise weapons against us.

Zakhar brushed past the sentries at the main doors, crossed the lobby, and entered the hall where the delegates were deliberating. At her arrival and that of her people, the speaker, one of Scandia's representatives, fell silent.

"What is the meaning of this?" He demanded.

"I am Chief Superintendent Zakhar of the Commonwealth Constabulary. We are executing arrest warrants, sir. It won't take but a moment." Zakhar gestured at her constables, who spread out among the back tables where the colonials sat.

And it didn't. In the space of about ninety seconds, they'd handcuffed the colonials and were taking them out of the hall to the silent glares of disapproval of the remaining delegates. I'd stayed in the lobby with my people and exited ahead of the Constabulary and their prisoners.

We made it back to the dropships and let them load while we simply marched to the main gate, where we let ourselves out while the dropships flew off toward Petras and the 55th Constabulary Group HQ. The entire operation took less than ten minutes. And I felt more than a bit dirty at having eased it. But Kal gave the order, and that was that.

The dropships came back to pick us up and return to Fort Monash. By the time I was back in my office, my ugly mug was already on the newsnets for having helped the Commonwealth Constabulary's arrest of innocent delegates. So much for being Mykonos' favorite son, who'd done good.

The Mykonos government had clearly released the information on the arrests and how they were done since the newsnets weren't allowed within two kilometers of the site. I wondered how that would affect Kal's cozy relationships.

"There's the man of the hour."

Speak of the devil, and he appears. A smiling Kal Ryent walked into my office and plunked himself in one of the chairs facing my desk.

"I guess I'm now persona non grata at the Celadon Resort and Spa."

"Yep. And in various other places, the presidential palace included."

"You seem remarkably sanguine about my banishment from society."

He tapped the side of his nose with an extended index finger. "In a good cause."

"You going to tell me what that cause is?"

"Not yet."

I gave him a hard look, but he remained unfazed. Instead, he climbed to his feet again, still smiling, and left.

Some days I just wanted to wring his neck.

# — Thirty-Four —

I hate getting woken in the middle of the night, especially when I was having a pleasant dream, but my communicator chimed at an ungodly hour, and I reached for it.

"Decker."

"Operations, sir. We have a priority one alert at the resort. They're under attack by an unknown but large number of tangos, many of whom dropped into the secure perimeter from above."

If I wasn't awake before, I sure was now. "Airborne troops?"

"Looks like it. The duty MLI company is fighting off the tangos outside the perimeter. The QRF company is getting warmed up and should be in the air in the next five minutes, while the 2nd MLI, the rest of the 1st MLI, and Ghost Squadron are being alerted. The latter two should be ready to go within the next fifteen minutes. The 2nd MLI will stand by as reserve."

It was my worst nightmare come true — an organized force, perhaps battalion-sized, attacking the resort in the middle of the night. And I had no one inside the perimeter, meaning two or three dozen cops were the only thing that stood between the attackers and the delegates.

"I'm on my way. Decker, out."

I climbed out of bed and slipped on my battledress uniform. Then, after a moment of hesitation, I dug into the closet and pulled out my combat armor, helmet, and harness. A few minutes later, my blaster strapped to my hip, I walked out of my suite and knocked on Kal's door.

He opened in under a minute, and I quickly got him up to speed.

"You look like you're headed out there, Zack."

"I am." With that, I turned on my heels and made my way out to a parade square now seething with activity as the 1st MLI's remaining two companies and Ghost Squadron were getting organized, ready to lift off as soon as the aviation squadron's remaining dropships appeared.

I'd switched my helmet radio to the emergency frequency and got plenty of chatter from the police, most of whom seemed to have barricaded themselves behind closed doors and were screaming for backup. There was a lot less from my duty company which was concentrating in platoon strength at four equidistant points along the outer perimeter, as they'd practiced in case of an enemy attack.

I flicked over to the regular frequency. "QRF, this is Niner-Niner."

"QRF."

"I want you to land inside the perimeter, the birds well spread out."

"Roger that."

"Niner-niner, out."

I had an overwhelming desire to be with them, but my place wasn't at the sharp end. Just then, Lora Cyone and Josh Bayliss, both armored and armed, appeared as if by magic.

"We're ready to go, sir," the former said. "You hear anything more about the tangos?"

"No." I shook my head. "Sounds like total confusion inside the perimeter right now. I ordered the QRF to land there, well dispersed. Lora, you go ahead and land the rest of your battalion inside. Josh, I'll have you set down a klick away to take the rest of the tangos in a pincer."

I touched my helmet and projected a holographic map of the area between us. I touched a few spots where roads and trails led to the resort. "There, there, and there."

"Got it. Got a question as well. How the hell did they drop airborne troops with no one noticing until they'd landed? And how did they move up what sounds like at least a company or two on the ground?"

"Your guess is as good as mine. Anything else?"

Both shook their heads.

"Then off you go."

I watched from a distance as both collected their company commanders to pass along what little orders they had. This one would be purely by the seat of our pants.

When the dropships showed up, I gave in to my desire and climbed aboard one of those assigned to transport the rest of the 1st MLI. As we lifted off, the first reports came in from the QRF, which had just landed inside the perimeter.

The cops were still holding the main building, but the tangos had breached it in one spot and were spreading out. It looked like we'd be facing room-to-room fighting — the nastiest combat of all.

The dropship I rode landed with a slight thump, and the aft ramp dropped to reveal a tableau of plasma flashes outside the fence, where the MLI duty company was holding off the attackers. I ran down the ramp after the platoon had left and oriented myself to the site while the dropships rose vertically before peeling off. Further plasma flashes lit up the windows of the main building as my QRF people hunted the attackers.

It was a completely confused clusterfuck, and I realized I had nothing to do while Lora deployed her third company to surround the building and attempted to get a clearer picture of what was happening from the QRF company commander. So, I found a spot at the foot of a tree, knelt, and watched as the tableau unfolded.

Then, the first explosion lit up the night and shattered out one of the ground-floor windows, and a voice on the emergency net said, "I had him cornered, and he blew himself up. Just like that."

A single word suddenly lit up my frontal cortex — Hashashin. It could only be them. Those fanatics who sold their services to the highest bidder never surrendered. They preferred death in the service of their deity.

I switched to the command frequency.

"Break, break. This is Niner-Niner. We could be facing Hashashin. I repeat, we could be facing Hashashin."

"Golf Niner, roger," Josh Bayliss replied almost at once.

"Mike Niner, roger," Lora Cyone chimed in a few seconds later. "That means we really need to keep the ones in the building away from the delegates' floors. Otherwise, they'll simply enter rooms and blow themselves up."

Moments later, the shadows of the troopers surrounding the building moved toward it as another explosion, this time on the second floor, blew out another window. The delegates were on the third and fourth floors and hopefully barricaded behind their room doors, but a few might stick their heads out, wondering what the fuss was.

The police commander finally broke through the radio noise and spoke with the captain commanding the QRF company to coordinate their activities. There was a lull in activities, and I turned toward the perimeter, but the firing had also decreased to almost nothing. It probably meant the Hashashin were attempting to maneuver around the duty company's positions.

Suddenly, a series of explosions rocked the main building — on the third floor — and I mentally swore. Then plasma flashed inside the hotel and along the perimeter, where armored figures were caught between Ghost Squadron and the duty company, which cut them down in short order. One last explosion lit up the third floor before everything fell silent.

I switched to the 1st MLI's frequency and listened in as the QRF company commander reported at least twelve tangos had committed explosive suicide, with another fifteen shot before they could trigger their charges.

"We're checking the third and fourth floors now," he said, "but I think that's it."

At that moment, one final explosion sounded on the third floor.

"Okay, now that's it."

I climbed to my feet and headed toward the open door to see for myself whether the tangos got to the delegates. When I reached the first explosion site, it was as nasty as I'd expected. Nothing was left of the man except a spatter of bodily fluids, and the force had been enough to damage stone walls and the marble floor and eviscerate the suspended ceiling.

I passed troopers standing guard and took the stairs up to the second floor, where more evidence of suicide bombers littered the hallways. Then I reached the third and saw several room doors simply blown away. I quickly found the captain commanding the QRF company, Captain Farhad, standing with a man in police armor wearing an inspector's rank badge.

"Any casualties?" I asked.

Farhad turned toward me grim-faced. "Looks like they took six delegates with them before we put a stop to it. I have eight wounded." His voice was level, but I could tell the adrenaline crash was coming.

I glanced at the inspector. "You?"

"Five dead, a dozen wounded." He sounded like a man keeping a tight lid on his emotions, a lid so tight it might pop any second. "Who were those animals?"

"You mean the self-detonating tangos? We call them Hashashin. They belong to a fanatical religious sect whose greatest sacrament is dying while taking unbelievers — everybody but their sort — with them. The Hashashin hire themselves out to the highest bidder and never, ever surrender."

I suppose I could have given the poor inspector chapter and verse about the origins of the Hashashin over a thousand years ago and their perpetuation under various guises over the centuries. But I figured he had different concerns on his mind at the moment.

Instead, I asked, "Which delegates died?"

The inspector quickly named them — one from Scandia, one from Cimmeria, one from Nabhka, both delegates from Cascadia, and one from Dordogne. All except the Nabhka delegate were from major star systems. That was going to cause no end of turmoil.

"Alright. I'll let you get on with it. Don't allow any delegates out of their rooms until Captain Farhad's people have combed through the entire hotel."

I made my way back downstairs and briefly spoke with Lora about setting up her battalion as inner security for the rest of the night, then headed for the main gate and the guard company. It also had a dozen wounded, but none seriously, so I had them pull into the perimeter and set up a first aid station for the battalion and the police while

Ghost Squadron, which had no casualties, took over the outer perimeter security.

Then, I spoke with Josh.

"How many tangos on the outside?"

"About a hundred or so. They went down in berserker charges. No survivors. Any idea of how many on the inside?"

"About thirty-five or forty. Self-detonating, though only half made the big jump into the Infinite Void by their own hand."

"So definitely Hashashin."

"I don't know of any other mercenaries who practice self-immolation in the service of their employer. This was clearly a one-way mission for the lot of them."

"But there are others of their sort still alive and running around free — the ones who airdropped the attackers into the secure zone, for example."

I nodded. "Yep. But finding them will be the Security Intelligence Service's job."

The first dropships come to evacuate the wounded, ours and the police's, appeared over the treetops and, guided by the MLI troopers, landed on the resort's front lawn, where the casualties were being concentrated.

"Did they get any delegates?"

"Six of them."

"Damn."

"Yeah, damn. If we'd had a company from your squadron inside the perimeter, they might still be alive, so that's on me playing games with the Constabulary."

"You couldn't have known."
"No. But it's still on me."
I suddenly felt exhausted.

# — Thirty-Five —

By the time dawn rolled around, I'd established my command post in a grounded dropship on the front lawn and was sipping a cup of coffee while standing on the downed aft ramp, keeping out of my subordinates' way as much as possible. A company of Ghost Squadron was retracing the steps of the tangos who'd come up against the outer perimeter to try to find the landing zones where they'd been dropped off while the other two patrolled.

I'd exchanged the 1st MLI for the 2nd, which now secured the inner zone while the Police Service's forensic teams were swarming over the resort. Other police teams were dealing with the delegates, trying to keep them calm and away from the sites of the explosions. Fortunately, none of my casualties turned out to be significant, though the police's were. They'd taken the brunt of the initial assault. All of them had been flown to the Petras General Hospital.

Shortly after oh-six hundred, an aircar appeared over the treetops and was immediately ordered down on the outside of the main gate. The driver tried to argue with the company commander running the 2nd MLI's operations cell in the dropship next to mine but got lit up with targeting sensors for his pains and told in no uncertain terms he was within seconds of being shot at. He landed on the main road and pulled up to the sentries at the gate. They inspected the passengers, then drew themselves to attention and saluted, which meant at least Kal was aboard, if not someone higher up the food chain.

I downed the last of my coffee and placed the cup on the nearest bench, then I adopted the parade rest position, eyes on the car as it came up the drive. As I expected, it came to a halt level with my command post dropship, and Kal, wearing a battledress uniform, complete with the two stars of his rank at the collar, got out from the left side of the passenger compartment.

President Eugenius Van Kirten, dressed in a somber business suit, climbed out on the right side, and I snapped to attention.

"Good morning, Mister President. General."

"Good morning, Zack," a grim-faced Eugene replied. "I hope we're not interfering with anything."

"No, sir. Things have settled. The Police Service has the resort itself and the delegates under control. We're merely providing external security."

"Your initial report mentioned Hashashin," Kal said. "Anything new to prove or disprove the theory?"

I shook my head. "No. The bodies we recovered had no identification and no markings, and their equipment was generic. But they were mostly of a similar phenotype, the sort we've seen with Hashashin before, and they're the only self-detonating tangos we know of. Almost two dozen blew themselves up rather than surrender. And they're not outstanding fighters. Between them, the duty company and Ghost Squadron wiped out a company's worth, many deliberately charging our lines to die gloriously and try to take some of our people with them. If you want to see their remains, we have them stacked outside the perimeter waiting for disposal."

"Why drop a platoon's worth into the perimeter and send a company's worth against the fence?"

I shrugged. "It could be they only had one shuttle or aircraft, which was only big enough for thirty-five. But I'll tell you one thing. They almost certainly had inside knowledge."

"How so?" Eugene asked.

"First, they knew the delegates were on the third and fourth floors, and second, they knew I'd withdrawn my people from the secure inner zone. Otherwise, they'd have never tried with just thirty-five."

A few thoughts occurred to me, and I wondered just how much success the tangos were hoping to achieve in the first place. Did they expect to overwhelm the duty company and reinforce the platoon that had been airdropped? If so, what gave them the idea MLI troopers would be pushovers?

Kal, who could tell I was cogitating, gave me a searching look, and I voiced those questions.

"This entire business seems a little off when you think about it. The Hashashin clearly weren't in sufficient numbers to overwhelm even the reduced security. At least not once our QRF arrived, and it was key to stopping the attack."

"Maybe they were all that was available for this contract. And I agree, if the QRF had arrived five minutes later, we'd have more dead cops and delegates. But on to the next set of questions — who commissioned the attack, and what were they hoping to achieve? Kill every last delegate?"

"Finding those answers will be a job for Ellie Pierce's people," Eugene said. "I guess we can be thankful that only eleven people died in the attack, and it seems that's mainly because of your folks, Zack. Please pass along a Bravo Zulu from me."

"Will do, sir."

Eugene glanced at Kal. "I'll see the delegates now. You can stay with Zack if you have more to discuss, though you're welcome to join me."

"I'll go with you, sir." He patted me on the arm. "We can speak later."

I watched them walk up to the resort's main building and pass between the sentries from the 2nd MLI at the front door. Just then, the urge to yawn hit me, and I went in search for another mug of coffee. It was going to be a long day.

***

"How are the wounded?" Kal asked as he entered my office later that day.

I'd returned to Fort Monash via the Petras General Hospital just after lunch, once the bodies of the mercenaries had been removed, and we'd resumed the security routine that existed before I sparred with the Constabulary. I doubted there would be another assault of the sort we'd witnessed in any case.

"In good spirits. Three will take a few days to recover, but the rest will be released on light duty by tomorrow morning. How are the delegates?"

"Shaken, angry, afraid, every emotion in the book. And they're clamoring to know who commissioned the attack. Have you looked at the newsnets yet?"

"No. Why? Are they doing anything more intelligent than spouting outlandish theories interspersed with condemnation of the police and the Corps for allowing this outrage?"

"I don't know." He gave me his usual smile, although it seemed tired. "I haven't seen them. That's why I asked."

"I'm sure the S-2 section is monitoring the main channels."

"Speaking of which, are they unraveling the mystery of the Hashashin yet?"

I shook my head. "No. The initial after-action report is on its way home, along with the biometric data on the dead Hashashin. Mind you, I doubt they'll be found in any database known to the human species."

"I doubt it as well. It's frightening to think people can be fanaticized to the extent that they'll gladly blow themselves up so long as they can take one of the enemy with them."

"It's nothing new. Zealots have been pulling that sort of garbage since time immemorial. What's the plan for the convention now?"

"Oh, they're more determined than ever to see it through. They'll hold a memorial for the murdered delegates tomorrow morning, before the start of the day's business, then get back to it. The home planets of the dead have been advised and will no doubt send replacements by the fastest means."

"Any rumors among them as to who's behind this?"

"Yes." Kal's smile became pained. "Who do you think they have as the primary culprit?"

"The Commonwealth government."

He nodded. "Indeed."

"And they'd likely be wrong. Call it a gut feeling. Sure, the Sécurité Spéciale has used the Hashashin before — not that we can prove it. But the more I think about it, the more this seems too ham-fisted for them."

"Then who?"

I made a face.

"The interstellar zaibatsus? They have the money and the underworld connections to hire Hashashin, and they're very much on the side of the Commonwealth government. Of course, it could always be another false flag by the secessionists."

"A costly false flag. One that could have seen a lot more delegates killed if it hadn't been for the speed of your QRF."

"Deadlier operations have been carried out in the name of deception." I chewed on the inside of my lip for a few seconds. "I'll bet you one thing, though. The Security Intelligence Service will be just as puzzled over this as they are over the fake SecGen speech and the attack on Saga and me, which was likely carried out by the Hashashin as well."

Kal cocked an eyebrow at me. "Are you saying the SIS is knowingly covering for the secessionists?"

A shrug.

"I don't know what I'm saying, to be honest. I just know they won't make any headway identifying the origin of the Hashashin or whoever piloted the aircraft or shuttle that dropped them into the secure zone. Which reminds me, he said closing the barn door after the horses escaped. We should have the Mykonos Regiment deploy an aerospace defense cell to cover the vertical axis above the resort."

"Agreed. I'll take care of it."

"Nah. Foster and I get along. He'll donate an aerospace defense cell on my say-so. Especially after last night's events." I reached for the display controls. "Want to see what the newsnets are saying?"

"Sure."

We stumbled on Eugene taking a press conference about the events, and, to my surprise, he had kind words to say about my troopers intervening quickly enough to prevent further deaths.

"Does that mean I'm in the presidential palace's good books again?"

"Did he mention you by name? No? Then, you're not." But Kal's little smile belied his words. "Don't worry, Zack."

"Oh, I'm not worried." I gave him a broad grin. "I'm just a Marine who does his duty. The opinions of others, especially non-Marines, don't worry me a bit."

"Glad to hear it." He climbed to his feet. "And if I thought it would do a damn bit of good, I'd tell you to take the rest of the day off. But I won't."

Kal left me staring at nothing in particular, my mind probing the idea the secessionists had hired the Hashashin. Considering the lead time necessary to import the secretive mercenaries, whoever did so must have let the contract well before the first delegates arrived. Meaning if it was secessionists, they'd have been intent on disrupting the convention from the get-go and driving the representatives into rejecting a new accord with Earth in favor of leaving the Commonwealth.

But was the damage now done? Six delegates lay dead at the hands of the Hashashin. Another dozen were under arrest in the 55th Constabulary Group's detention cells, waiting to appear before a judge. Whether both had been commissioned by the same entity, they might well achieve the same goal — turn the delegates against Earth and kibosh a last attempt at reconciliation.

I figured I needed to hash this out with someone smarter than me and went to look for my daughter.

# — Thirty-Six —

"I agree with you that the Hashashin had to have been contracted before the delegates' arrival, pretty much within days of the convention announcement, Dad."

We were sitting at a quiet table in our mess, having a pre-dinner drink — Shrehari Ale for me, gin and tonic for Saga — and discussing my thoughts.

"We don't know where they're from, but it's certainly not Mykonos. Nabhka is one of the potential places for their lair," she continued. "Which means three weeks at top speed, minimum. Longer if they're traveling commercial. Not that we're likely to ever find out. There's enough traffic coming through this star system to let plenty of ships fall through the cracks and never be inspected. I doubt the SIS will ever find out how they came to Mykonos. But I figure they've been here at least a week or two, reconnoitering, watching, and waiting. And you're right. They almost certainly have someone on the inside."

She took a sip of her drink.

"And yes, they could well be behind the attack against us. This, of course, brings us to the question of whether the Mykonos secessionists commissioned the Hashashin. Would they sacrifice the lives of delegates to advance their cause? In a heartbeat. The more I learn about them, the more I'm convinced they're hardcore players. Will we be able to prove it? Doubtful. The Mykonos government is riddled with secessionists, including its Police and Security Intelligence Services."

"So, where does that leave us?"

Saga shrugged.

"Nowhere in particular. Notwithstanding our stellar intervention, the site's security remains a police responsibility, and the investigation of the attack remains a police and SIS matter, just like the assault on us and the fake SecGen speech. We have no legal standing whatsoever. Which," she smiled, "doesn't prevent us from looking into the three matters, nonetheless. I redirected Hera's agents onto the Hashashin."

"If they find anything, will you share it with the SIS?"

Her smile turned into a grimace. "I don't know. It's better to play my cards close to the vest, especially where the results of intelligence from Hera's agents are concerned."

I nodded. "Agreed. The more I think about it, the less I trust the locals. They're all smiles and nods up front, but…."

"But they're keeping a lot from us. My relationship with the SIS has been mostly a one-way thing — they get from me but give little, if anything, in return."

"Why am I hearing about this only now?"

"It isn't important enough in the grand scheme of things, Dad." Her smile returned. "Besides, they haven't been getting any good stuff, so we're practically even."

I wagged my finger at her. "You're channeling Hera way too much, young captain."

She winked at me. "I thought that was the idea."

"So, you weren't comfortable with the locals from the get-go?"

"No. I get these gut feelings from time to time. Not often, but enough so that I pay attention to them. And they're always right."

I took a sip of my Shrehari Ale. "Funny you should mention that sort of thing. I get those as well. Also, not often, and I pay attention to them too. And yes, they turn out to be on the mark most of the time. I figure I have a touch of the gift. It could be you have it as well, being my daughter. You ever meet a Sister of the Void?"

"No."

"The Sisters, they have the gift in spades. They call it their talent. Only females of the human species are supposed to have it. I've got it too." I tapped the side of my head with an extended index finger. "Or at least a version. I can sense Sisters of the Void entering my mind, and I can make them fear me with my thoughts. Nobody else, mind you. Just them. Or at least that I know."

I related my contacts with the Sisters, including one who'd gone rogue and was experimenting on the minds of others.

"So, I figure my gut feelings mean something real. And we're both getting some bad ones about the locals."

"Not bad as such, Dad. It's just that they feel off somehow. Like we can't trust them. Ellie Pierce, for instance. I got the feeling that she's playing her own game, and it's not the one we signed up for."

Then, it hit me. "We're being used as cat's-paws."

I met my daughter's eyes and saw the same conviction in them I felt.

"Yes," she said, slowly nodding. "Of course. By the secessionists."

"But how to prove it?"

"Should we even attempt?"

"Why do you ask?"

She grimaced. "My gut's telling me this is bigger than we imagine. There are things afoot we can't control, let alone stop, and the best way to survive is simply stepping aside and letting the tide of history roll in."

I chuckled. "Now that sounded dramatic, almost like something I would have said."

Her smile returned. "I am your daughter. And it seems like we share more than just genetics."

"The gift you mean."

Saga nodded. "I'll be honest with you. Sometimes, I get unexpected insights that plain scare me with their clarity. And they're always on the mark. It's what got me through the master's and Ph.D. programs so quickly and helped me become captain the moment I became eligible. I'm not supposed to know this, but I'm nicknamed the Intelligence Witch because I have a habit of coming up with conclusions instinctively and figuring out issues before anyone else. Like predicting this constitutional convention before anyone else had an inkling. So yeah, I'm pretty sure I have a good touch of the gift, or talent, as your Sisters of the Void call it."

"They're hardly my Sisters. I have met none that I didn't scare in some way. Well, other than that sociopathic mind meddler Anca. And there was Delia — not your aunt but the one I met on Parth — who was what they call a wild talent, someone who has a Sister's gift but wasn't roped into the Order of the Void."

Something in my tone when I talked about Delia must have caught Saga's attention because she briefly frowned at me.

"It's a long story. Most of it is still classified. Let's just say she and I had a brief but intense romantic relationship. This was before Hera and I got serious about each other." I took a sip of my ale. "Intelligence Witch, eh? Funny. I always figured you were more like a Viking shield maiden circa seventeen-hundred years ago. At least going by your looks."

"Hey, I didn't come up with the nickname. I merely overheard Hera use it once when she thought I wasn't listening."

"And you're sure she meant you?"

She put on a sour expression. "Oh, yeah. No doubt about it."

How did I feel about my daughter having a touch, or perhaps more than a touch, of the gift? Could she be a wild talent?

"Is this a private party, or can anyone join?"

I looked up to see Kal approaching our table, glass in hand.

"We'll make an exception for you, *mon général*."

He sat and placed his glass on the tabletop. "You were having quite an intense conversation. Anything that might interest me?"

"I was discussing my misgivings about the secessionists and the Hashashin attack with the Intelligence Witch here."

Kal gave me his little smile. "And how did you find out about Saga's nickname?"

"From Saga." I nodded at her. "How did you know about it?"

"From her superiors. So, what misgivings do you have?"

"The more I think about it, the more I figure the secessionists are behind the attack. Take the timeline, for instance. Let's assume the Hashashin originate on Nabhka — Saga figures it's as good a spot as any. That's a long way from here. Yet they've been on the ground for a while. Which means someone hired them well before the convention started."

Kal shrugged. "Someone, a zaibatsu, for instance, if you want to discount the Sécurité Spéciale, got nervous early on when the convention was still being discussed."

"It's a possibility," I admitted. "Then there's the fact that they weren't in sufficient numbers to do more than glancing damage. And if I hadn't withdrawn my troopers from inside the perimeter, they might not have done any damage, period."

"If they were hired early on before the security arrangements took shape, then a company and a half might have been considered sufficient."

"Perhaps, but come on, Kal. Anyone would have figured out something like a constitutional convention involving delegates from more than half of human-settled worlds would have had security up the wazoo. If not by us, then by the locals. How about the numbers weren't sufficient because they weren't meant to wipe out the delegates but scare them, then make them angry at Earth for daring to commission an assault. That six of them died — plus the police members — were collateral damage. Like I said, the more I think about it."

I let my words hang between us while I watched him for his reaction.

He looked at Saga. "And what does the Intelligence Witch think?"

"She thinks her father might be onto something. But as I told him, proving it will be next to impossible."

I let out a faint grunt. "You also said, and I quote, there are things afoot we can't control, let alone stop, and the best way to survive is to simply step aside and let the tide of history roll in. In other words, Kal, Saga figures we might as well forget about proof or even attribution."

Kal nodded wisely. "And I think she's right. Best if we make sure the rest of the convention passes without further incident and leave the investigating to the locals."

I knew he was the voice of reason, but something bothered me about his words, if not his tone.

"Why? Why should we, the best Marines in the Corps, back away from investigating a Hashashin attack and leave the aftermath to the cops and the SIS?"

"Because we have no jurisdiction," he replied in a mild voice.

"That's never stopped us from doing what's necessary."

"Okay. Because of me saying so?"

I gave him a hard look for a few seconds before nodding. "Aye, aye, General, sir."

"The thing is, Zack, the convention is navigating an increasingly hard path. They don't need us to make it even more onerous by meddling in things that belong to local law enforcement."

"Why is their path getting more burdensome?"

"Because this incident will have triggered many delegates into abandoning the idea of constitutional reform altogether, even though they still need to go through finalizing a proposal for Earth."

"You mean it's driven them into the arms of the secessionists." I raised my bottle of ale in salute. "And that, my friends, confirms my suspicions."

# — Thirty-Seven —

Yet I couldn't let it go. As much as the old Commonwealth stank on ice, I'd still sworn my oath to its constitution. And the secessionists, no matter how much of a faint, nagging sympathy I might have for them, were, if not quite the enemy, then part of the opposition if they'd commissioned the Hashashin attack.

The following day, after I made the rounds of the Caledon Resort and Spa to check up on my people, I decided to see what I might extract from my family, well-known secessionists that they were. If anyone put together the financing for a hundred and fifty Hashashin — an expensive undertaking — they would have surely been involved considering our clan was among the wealthiest in the star system.

Of course, I couldn't simply go up to my father and ask him directly. That would cause me more heartache than I needed. But perhaps Delia might be a decent way into the family's involvement. After all, she had a soft spot for me.

How to approach her was the problem. I couldn't call her and ask if the family's been financing off-world mercenaries to conduct a false flag strike against the convention center.

On the other hand, why not?

The next morning, I called Delia and invited her for lunch at the restaurant of her choice. She immediately knew I had something on my mind but merely agreed to meet me at Raskin's, which was downtown Petras near her place of work, at noon.

I got there five minutes early, wearing civilian clothes, and took a corner table far from prying ears. Raskin's was an understated yet sophisticated restaurant whose cheery, open atmosphere made it pleasing to the eye. The price list, though, brought a tear to said eye, but I could afford it.

Delia showed up at twelve-hundred hours precisely, waved at me from the door, and made a beeline for our table, smiling at the hostess along the way as if she was well known in the place, which turned out to be the case.

I stood to greet her, and we exchanged kisses on both cheeks.

"How are you after that to-do at the convention site?" She asked.

"I'm doing fine."

She took a seat across from me. "Isn't it terrible? Those delegates and police members dead, and then there are the injured?"

"Oh, that it is."

A waiter approached our table to take the drinks orders, and we both opted for club soda with a slice of lymon, a local fruit somewhere on the same spectrum as lemons, limes, and oranges.

"Fortunately, the injured will make full recoveries."

"Good. At least there's that."

The drinks arrived, and I raised my glass. "To your health, Delia."

"And to yours." We both took a sip, then placed our glasses on the table. "So, to what do I owe the honor of lunch at one of the government upper crust's favorite bistros?"

"I wanted to pick your brain."

"So, pick away."

Before I could do so, the waiter returned and asked if we'd chosen our meals. Delia queried him about the specials, and we both ended up taking the sole meuniere on rice with wilted greens.

She picked up her drink and took another sip. "Let me guess what you're after — something about the family?"

"Yes. They're conspiring with the secessionists, right? My father foremost among them."

"Pretty much, though Richard is lukewarm, and your grandfather is mostly silent on the matter, as are the Khanjans. But their sympathies lie with the secessionists."

"How about you?"

A faint smile briefly lit up Delia's delicate features. "Oh, I'm torn. I can see both sides having a point. The Commonwealth definitely has serious issues that affect the OutWorlds disproportionately. Yet is splitting it up the answer? I don't know. And I suspect many people, perhaps a plurality, maybe even a majority, are in the same head space. The hardcore secessionists like your father are definitely a minority. But they have a lot of sympathizers and plenty of clout where it counts. Why did you ask about my views on the matter?"

"Because I think the attack on the convention center was a false flag event commissioned by the secessionists to push the delegates away from constitutional reform, but I have no proof and no way of finding any."

Her eyebrows shot up. "Really? And what makes you think so?"

"That it was designed to fail. If I hadn't withdrawn my troopers from inside the perimeter, I doubt a single delegate or police member would have died. As it was, the police and my quick reaction force kept casualties to a minimum."

"Are you sure it was designed to fail?" She sounded skeptical.

"Believe me. Those mercenaries were expensive, the kind we call Hashashin, because they carry out one-way missions, like their spiritual forbears more than a thousand years ago. They were to get through the first line of defense before dying while trying to get through the second, whether because of defensive fire or by their own hand. There weren't supposed to be any survivors to finger their employers, and guess what? None of them survived, many because they blew themselves up rather than surrender. So yeah, the attack was designed to fail. And the only people who would launch something of that sort are secessionists."

"I'm still having a hard time wrapping my head around this," she said after a moment of silence.

"Then there's the fact someone hired them before the convention started, probably within a week of the announcement it would be held on Mykonos. Contracting this sort of mercenary takes time, and their world of origin is a fair distance away. More evidence pointing to an inside job. So, I'd like to know whether the Decker-Khanjan clan was involved somehow."

"And you expect me to tell you that?" Delia frowned. "How should I know?"

I gave her a smile. "Because you're the smartest of the bunch, the most aware, and you're well placed in the Mykonos government."

This time, she let out a little laugh. "What does my being in the government have to do with this?"

"It's riddled with secessionists. Heck, there may even be colleagues of yours involved."

"Trust me on this, Zack. If anyone in the family or the government is engaged in hiring mercenaries, I wouldn't know thing one about it."

Our meals arrived, and we changed the subject while eating because it was polite to do so if nothing else.

But when the dessert plates were removed and we sipped our coffees, I returned to the reason we'd shared a meal.

"Now that you've had some time to think it over, do you still figure there's nothing to show the family was part of hiring the mercenaries?"

"Why are you pursuing this, Zack? Isn't it a matter for the police and the Security Intelligence Service, not the Fleet? After all, Mykonos is a sovereign world, and anything that happens on the planet's surface is for us locals to sort out."

It was more or less what Kal had said.

"If secessionists are behind the attack, it becomes more than just a local issue. The secessionist movement is growing on every OutWorld and colony, and until further notice, the Fleet works for the Commonwealth."

She laughed again. "I guess you're not a secessionist. Tell you what, if I hear anything, I'll let you know. And with that, I'm afraid it's back to work. Thank you for a most interesting lunch."

Oh well, perhaps it had been a long shot.

I parsed our conversation on my way back to Fort Monash but found nothing that might be construed as evasiveness, let alone falsehood. But then, senior bureaucrats were quite adept at allowing people to see only what they wanted them to. That's why they were senior bureaucrats.

Still, I wondered why I was so adamant about getting to the people behind the Hashashin. In the end, it was no skin off my nose, except for the injured under my command. But I didn't like those who used mercenaries, especially those of the vicious kind like Hashashin.

The next day, I unexpectedly received an invitation — text only — from my father to join him and mother at their town house for supper. Only me, not Saga. Intrigued, I accepted. The town house was where I spent most of my childhood, and I wondered how much it had changed over the decades.

Mind you, it wasn't a simple house in some suburb, but a small mansion on a hectare of parkland in one of Petras' toniest precincts, surrounded by a tall wall and a security suite.

The appointed hour was later than usual, so I had a heavier lunch to tide me over. I warned Saga about the invitation and left aboard an unmarked staff car at dusk with plenty of time to get there.

It took little for me to find the old neighborhood, which hadn't changed much. At least what I saw in the darkness. There were no streetlights, and the houses were far removed from the curb. Nor was there any star or moonlight — a thick cloud cover had hovered over Petras all day, threatening rain that so far hadn't come. Of course, the staff car's AI could see everything bright as day.

I pulled into the drive leading to the house and came up against a closed gate. Maybe they weren't expecting me to be five minutes early, but the security system AI would tell them I was there. However, after more than a minute of waiting without the gate budging, I shut off the car and climbed out, intent on looking for a manual override or a direct link to the house, something that would get me through.

The moment I stepped away from the car, I thought I saw shadowy movement out of the corner of my eye. Seconds later, I felt a sting on the back of my neck, and I realized I'd been hit by a needler. The last time that had happened, many years ago, I'd woken up in a highly uncomfortable situation indeed.

Then, everything went black.

# — Thirty-Eight —

"General?"

Kal Ryent looked up to see Saga Decker standing in the open door to his office the next morning. He waved her in.

"What's up?"

"Dad hasn't returned from supper with his parents last night, and I can't raise him on his communicator. Do you know where he might be?"

A frown creased Ryent's forehead. "He didn't mention that he'd be going out. Is there any reason you want to speak with him?"

"Yes. The agents Hera sent found traces of surviving Hashashin. I just got a message through the anonymous drop."

"Hmm. Why don't you try contacting your grandparents and ask whether Zack's still with them?"

"Will do."

Saga returned ten minutes later, looking deeply troubled.

"I finally tracked them down. They're not in Petras and haven't been for three days."

"Where are they?"

"On Karinth, in a place called Issos, where the family has extensive vineyards. My grandfather is on an inspection tour. He sounded appalled that someone had impersonated him and invited my father to a house that was not just empty but locked with tight security measures. He wasn't quite as dismayed by the idea Zack has gone missing."

"Are we sure they're one continent over?"

Saga nodded. "I had one of our satellites track his end of the conversation. His communicator is in Issos. Mind you, it's not a big hop. A few hours maximum across the Boetian Sea, so they might have been home last night."

"What about his staff car? I presume he took one from the pool."

She nodded again. "I checked, and all staff cars are accounted for, sir, including the one he borrowed. It's sitting in the compound like it never left."

Kal dropped his hand to the desktop and began drumming with his fingers, eyes losing focus as he stared at a point over Saga's shoulder.

"Okay," he finally said, turning his gaze back on her. "Zack's not one to vanish for fun, so we have to assume someone's abducted him near his parent's place and returned his staff car. Might it be the Hashashin?"

"It could be anyone, sir, but yes, if there are more of them in Petras, then they might have kidnapped dad. But they'd only have done so under orders."

"Which means they're more than likely controlled from Mykonos. Perhaps Zack was right to blame the secessionists for the attack on the resort."

"I'll try to get surveillance recordings from my grandparent's house and the motor pool. Maybe we'll see something useful."

By noon, with no trace of Zack Decker, Kal Ryent called a command team meeting and briefly got the unit commanding officers up to speed.

"And that means, Josh," he said, looking at Lieutenant Colonel Bayliss, "you're in command of the brigade until Zack resurfaces."

Bayliss nodded gravely. "Aye, aye, sir."

"Now, let's see what Captain Decker has uncovered so far. Saga?"

"Yes, sir. Recordings from the surveillance suite at the Decker house show nothing. Now that doesn't mean it didn't pick up anything. Someone might have tampered with them. I'm putting the recordings through in-depth analysis right now to detect just that. The colonel's car has definitely been tampered with, and the log of its operation last night was erased. However, Fort Monash's main gate recorded it as leaving at eighteen-thirty and returning at nineteen-thirty. The recordings of the motor pool surveillance picked up a male in uniform leaving the car. He vanished moments later. We have images of his face. But not good ones since he was clearly trying to hide it.

"So, the only thing we know is that the colonel disappeared sometime between eighteen-thirty and nineteen-thirty at an unknown location, but perhaps by the main gate to his parent's house, the only place he'd have stopped, which corresponds to the timings. It takes approximately thirty minutes from here." She paused as her communicator vibrated and glanced at its display. "And yes, the surveillance recordings from the house were tampered with at approximately nineteen-hundred hours, which indicates either the family or their security contractor is involved."

"Are you calling the police?" Lieutenant Colonel Cyone asked.

Saga and Kal exchanged a glance, then the former shook her head. "No. At this point, I think both the police and the Security Intelligence Service cannot be trusted."

Cyone nodded once. "Roger that."

"We have undercover officers from Naval Intelligence operating on Mykonos. I've contacted them with the evidence we have so far, and they'll be looking for the colonel along with any remaining Hashashin, but we'll need Ghost Squadron to back them up." Saga turned to Josh Bayliss. "If you could free one of your companies, put them in mufti and have them stand by, sir."

"You got it. Major Delgado and his Erinyes will be ready to go within half an hour of the time we end this meeting."

"As you may have noticed," Ryent said, smiling, "Captain Decker has put herself in charge of finding her father. She has my full support in this matter. Needless to say, Colonel Decker's disappearance is to remain closely held. If the abductors want a big spectacle over a hero of

Mykonos going walkabout, they'll have to be disappointed."

He looked around the table to nods of understanding from the unit commanders and principal staff officers.

"Not even the CO of the Mykonos Regiment is to know about it."

"You don't trust him, sir?" Cyone asked.

Kal looked at Saga, who replied, "Let's just say that the staff car returned by a mysterious person in uniform who disappeared is the second time the Mykonos Regiment may have been involved in matters about the colonel, the first having been the missile attack. Or rather, that the missile might have come from Mykonos Regiment stocks, although we've found no evidence of one missing. But that too could have been falsified, just like the surveillance recordings of the Decker family home's main gate."

"Understood."

"Does anyone have questions or comments?" When everyone around the table shook their heads, Saga turned to Kal. "Sir, with your permission, we will proceed."

"Carry on, Captain."

***

"Huh. So the colonel has vanished." First Sergeant Emery Hak, Erinye Company, Ghost Squadron, said with a faint air of incredulity when Major Curtis Delgado informed him and his troop leaders of their new mission. "Where the hell to?"

"No idea. Finding that out is the job of the undercover agents Naval Intelligence planted on Mykonos about the same time we showed up. Once they find the colonel, our job is to recover him."

"Big planet, and although the colonel ain't a small man, he's still man-sized," Sergeant First Class Metellus Testo, the company operations NCO, said. "Good luck to the agents. We might be better off being out there, looking for him as well."

"Okay, but where do we start?" Delgado asked. "Considering General Ryent — or more likely Captain Decker — decided we wouldn't bring in the cops or the SIS."

Testo shrugged. "We could start by looking at the most likely spot where he might have been abducted, in front of his folks' place. Who knows what clues the bad guys might have left behind?"

"I'm sure the agents are looking there as we speak."

"There's more of us than there are of them, Skipper. Besides, someone needs to check with the neighbors. Their security systems may have picked something up that wasn't erased."

"In other words, you want us to play the part of the police."

Testo snapped his fingers and pointed at Delgado. "That's exactly what I was thinking."

"Okay. I'll run it by Colonel Bayliss and Captain Decker and see what they say."

# — Thirty-Nine —

I woke with a start, the way one does after being knocked out by a needler, and quickly concluded I had another gift of the needler — a massive headache. The good news was I wasn't tied up or manacled. The bad news? I was in total darkness, lying on a firm surface, probably a concrete floor. Since I was blind, I let my other senses do the arduous work, and I inhaled steadily through the nose, getting the smell of old lubricants, dust, and a faint tang of ozone. I touched the ground with my fingertips and found it indeed to be concrete. At least I didn't wake up on a starship headed for the unknown like I had so many years ago.

I gently eased myself into a sitting position and checked my pockets. Empty, of course. And my timepiece was missing from my left wrist. But otherwise, I was fully clothed and wore my shoes. Once my head stopped pounding, I went into a crouch, then stood and waited for the renewed intracranial thumping to stop.

The darkness was complete. No matter where I looked, I saw nothing. Not even a faint line showing the bottom of a doorway. I held out my right arm in front of me and took a few careful steps before touching a concrete wall. I followed that wall to the right and quickly came to a corner. By the time I'd finished pacing the outline of my cell, I'd found a wide, smooth metal door, locked with no handle and nothing else. The space was roughly three meters by four, its walls made of concrete. It was probably a storage room in an industrial structure. The faint tang of ozone could indicate it being close to a spaceport, whether the one in Petras or another city.

Judging by the stubble on my chin and cheeks, I'd been out of it for almost a day, something that was confirmed by a faint rumble emanating from my stomach. And I was thirsty. Massively so. As they said, nothing ventured, nothing gained.

"Hey, if someone is listening," I said in a loud voice that sent my brain a-thumping again, "I need water and food. Especially water. Something to help with a headache would be nice as well."

I retreated across the room from the door, presuming whoever had captured me saw in the dark and wouldn't dare open it if I was too close. First things first. And the first thing I needed was water. But no one came. I let myself slide down the wall until I sat again and stared at the dark space where the door lurked. For how long, I didn't know. My usually reliable internal clock was still off kilter because of the needler. After what seemed like ten or fifteen minutes, I repeated my entreaty for water and food twice, still without effect.

And so, I composed myself and fell into a meditative trance. The sort that conquers pain, thirst, hunger, and many other earthly needs and desires. It was something I picked up as a field operative, part of my abbreviated training before jumping into missions with both feet alongside Hera.

Finally, about an hour later — my internal clock was coming back online — I heard a noise outside the door and snapped out of my trance. I opened my eyes halfway, knowing that any light on the other side would blind me after so long in total darkness, and waited.

The door opened suddenly, almost startling me, and light filled the room with an unbearable brightness that forced both of my eyes shut. I sensed movement, and when I finally cracked one eye open, I saw two figures dressed in black, with black scarves wrapped around their heads, leaving nothing but a slit for eyes that were both dark and devoid of any humanity.

Somehow, I instinctively knew they were Hashashin.

One of them kept a blaster pointed at me, while the other placed a large bottle and a ration bar on the floor. Then, they withdrew, and the door slammed shut again, leaving me in darkness. The ozone tang had increased slightly, lending credence we were next to a spaceport. But sadly, of the corridor beyond the open door, I saw nothing.

I scooted across the floor until my outstretched fingers met the bottle, which I quickly uncapped. I sniffed its contents, which seemed to be plain water, and then took a tentative sip. It was water alright, cold and refreshing, just what I needed. I chugged approximately half of the bottle, then reached for the ration bar, which I unwrapped and sniffed as well before taking a bite. Sweet, salty, sticky, and crunchy, it was a standard-issue ratbar, containing enough calories to sustain a grown human for at least eight hours. I ate the whole thing in short order, then washed it down with another swig of water.

And then, my bladder made itself known. Wonderful.

"Hey, guys. I need to take a piss. Either come and take me to a bathroom or give me a bucket and some light. Otherwise, it might get messy in here."

I moved back, away from the door, with the water bottle, and composed myself to wait again. This time, it didn't take quite so long. The door reopened, and the same two men — at least I figured it was the same duo, based on their eyes — appeared, both carrying blasters aimed at my midriff. One of them tossed ankle shackles at me and gestured that I should put them on, which I did. They would confine me to a slow shuffle. Then, he produced manacles and, once I stretched out my arms, wrists almost touching, entered the cell and snapped them on.

"Nice of you guys to take me to the loo," I said, giving them a smile. But they didn't answer.

Instead, they gestured with their guns that I should leave the cell and turn left, which I did. I found myself in a bare corridor with concrete walls and floor and a suspended ceiling. Light globes floated above our heads at regular intervals, some looking distinctly worn out. The passage was a good three meters wide by two and a half meters high, and dull metal doors pierced its grimy walls at regular intervals. It had the atmosphere of an abandoned warehouse and none of the charm.

We came to an open door, and one goon gestured that I should enter what turned out to be a dirty washroom with a single toilet and sink, no windows. With the men watching me closely, I relieved myself, though surprising me none, there was no water to flush or wash my hands. They then returned me to my cell but left the restraints on. Before I could protest, the door slammed shut behind me, and I was back in the darkness, so I returned to my by-now usual spot on the floor across from the entrance.

I supposed they left me shackled because now that I was awake and seemingly in good fettle, I could be dangerous the next time they opened the door to my cell. It made sense.

So why did what I presumed were Hashashin kidnap me? I simply couldn't see much sense in it. They were keeping me alive for a reason, that was certain. If they wanted me dead, I'd be merging with the Infinite Void. Of course, it wasn't really the Hashashin who wanted me alive but confined. It was whoever employed them.

The secessionists, for instance. Though what they had to gain by my abduction was beyond me. Unless I was wrong, and it wasn't the secessionists but our usual opposition, the Sécurité Spéciale. Though they had nothing to gain either. I couldn't be interrogated because I was conditioned. Any attempt at using torture or drugs would cause a fatal heart attack, and they knew it. And removing me from command? I was sure Josh Bayliss had taken over the brigade by now, making me irrelevant to current and future operations.

It was a puzzler, alright.

At least I'd been fed, watered, and used the facilities. And I was no stranger to being held prisoner. Shackled, manacled, and kept in the dark? How could I resist the temptation to find a way out?

# — Forty —

"We keep changing priorities like that, we'll get whiplash." The Naval Intelligence agent, an unremarkable man in his late thirties who went by the name Sam Small, said in a mock grumble to his partner as they ambled along an insalubrious street near the Petras spaceport. Evening had settled over the capital, though judging by the amount of activity around them, it might as well have been high noon. They'd been visiting the poorer quarters surrounding the spaceport ever since the attack on the Celadon Resort, looking for traces of the remaining perpetrators.

"If the Hashashin are responsible for Decker's abduction, then it won't be a change in priority but merely an add-on to our operation," Small's companion, an equally unremarkable woman in her early forties, calling herself Loni Tremaine, replied.

"If. How many intelligence failures stem from that single two-letter word?"

"Aren't you in a mood tonight?" She smirked at him.

"This entire mission has been screwy from the get-go. I'm not sure what we should believe between the secessionists being overactive and the Sécurité Spéciale being inactive. And don't get me started on the constant change in priorities. They might have nicknamed Saga Decker the Intelligence Witch, but she's clearly never spent a day in the field."

"Now you're just being unfair."

After a moment, Small grimaced. "I suppose I am. It's just the sense we're trying to grasp water with our bare hands that's irking me. We don't really know who the opposition is this time."

"No, we don't. But we know they're ready to deploy the big guns against the convention and against Colonel Decker." Something caught her eye, and she glanced sideways at a pair of black-clad men with swarthy faces, short black hair, and black mustaches who'd come out of a dark alley leading off between old warehouses. Something about the way they moved and their eyes never stayed still told Tremaine that these weren't the usual sort of people who frequented Petras' lesser neighborhoods. "Two men, three o'clock, similar looks, wearing black clothes, and moving like fighters."

After a second or two, Small replied, "Seen."

"What do you think? They could fit the profile for Hashashin."

"Possibly. Let's follow them. It's not like we have better things to do at the moment."

***

Staff Sergeant Salford Lambrix and his winger, Corporal Leroy Taggart, both of D Troop, Erinye Company, Ghost Squadron and wearing civilian clothes that wouldn't mark them as much different from the usual spaceport rats, stopped at an open-air refreshment stand. Like the rest of the street, and indeed most of the streets in that part of the spaceport precinct, it was lit up bright as day even though it was past twenty-hundred hours.

"Get you a beer, Sal?" Leroy Taggart asked.

"Nah. A soda will do just fine."

Taggart turned toward the stand's keeper and held up a cred chip. "Two cran-sodas, my good man."

"Coming right up."

A few moments later, the cred chip vanished, and two uncapped fizzing bottles appeared in its stead. The Marines picked up one each and took a long pull, eyes on the crowd surging and ebbing around them. After that first sip, they walked away from the stand and headed for a recessed spot by the opening of an alley. There, they leaned against the wall and observed people going by, looking for something that could indicate Hashashin.

Taggart was the first to see a pair of black-clad, swarthy men with mustaches who moved like warriors and whose eyes were never still, appear to their left on the main drag.

"Nine o'clock, twenty meters, two guys in black."

After a few seconds, Lambrix said, "Seen."

Then, Taggart noticed a pair — man and woman — keeping pace with the men.

"Check out the two about five meters behind them. Brown clothes, short hair, look innocuous as hell. They're also moving like pros with their eyes everywhere. Looks like they're following the men."

"Seen as well. If the guys are Hashashin, does that mean the others are operatives? Either ours or the SIS?"

"Could be. Let's follow them."

"Sure."

Lambrix and Taggart pushed themselves off the wall and merged with the stream of humanity flowing down the street, keeping a few meters behind the man and woman. The two men the latter were following entered a small restaurant approximately five hundred meters further on, and they went past it, stopping at a stall serving up kebabs. However, the two Marines entered the restaurant and found a small table near the door from which they could see both the two men and the man and woman.

The former had taken a corner table near the back and intently observed their surroundings, hunched over, unlike most customers, who were staring into their drinks or aimlessly around them. Lambrix and Taggart sat with relaxed postures and made small talk, careful to not meet the eyes of either the two men or the man and woman. They ordered small plates and more sodas when a human waiter approached them, paying in advance.

"Well, this is nice," Taggart said once a waiter had delivered their food. "We're watching people who are watching people who we're also watching, and all of us are eating separately but at the same time."

***

"So, what do you think about the two jokers sitting just inside the restaurant door?" Small asked Tremaine between bites of his kebab. "They were following us for the last five hundred meters."

"If I were a betting woman," Tremaine replied, "I'd say Marines, some of the Special Forces operators from Ghost Squadron. They carry that aura."

"And they glommed onto us and the possibly Hashashin?"

"They may have glommed onto the Hashashin and not us." At that moment, the older of the two briefly glanced in their direction, and she knew he and his companion were aware of them. "Cancel my last. They've definitely made us as persons of interest."

"Hmm. So, what do we do? They must be out here looking for their colonel. There's no other reason Marines would hang around the spaceport on a weeknight, looking scruffy enough to blend in and hide from everyone except for people like us who can recognize fellow predators."

"Why not simply approach them and compare notes? They're aware of our presence on Mykonos. If those are indeed Hashashin, doubling our numbers would be better."

"Do you think they gave them the recognition words?"

"If they set them loose to find their colonel alongside us, I'm pretty sure they have." Tremaine finished her kebab and disposed of the skewer in a nearby refuse receptacle. "Shall we?"

***

"Don't look now, but the people who were tailing our friends in the corner are headed in our direction," Taggart said after polishing off his last dolmade. The stuffed grape leaves were surprisingly tasty. "And they're staring squarely at us."

"Which means they made us," Lambrix replied as he wiped his mouth with a napkin. He put it down, sat back in his chair, and turned to face the approaching man and woman, appraising them as frankly as they did him and Taggart.

Both took the remaining chairs when they reached the table and sat without so much as a by your leave.

"I understand we might have the same uncle," the man said.

Lambrix and Taggart exchanged glances. Then, the former asked, "You mean Uncle Josiah?"

"He's the one. Aunt Hera says hi. You two are Ghost Squadron, right?"

"Yep. Salford Lambrix at your service." He gestured at his winger. "And that's Leroy Taggart."

"I'm Sam Small, and this is Loni Tremaine. Not our real names, of course, but they'll do for now."

"To what do we owe the honor?"

"Since we apparently recognized each other for being on the same team, I figured we might as well combine our forces. The two swarthy men in the far corner might be suspects in the disappearance of your colonel."

"How do you figure they are?"

"We've been looking for Hashashin since the attack on the resort and narrowed it to the spaceport precinct, where anything goes, and people can be as anonymous as they want. Those two fit the description of the Hashashin who died during the assault and move like trained fighters. There aren't many of that sort around here, and Captain Decker said Hashashin were high on the list of suspects for the abduction of her father."

"Okay. I guess it's as good a place to start as any. By the way," Lambrix grinned at them, "we figured the spaceport precinct was prime territory to stalk the opposition, mainly because we've used its like on many worlds to hide in plain sight. So it stands to reason they'd be using it as well. We've got a lot of buddies wandering around right now, looking, watching, sniffing. Tell me, are the men in black the first suspects you've seen?"

"Yes." Small nodded. "Which is why we cannot afford to lose them or get made by them. What we'll do now is Loni, and I will leave. You and your mate will leave after the suspects."

"Who seem like they're about to go," Taggart said in a conversational tone.

"Well, goodbye then." Small smiled at the Marines and casually rose from his chair, imitated by Tremaine.

Lambrix and Taggart smiled back, the latter wiggling his fingers at them in farewell.

They watched the agents leave and vanish in the crowd, then the two men, heads on a pivot, eyes everywhere, went and headed back the way they'd come.

Lambrix glanced at Taggart and nodded once. Both Marines stood, stretched, and ambled out of the restaurant, hands in their pockets, looking like well-fed customers pleased with their meals.

Once in the street, they got a fix on the targets. However, neither could spot the agents and followed at a distance of twenty meters for almost a kilometer until the men turned off into a darker side road aimed straight at the spaceport and numerous old warehouses, many of them disused. When Lambrix and Taggart reached the road's mouth, they could see their targets walking alone beneath weak glowglobes.

"Not going to be easy hiding from them now, is it?" Taggart said.

They let the men open their lead to over fifty meters before venturing into the road behind them, hoping that they wouldn't be perceived as threats at this distance. Just as they did so, the targets vanished into a left-hand alleyway. Lambrix and Taggart broke into a fast jog, but before they made it halfway, two shadows appeared at the far end, headed in their direction — Small and Tremaine, who'd obviously gone ahead of the targets and knew which side road they'd come from, but not which of the alleyways bisecting the area.

All four reached the alley simultaneously, but the two men had vanished.

# — Forty-One —

I must have fallen into a much deeper meditative trance than I ever did before that evening because I began to get visions. Or I fell asleep and experienced strange, vivid, and utterly realistic dreams. There was no way for me to tell which.

In my vision or dream, I was a lieutenant general, commanding a corps of three crack divisions, 30 Corps. An imperial lieutenant general at that, with the imperial crown topping the crossed swords and starburst insignia on my beret, which was still the same sky blue.

I saw images of my divisions embarking aboard interstellar transports in orbit around Caledonia, destination Earth. They were freeze frames rather than a continuous stream of consciousness. I remembered a similar vision I'd had many years ago of a future me wearing stars on my collar.

The images jumped forward by several days and became a continuous video of my staff and me, armed and armored, climbing aboard dropships and shuttles along with thousands of troopers on my transport alone. And there were three dozen transports in my fleet. We were about to invade Earth and destroy the Commonwealth government once and for all.

Once our dropship was buttoned up, a warning klaxon came through the speakers, announcing our imminent transition from hyperspace to normal space. Shortly afterward, emergence nausea gripped us, but it was like never before. The malaise was violent, wrenching, turning us inside out. But when it finally subsided, we were orbiting Earth — beneath Starbase One and the defensive fleet preparing to engage with the imperial task force.

It was as if I could hear the distress of the starship hulls at the wrenching from an emergence so close to a gravity well. I realized then that half or more of the transports would never jump to hyperspace again after this, yet if we succeeded, they wouldn't need to. And we'd not only taken the Commonwealth forces entirely by surprise, but they couldn't fire at us without endangering civilian populations on the ground.

Then, the transports released thousands of dropships and shuttles aimed at the Commonwealth capital, Geneva, which was 30 Corps' objective. My objective. Seize it, and the Commonwealth ends save for a few diehards. Once that was achieved, we would reunite humanity under the imperial crown, though Earth would become a backwater world, stripped of its pretensions to rule our species.

Why did I get the assignment? Because seizing the capital was just the sort of thing I could do better than anyone else.

I was the expert in quick insertion, hard-hitting raids that bypassed the enemy's defenses. This one was merely the largest ever planned. And because 30 Corps comprised the most daring, best-trained Marines ever fielded in humanity's long and strife-filled history.

Our dropships and shuttles spiraled down at the maximum rate of descent. They landed around Geneva, with mine landing atop the Montagne de Vuache, south of the city, from which I could see the entirety of its surroundings. Within moments of our shuttles settling, we deployed an aerospace defense dome covering the corps and the city, effectively isolating it and us from the rest of the planet. The shuttles themselves were the anchors of this dome, having been specially prepared ahead of time.

My point of view shifted, and I realized time had passed since our landing because I stood on the mountain, watching columns of smoke rise from the city in many places. They marked the defensive emplacements of the 1st Commonwealth Marine Regiment, which was fighting an increasingly desperate battle.

Then, suddenly and without warning, a brilliant flash of light filled the horizon from side to side, blanketing the city. The visor on my helmet slammed shut automatically, and I instinctively threw myself behind a small mound of crumbling rocks. The shock wave from the antimatter explosion reached me seconds later and slammed my prone body against the mountainside, winding me even though the armor absorbed most of the energy.

"God damn it. The fuckers blew themselves up instead of surrendering. Damn them to hell."

I didn't know whether I'd spoken the words out loud or even shouted them, but they broke me from the vision. Or dream. Whichever it was. I didn't have time to mull over what I'd experienced. However, the last bit, the antimatter explosion turning Geneva into a gaping hole in the ground, one which quickly filled with the waters of the lake, was eerily familiar because I'd seen it in a dream before. My eyes snapped open just as my ears picked up the sound of the door being unlocked.

Bright light flooded into my cell, and I saw the same two black-clad men wearing headscarves to hide all but their eyes. One of them, blaster pointing at my midriff, entered and stepped aside. The other stayed in the hallway but stood away from the door.

Moments later, a third man wearing a business suit appeared. His face was hidden behind a blurring field, but he was a big man, especially compared to the smaller, wirier guards, about my size, if less muscular.

"Well, well, well. The famous, or should I say infamous Colonel Zachary Thomas Decker." His voice was equally distorted. He had his left hand in his trouser pocket, but the right one, hanging at his side, twitched in a somewhat familiar way. "How the mighty have fallen. It's nice to see you helpless, a prisoner awaiting execution."

"You're going to kill me. How original. Do you understand how many have tried and failed? And when I mean failed, I mean they died instead." I pushed myself up against the wall until I was standing.

He chuckled. "I think your luck has finally run out, and I'm going to enjoy watching you die."

"Who the hell are you, anyway? You have to be someone I know. Otherwise, why the blurred face and voice, especially if you'll have me killed." I watched his right hand twitch again. "It speaks of a certain lack of courage if you ask me. A man sure of his convictions wouldn't be hiding."

His voice hardened. "Don't you dare speak of courage to me, you cowardly lout."

I shuffled forward, closing the gap between myself and the guard in the cell.

"Cowardly lout." I let out a bark of laughter. "Not a very original insult."

I took a few more abbreviated steps, eyes focused on the man, though I kept the Hashashin in my peripheral vision. Like most trained people, the latter held his index finger along the blaster's trigger guard rather than on the trigger itself, signaling he didn't consider me an immediate threat. And that was a mistake.

"I didn't know you were strong on originality, Colonel. A man of your base intellect?"

"Ah. Base intellect. Yes, definitely a better insult. I also have base appetites." I shuffled closer. "The sort that would get me punted from the Town and Country Club if only they knew about them."

"Oh, you won't be disgracing the club with your presence again, so no worries."

"Is that a fact?"

At that moment, I turned hard toward the guard in my cell, who by now was less than half a meter from me, wrapped both hands around his gun hand wrist and forced it upward. My knee connected with his groin, and his grasp on his blaster loosened. I let go of his wrist and grabbed the weapon, juggling it to get a handle on its grip while the man collapsed.

The moment I had the gun in my hand, I turned toward the other guard, who was only now reacting to my actions and moving his finger from the trigger guard to the trigger. I fired three times, two of the shots singeing the one who'd been taunting me. The guard dropped.

I turned the blaster on the first man and fired three times, again, and any ambitions he might have had to take me on after recovering from the knee in the goolies vanished into the Infinite Void along with his soul. Or whatever he had instead.

The third man, who'd been hiding his face, turned and ran down the corridor while I crouched and grabbed my jailer's hand, intent on using his thumbprint to release my manacles before his vital signs dropped to zero. I fumbled with his hand a few times before I could apply the thumb to the reader, but then the manacles fell away. I did the same to my leg shackles and rose again, feeling much better now that I was free.

The sound of running footsteps drew me back to the immediate, and I burst out of my cell and on the heels of the third man, who disappeared around a bend in the corridor. But by the time I reached that bend, he'd vanished, replaced by two more men in black, this time without headscarves. They immediately opened fire on me, and I felt the burn of a plasma round creasing my right upper arm. I withdrew, wondering what to do next.

# — Forty-Two —

"They can't be far," Small said, eyes flicking over the dilapidated warehouse fronts lining the ill-lit alley.

"No, they can't," Lambrix replied. "Leroy, pull out your sensor. Let's scan these buildings and determine which ones have life signs."

"Sure thing." Taggart produced a Mark X handheld battlefield sensor from the pouch at his waist and switched it on. Then he slowly entered the alley, pivoting from side to side as he scanned the first small warehouses. "Nope. Nothing alive in them."

They moved deeper into the alley, senses alert for the slightest hint of their quarry, when suddenly a door a few buildings away burst open, and a tall man in a business suit ran out. He took one look at the foursome and sped away from them.

"Was that guy's face blurred, or am I losing my eyesight?" Lambrix asked.

"He was blurred all right," Tremaine said. "And in a hurry to get out of here. A little overdressed for the area, too."

"Should one of us pursue him?"

"No. Besides, he's got a good head start. Let's check out the place he came from instead."

They cautiously approached the open door, Taggart still scanning.

"Got three life signs in there."

By common, albeit unspoken accord, the four drew weapons from concealed holsters, then Lambrix and Taggart entered first.

They found themselves in a wide corridor whose grimy, bare concrete walls and floor hinted at long abandonment. Weak, ancient glowglobes hovered near the ceiling, dispensing faint light that gave their skin a sick cast. The corridor ended with an open metal door five meters in, and they cautiously approached it.

Lambrix stuck his head through and withdrew it almost immediately.

"Two tangos, probably the ones we were following, twenty meters ahead, at a bend in the corridor," he whispered to his winger. "They're both armed, and it looks like they're tracking someone or something."

Taggart glanced at his sensor readout. "The third life sign. It's backing away from the other two. Could it be the colonel?"

"Not a clue."

Lambrix looked again, this time long enough to catch sight of an almost silent exchange of blaster fire. Three rounds splashed against the wall behind both men while one of them returned the favor.

Small and Tremaine joined the Marines, and Lambrix quickly explained what was happening. "What should we do? Simply going in there and opening fire on them seems a little excessive, seeing as how we don't know who they are or what's going on."

"Challenge them."

"Okay." Lambrix raised his gun, edged around the door frame, and shouted, "Police! Drop your weapons."

One man turned toward him, gun raised, and fired off two rounds, both of which missed as Lambrix pulled back.

"Well, that answers the question of whether they're hostile. They might also be suicidal, opening fire on the police without a second thought, pegging them as Hashashin. Leroy, on the count of three. I take the one on the left. You take the one on the right."

"Roger that." Taggart put his sensor back into the pouch and gripped his blaster with both hands. "Ready."

"One, two, THREE."

The Marines leaned into the open doorway, squeezed off three rounds each, and withdrew. A few seconds later, Lambrix peeked around the door frame again, only to see both men on the ground.

"That took care of them. Come on, Leroy."

Lambrix and Taggart cautiously headed for the downed figures, weapons at the ready. One of them raised his head and tried to aim his gun, but Lambrix fired again, this time getting him squarely between the eyes.

They stopped just before the bend, and Lambrix shouted, "Whoever you are, the guys shooting at you are dead. I'm going to come around the corner with my weapon pointing downward. Please don't open fire."

"Why should I open fire on the one and only Salford Lambrix?" Colonel Zack Decker replied.

"Colonel! It is you."

Lambrix and Taggart rounded the corner in time to catch Decker stepping out of a side room. He was clutching his right upper arm with his left hand, though a gun dangled from his right hand. Blood was seeping through his fingers.

"Who the hell else would it be? Did you spot a man with a blurred face race out of here?"

"Yep. We didn't give chase. Who was it?"

"My father."

# — Forty-Three —

The Petras General Hospital patched me up nice and tight and thankfully let me go back to the Fort instead of keeping me for observation. Both agents had vanished into the night shortly after making sure I was alive and well, and Salford and his winger Leroy Taggart had escorted me to the emergency ward. I was able to talk the hospital administrators out of calling the cops, which is the standard procedure when a shooting victim walks in by invoking federal government secrecy. I don't know whether they bought it or were glad not to deal with the lengthy and involved police procedures.

A staff car took us back to Fort Monash, and I found Kal, my daughter, and Josh Bayliss waiting for me in my quarters, having been warned by Lambrix once we were underway.

"The conquering hero returns!" Kal stood as I entered. "The way Staff Sergeant Lambrix put it, they arrived just in time for the grand finale, seeing as how you liberated yourself."

He picked up a glass half full of an amber liquid I recognized only too well and handed it to me.

"Glen Arcturus. Get that inside you, stat."

I took a healthy slug of the whiskey and leaned against a dresser. "How did you know I needed this?"

"Josh suggested it. So, any idea who kidnapped you and why?"

I nodded. "Yep. I'm not a hundred percent sure, but mostly so. Would you believe my father wants me dead?"

Kal's eyes widened. "Your father?"

I recounted my exchange with the blurry-faced man and mentioned the strange twitch in his right hand, the same sort I'd seen with my father.

"Why would he want you dead?"

I shrugged. "Search me. But the four guys we put down are almost definitely Hashashin, or at least similar enough to the ones who attacked the resort to make it obvious they're of the same ilk. Perhaps they piloted the shuttle that inserted the airborne platoon. And that means my dad is one of those responsible for the attack. Unfortunately, we have no evidence."

Saga raised her hand. "Dad, I realize it's late, but I'd like to debrief you now rather than in the morning while the events of the last twenty-four hours are still fresh in your mind."

"Sure. But Kal and Josh can go off to bed. I wouldn't want to deprive Kal of his beauty sleep before another day of monitoring the convention and schmoozing with notables among the delegates."

Kal gave me his usual crooked smile. "The convention is, for all intents and purposes, over. They voted on the final draft of the proposed constitutional amendments this afternoon and fired it off to Earth."

"So, we can go home."

He shook his head. "Not just yet, Zack. Everything stays in place until the delegates receive a reply from the Commonwealth government and the Senate."

"Oh?" I cocked a questioning eyebrow. "Is there a second phase to this whole business?"

"Yes. If Earth refuses to consider the proposed amendments. Now give your daughter the rundown on your abduction so we can go to bed."

"*Oui, mon général.* Right away."

When I fell silent after talking and answering questions for half an hour and sipping on a second glass of Glen Arcturus. Saga contemplated me with a thoughtful expression.

"You know, Dad, I don't think your father was aiming to have you killed. Otherwise, he'd have shown his face, as would your jailers. You were going to find yourself alone in the warehouse, doors unlocked, one morning. Perhaps even tomorrow morning. If it was him, Grandfather Jack wanted to humiliate you and put you in fear of your life as revenge."

"Well, like so many other things when it comes to me, my father simply couldn't get it right. Again."

"That's because he doesn't understand who you are, Dad." She gave me a sad smile. "He never did. You're a complete stranger. Will you confront him?"

"I have no idea. Is there a point? We're almost done here. I never have to see him or anyone else in the family again." I glanced at Kal and Josh. "If you don't mind, how about you gents bugger off? I'd like to talk about something with Saga."

"Sure, Zack. Rest up, okay." Both stood, emptied their glasses, and left.

I poured myself another dram, then sat across from my daughter. "You remember how I said I might have a touch of the sight?"

"Sure."

"Well, I sometimes get very vivid dreams or visions. I don't know which. They feel so real it's almost scary. And I got one earlier tonight, just before my father showed up." I related the dream about the assault on Earth and the destruction of Geneva. "It's the second time I saw the capital blown up in precisely the same way."

"That's pretty wild, Dad."

"What's wilder is me wearing three stars as an Imperial Marine officer. I know the Commonwealth is far from ideal, but we've sworn our oath to its constitution. I wonder. Is my dream trying to tell me it's time I threw in my lot with the secessionists?"

She gave me a half-shrug. "Not a clue. But everything I see tells me the Commonwealth government will reject the constitutional amendments, leaving the OutWorld secessionists in charge of deciding what happens next. And Caledonia is technically an OutWorld.”

“Plus, most Marines are OutWorlders or colonials.”

“Us included.”

“All right. Thanks for listening to your old man go on about his fears.” I smiled crookedly at her. “Off to bed with you.”

# — Forty-Four —

"What am I supposed to do with this mess?" Brodrick Brüggemann demanded as Andreas Bauchan took a seat across from his desk.

"I presume you're referring to the demands issued by the so-called constitutional convention, sir?"

"What else?" Brüggemann sounded testier than usual.

"As I might have mentioned before, sir, you assign it to the Senate who'll strike a committee to study the document ad nauseam until the election cycles on the OutWorlds have come and gone, and other issues preoccupy their governments."

Brüggemann let out a bark of humorless laughter. "The Speaker of the Senate refused to consider the demands on the grounds that they weren't produced by a duly constituted convention. Of course, the OutWorld senators are up in arms at that decision, but the fact is that he kicked it back to me, and I'm stuck with it."

"How unfortunate."

"Tell me, Andreas, what is your estimation of the reaction if I simply turn them down outright?"

Bauchan thought about the question for a bit, then cautiously replied, "Initially, there will be anger, dismay, perhaps a renewed interest in secession. Will there be a political crisis? Probably. At least a minor one. Will it be survivable? Assuredly. The indications we're getting from the outer sectors are that most people, including politicians, don't much care about the convention and its goals."

But even as he spoke, Bauchan felt uneasy about his words. Yet what else could he say? Britta Trulson, whose intelligence had been correct so often over the last two years, didn't think the consequences of an outright refusal to consider the convention's demands that alarming. It would occupy newsnet time for a short while, then be forgotten as more immediate concerns captured OutWorld government attention.

Still, the sense that Brüggemann might cross a Rubicon of sorts with his reply to the convention nagged at him.

"Well," Brüggemann said, standing and walking over to the tall windows giving out on Lake Geneva, "it's not like I have many choices in the matter anyhow. I've been told in no uncertain terms that any sort of agreement with the OutWorlds on this matter might lead to my impeachment."

Bauchan's eyebrows rose fractionally. "It's that drastic, sir?"

"Yes, it is."

Bauchan felt something akin to fear for the first time as the full import of the hardening positions on Earth and the Home Worlds toward the OutWorlds struck him. And there was nothing he could do about it.

# — Forty-Five —

As I stepped out on the mezzanine overlooking the convention center's main hall, I heard Secretary Liang's gavel calling the delegates to order below. I joined Kal, leaning against the railing, watching the mood in the room.

"This place is locked down tighter than a black hole's exit terminus, General. Nothing is getting in or out, not even from above. The Mykonos Regiment's aerospace defense people have us covered by an impenetrable dome."

He turned his head and glanced at me. "I wouldn't have expected anything less."

At that moment, Saga came through the same door as I had and joined us. "Has the final vote started?"

"Not yet," I replied. "Gudrun Liang is trying to calm the excited delegates."

Said delegates included the colonial representatives, who'd been released on their own recognizance with the condition they do not rejoin the convention, a stipulation they immediately ignored. For some reason, Chief Superintendent Zakhar didn't seem in a hurry to re-arrest them, which suited me just fine. They also included the replacements of the six killed in the Hashashin attack, the last of whom had arrived just twelve hours ago.

A few minutes and much gavel pounding later, silence fell over the room as the representatives of the OutWorlds and the colonies settled at their tables and faced Liang with expectant airs. Kal, Saga, and I weren't the only observers on the mezzanine, but we were the only ones in uniform. Every other Marine on Mykonos was making sure nobody and nothing could interfere. Even personal communications were being jammed by my people so that only official channels could transmit and receive.

"Delegates," Liang's voice reached the furthest corners of the room without amplification, "Earth and the Home Worlds have rejected our grievances and proposals to restore star system sovereignty as envisaged by the drafters of the current constitution after the Second Migration War. We now face a decision.

"We can either accept defeat in our attempt to revitalize the Commonwealth by strengthening its members, both independent systems and colonies and continue to work within an increasingly tyrannical status quo."

As Liang expected, her words drew a chorus of boos, and she paused. After a few moments, she raised her hands, silently asking the delegates to let her speak. When the sounds of derision finally faded away, she lowered her hands.

"Or we can form a new Federation, separate from the Commonwealth, one based on the equality of the sovereign star systems and under a federal government whose powers will be limited to those necessary for the prosperity, safety, and expansion of our species. In other words, under the constitution we wrote here over the last few weeks, and which has been accepted by all OutWorld legislatures and the colonial citizens' assemblies. It is a stark choice, my friends. Secession is fracturing humanity into two polities whose aspirations are at odds. But a new Federation would surround the Home Worlds and keep them prisoners of a small sphere where they can live under Earth's tyranny until, one by one, they too seek escape and secede to join that Federation."

She paused again for effect, her eyes meeting those of delegates who knew they would make history in the next few minutes.

"You have instructions from your governments regarding your vote in case of Earth's refusal. Or with the colonies, your citizens' assemblies. I will now call upon you in order of your world's accession to the Commonwealth or, in the case of the colonies, your date of founding. The options are status quo or secession. You know what either entails."

A final pause, then, "We begin with the OutWorlds. Wyvern."

"Secession."

"Dordogne."

"Secession."

"Novaya Sibir."

"Secession."

And so it went, one OutWorld after the other declaring its intent to leave the Commonwealth and join what I knew would be announced as the Federation of Sovereign Star Systems if the vote for secession was unanimous. When the final OutWorld declared it would secede, Liang spoke again.

"And now the colonies. I know we discussed this in the plenary, but I will state it again for the record. A vote for secession by a colony is an automatic unilateral declaration of independence under the constitution this convention voted into existence and, therefore, unlawful under the existing Commonwealth constitution. It means civil strife could ensue where a citizen's assembly is at odds with the colonial administration on the matter."

Again, Liang paused for effect, and I couldn't help but be impressed by her acting skills. I wouldn't have been surprised if she told me she was the lead in one of Petras' community theater groups.

"We begin with Mission."

"Secession."

"Marengo."

"Secession."

And like the OutWorlds, the colonies, whether federally administered or owned by one of the Home Worlds, voted to leave the Commonwealth until only one remained.

Liang looked up at where we stood on the mezzanine. "Caledonia."

Kal drew himself to attention and said in a calm voice that carried, "Secession."

The hall erupted in cheers and applause. With the Fleet's home world renouncing the Commonwealth, the secessionists could count on at least half, if not two-thirds, of the Armed Forces changing their allegiance to the new Federation.

I leaned over so Kal could hear me over the din. "So, you were the Fleet's delegate all along, you sneaky bastard."

He gave me an ironic smile.

"My parents were married, Zack. But yes. Grand Admiral Larsson and the governor general made me their secret representative. I only told Liang when Earth rejected the convention's demands, and a vote for secession became inevitable. She then made it quietly known the secessionists could count on a large part of the Armed Forces to go with them because that's what Larsson decided when it was clear Earth had signed the Commonwealth's death warrant by being obstinate."

It took several minutes for the delegates to regain their composures. And I could only imagine what would happen to the composures of the SecGen and the Home World senators once the recording of this session reached Geneva via a special subspace packet. With Kal's vote, the Armed Forces had, in effect, mutinied against the government of the Commonwealth.

"Delegates," Liang said once silence had fallen, "since every star system represented in this room has voted to leave the Commonwealth, I will now ask for a vote on whether they will join a new federal state to be known as the Federation of Sovereign Star Systems whose constitution will be that which we voted on earlier this week. The responses are aye or nay. We will proceed in the same order as before. Wyvern?"

"Aye."

"Dordogne."

"Aye."

And once again, the OutWorlds were unanimous. The former colonies, now independent, although with the subspace radio time delay, they wouldn't know yet back home, also voted to join the Federation.

"Caledonia."

Kal nodded once. "Aye."

And it was done. Almost half of the independent star systems had united under a new banner along with every last colony. The new Federation now had more members than the old Commonwealth. But it wasn't over yet.

Liang banged her gavel a few times.

"As delegates of our home systems, we are the closest thing to a provisional legislature the newborn Federation has until a capital can be determined and a Senate created with senators chosen by the star systems under their own processes. I need a proposer and a seconder to open the provisional Senate's first session, after which we will elect a speaker."

Kal raised his hand.

"I propose we open the session."

The delegate from Wyvern raised hers.

"I second."

"Does anyone demand a vote, or is everyone in agreement?" When no one moved or spoke, Liang banged her gavel again. "I now declare the first session of the Federation's provisional legislature open."

A spontaneous round of applause erupted, and Kal turned to me.

"I guess I should join my fellow provisional senators on the main floor."

Then he left Saga and me to stare at each other with bemusement. A major general of the Commonwealth Marine Corps, in uniform, had suddenly become the senator for Caledonia. And none of us were actually Commonwealth Marines anymore.

As expected, Gudrun Liang, Federation senator for Mykonos, was elected speaker on the first round of balloting. Then, surprising me again, Kal rose to propose the Senate debate the location of the Federation's new capital so its member worlds could move as fast as possible to set up the new star nation.

"I have a proposal from Major General Ryent, provisional senator for Caledonia, that this assembly debates the location of the new capital. Do I have a seconder?"

The senator for Cimmeria rose.

"I second."

"Does anyone call for a vote? No?" Liang wielded her gavel. "Adopted. The floor is open for proposals. Since General Ryent proposed the provisional Senate debate the matter, will he put forward a candidate?"

Kal stood again.

"I nominate Wyvern as capital. It is the oldest among the Federation's worlds and thus primus inter pares. It has the infrastructure to absorb a federal administration, is home to what will become the Federation Constabulary once these proceedings are broadcast, and is the most centrally located star system."

Saga chuckled softly, and I glanced at her.

"What?"

"Everything that happened so far today was carefully choreographed, probably even before we received Earth's refusal to negotiate, Dad. It's so obvious. And Kal was one of the instigators to ensure it went the way Grand Admiral Larsson wanted. I'll bet the key players agreed on every item beforehand. These proceedings are merely to formalize things and produce a show of unity. Watch. They'll confirm Wyvern as the capital and nominate a provisional president. And I bet it'll be the current president of Wyvern, Aline Rostov. She's an ardent secessionist and well-liked by a majority of Wyvernians."

I knew Saga was right when I heard her words, and my respect for Kal Ryent grew by leaps and bounds. He was not only one of the ablest leaders I'd ever met but an astute politician as well, one who enjoyed the total confidence of humanity's top military leader.

"As long as it's not obvious to anyone else."

"Oh, I figure those who draw the right conclusions won't say a word, at least not beyond confidential circles. There's nothing to gain by accusing the delegates of deciding all the big moves in private beforehand. Yes, some might decide secession was always the outcome, no matter what. But I believe that had Earth come back with a reasonable counterproposal, we wouldn't be listening to the Federation's provisional Senate debating the new capital of humanity's second star nation."

I watched the various senators rise as they discussed the merits of one star system or another compared to Wyvern.

"I think it was preordained that Earth wouldn't listen and that we would go down this path, Saga. If Kal came here with the sort of orders from the Grand Admiral I suspect he received, then it means there's nothing anyone could have done to prevent it. Not when Larsson himself had made his choice. And that being the case, I agree the Commonwealth's time was up. Perhaps even long ago, before I was born. All we did was finally ignite the funeral pyre Kathryn Kowalski saw in her visions of the future. What happens next is up to the Almighty."

"Agreed." She paused, lost in thought for a second or two. "I don't figure reforming humanity's contract with itself will be as easy as Grand Admiral Kowalski hoped. But I hope it won't be as bad as she feared in her worst nightmares."

"You studied her that closely?"

"It's a foundational course at the Intelligence School, Dad, and classified top secret special access. We've been protecting her legacy until we were ready for the inflection point she saw when everything would change forever."

"And are we ready?"

My daughter made an anxious grimace. "I don't know. Nobody does. But there's no going back."

"No, there isn't. Which means we shouldn't fear the darkness but welcome it as the precursor to a second dawn. The second age of interstellar humanity."

In the end, it took just over an hour for the provisional senators to name Draconis on Wyvern as the Federation's new capital. And as my scarily perceptive daughter predicted, the provisional Senate appointed Aline Rostov as interim president of the Federation. When I wondered whether she knew she was being volun-told, Saga chuckled.

"Arranged beforehand, Dad. President Rostov is merely waiting for the recording of this session to cross the subspace network. I'll wager next month's pay on it."

"No bet."

# — Forty-Six —

"What happens to the Fleet now?" I asked as Kal poured a good dram of whiskey into our glasses. Saga and I were in his suite at the Caledon Resort, which remained under military protection until we knew how Earth would react to the OutWorlds seceding and the colonies issuing UDIs. It meant Saga and I had rooms close to Kal's while my entire command patrolled the perimeter. "You're the one who knows everything Larsson's planning."

He handed us our glasses, then took the chair across the coffee table from the sofa where Saga and I sat.

"It gets split up. Eventually. For now, Larsson will issue stand-fast orders telling everyone the Fleet remains under the current command structure while we work out the exact mechanics. However, that won't be long since we have already drawn up plans. The easiest is the Army. The units on Earth and the Home Worlds remain part of the Commonwealth Armed Forces. The units on the OutWorlds and colonies become part of the Federation

Armed Forces. Individual members who are part of one and wish to serve in the other will eventually be sorted out.

"The Marine Corps is almost as easy with the 1st and 2nd Marine Divisions remaining under Commonwealth command and the rest of the Corps going to the Federation. But I suspect we'll have a lot more people wanting to exchange than the Army will. The Navy will be the trickiest. Grand Admiral Larsson fears crews might mutiny if captains decide they won't follow the partition plan. And there will be large-scale exchanges, though posting plots over the last ten to fifteen years have ensured Home Worlders serve mostly in 1st Fleet. We shall see. There's a historical precedent from the twentieth century I studied when it became clear this convention would go ahead."

He grinned at me. "Let's see if you can dredge it from that capacious fund of historical data you carry around in your head."

I thought for a moment, then snapped my fingers. "The partition of India, nineteen-forty-seven, along religious lines. The Indian military under colonial rule was huge, and units were often of mixed religions or ethnic groups."

Kal nodded. "And yet they separated it into two armed forces, one for each successor state, with relatively few major difficulties under the circumstances. We will do the same."

I eyed him with suspicion. "You had a hand in drafting the partition plan?"

He gave me his usual crooked smile, then raised his glass. "Of course. Now, how about we toast our new star nation? I give you the Federation of Sovereign Star Systems."

Saga and I imitated him. "The Federation."

After taking a sip of the Glen Arcturus, Kal sat back.

"Once this is over and we return home, a few things will change. First, I'm not returning to the division. Grand Admiral Larsson is setting up a political planning and analysis office reporting directly to him. Its mission will be ensuring the Federation's political stability so it can become what it has to for humanity's long-term security."

"Let me guess. You're heading that office as a substantive major general."

Kal nodded. "And I'm taking Saga as one of my analysts, which is why she witnessed today's events instead of sitting in the S2 command post."

"Good choice." I smiled at my daughter, whose delight was evident.

"You, my friend," Kal continued, "are getting your first star and taking my job as deputy division commander."

"I'm flattered, but I'm no general officer, Kal."

"On the contrary. We might get through partition without triggering another civil war, but the Commonwealth will never forgive us. They'll look for every chance to stick the knife in, especially since it'll likely become an authoritarian state absent the OutWorlds' resistance to the centralists. This means your expertise in irregular warfare will become vital on a large scale since the Commonwealth can't afford to confront us head-on. And, in the longer term, we'll reunite humanity under Wyvern's leadership because we can't afford a discontented star nation at the heart of ours as we expand."

I thought about it for a moment while taking another sip of the Glen Arcturus. "Okay. I'll take your word for it."

"He's right, you know, Dad. We might have avoided a full-scale civil war, but that doesn't mean we'll avoid conflict altogether. On the contrary. General Ryent's example for partition saw both successor states engage in several wars and almost constant conflict over disputed borders."

"Yeah, I recall reading about that. Let's hope we keep wars to a minimum."

"Which is why we'll need our Special Forces more than ever, Zack." He raised his glass again. "Congratulations on the promotion."

"Oh, is it already effective?"

"It will be once the Grand Admiral sees the record of today's events and sends me an acknowledgment."

I scowled at him. "Don't tell me you had that planned out in advance as well?"

"No. I'm not prescient. But Larsson and I were exchanging subspace messages daily once the convention started, so things evolved quickly along the way. He was undoubtedly being advised by Hera, among others, since her people have been watching Earth and the Home Worlds for their reaction from the get-go."

"I wonder what the mood at Fleet HQ feels like these days."

Kal shrugged. "Whatever it is today, it'll be totally different tomorrow when word gets around that we now serve the Federation. There will be much turmoil, I have no doubt of that, but the service chiefs will be ready to deal with it. They've been briefed every day."

"Since you know everything, what'll happen to the Constabulary?"

"They change allegiance just like the Armed Forces. Besides, the number of Constabulary members in what's now the much-reduced Commonwealth is pretty small, and I doubt Earth will want to create a federal police force to replace it. Our old friends from the Sécurité Spéciale will gain from the OutWorld secession, but not in the way they might want."

I shook my head before taking another healthy sip of the Glen Arcturus.

"You know, I still can't believe it happened, let alone so quickly and suddenly. It'll take me a bit to readjust my thinking after spending my life fighting for the Commonwealth, especially the last decade or two when I was doing my best to help prolong the Commonwealth's life."

"Zack, let me put it in words the historian in you will appreciate. You are the last surviving legate of the Western Roman Empire. This, right here, is the new Constantinople. The heir of a long legacy. The historical Constantinople existed for another thousand years after the Western Empire collapsed forever. It protected the West long enough to allow a rebirth of civilization on the foundations of Rome. One alive today. This is why the Fleet has done what it's done since Kathryn Kowalski's day. She saw the end of the Commonwealth but knew it must not happen before the new Constantinople arose. And now it has — a Federation of star systems looking toward the future rather than the past. One which will be led with a light touch by Wyvern instead of ruled with a heavy hand by Earth."

I drained my glass. "We hope. But your simile with the Byzantine Empire has one flaw."

"Oh?"

"It might have survived the Western Roman Empire by another thousand years, but for the last four centuries of its existence, it steadily shrank from what wasn't a sizable chunk of the old Roman Empire at its maximum expansion, to begin with. Its obsolescence was built in. Let's hope our new Federation finds its way back to glory rather than suffer a steady decline."

Kal picked up the bottle and served us another round.

"So, what would you propose as a more reasonable lesson from the past?"

After taking a slow sip, I placed my glass on the table again.

"If we want to stay with the same theme, the Holy Roman Empire would probably be a better example. But it's still imperfect." I shrugged. "It doesn't really matter, though. I suspect that your Federation—"

"Our Federation," Kal interjected.

"Right. I suspect our Federation will eventually commit the same mistakes as the Commonwealth. The allure of centralizing control, even though it's impractical over hundreds of light years, will always resurface. It's part of the human curse."

My daughter gave me a wry smile.

"True. Let's just hope we take a long time before another shakeup becomes necessary. In the meantime, and for a good chunk of our lifetimes, we'll be protecting our sphere while the politicians figure out the new construct. Who knows?" She winked at me. "We might even lay the foundations of an empire that will last a thousand years."

My communicator gently buzzed for attention at that moment, and I fished it from my tunic pocket.

"Well, well, well. Saga and I are invited to Carnarvon Manor tomorrow evening to celebrate the secessionist cause's victory. Dress is formal, and we're asked to wear our uniforms." I glanced up at my daughter. "You game for another visit?"

"So long as there's no idiot with a missile waiting for us, sure."

# — Forty-Seven —

The manor was fully lit up when we arrived at dusk the next day, and the forecourt was already crowded with fancy ground cars. Saga parked our staff car among them, and we alit, leaving our berets behind. The front doors were wide open, spilling a carpet of light over the steps, and we could see many heads through the formal reception room's mullioned windows, the women's bejeweled, the men's perfectly groomed. The sound of voices and laughter grew as we neared the doors, and the butler met us the moment we entered.

"Colonel, Captain. Welcome." He gestured toward the reception room. "It's in there."

"Thank you."

We stepped through the open door and stopped, eyes searching for familiar faces. Perhaps fifty or sixty people were in small groups, glasses in hand, having a grand old time. All were elegantly dressed in formal wear.

I finally spotted the Old Man and grandmother, and we made a beeline for them, snagging glasses of champagne from a passing waiter with a tray. When he spotted us, an unexpected smile lit up his face.

"Our Federation Marines have arrived," he said, raising his glass. "I understand you're to become a brigadier general shortly, Zachary."

"That's the rumor, sir."

"It'll be only what you deserve. And now that you're here, we can toast the future."

A chime began sounding, slowly stilling conversation after conversation along with the background music, until everyone in the room was silently looking at the Old Man.

"Ladies and gentlemen," he said, "what an auspicious night. A night of new beginnings, untold futures unfolding, and celebration. We finally left behind the rotting carcass of the Commonwealth. Please join me in raising your glasses to the Federation of Sovereign Star Systems. Long may it lead our species to its destiny. I give you the Federation."

"The Federation," sixty-odd voices replied, mine and Saga's included. I was a bit surprised at how easily the toast came to me, proving once again that I was anything if not adaptable. The Commonwealth had my loyalty, however strained, yesterday. The new Federation had it today.

The music and the conversations resumed, and I spotted my father and mother. I excused myself to the Old Man and grandmother, leaving Saga with them, and headed across the room.

My father's face, flushed with alcohol, hardened as he noticed my approach, and his jaw set in the stubborn

Decker fashion. I glanced at his right hand, and sure enough, it was twitching.

"Mother, Father. How are you this fine evening?"

"Doing well," my father replied. "That is until you showed up."

"Jack!" My mother slapped his forearm.

"No, that's all right," I said. "I won't keep you long. Tell me, *Dad*, did you get singed that evening when I broke out of your mercenaries' custody, or did I crease your arm?"

My father's face darkened, and I saw the fury in his eyes.

"Hiring Hashashin — at least that's what we call them, we don't know their real name — must have set you and your colleagues in the secessionist movement back by a pretty cred. And for what? A foreordained conclusion that didn't need the deaths of those delegates and police officers. Well done. I suppose your Hashashin fired at Saga and me after we left Carnarvon Manor the last time. Care to tell me why? After all, we're on the same side."

"We will never be on the same side," he replied through clenched teeth.

"That's quite clear to me by now. I just hoped you'd have the courage to own up to your actions, but I guess not."

His jaw muscles worked for a few seconds. "Yes, I'm part of a consortium that hired the Holy Shadow Warriors, who you call Hashashin. And yes, I had them fire at your car, hoping to hurt you. Incapacitate you. Make you helpless."

"And Saga, who's an innocent in this?"

"She's your spawn," he spat out in a quiet growl.

My mother slapped him on the arm again. "What do you mean, Jack?"

He ignored her. "But you came through it with flying colors."

"So, it had nothing to do with advancing the secessionist cause?"

"No. It was just me."

"And the abduction?"

"Also me. You weren't supposed to get hurt."

"Yet four Hashashin died nonetheless."

He shrugged. "They were expendable from the get-go."

"They were human beings. But thank you for finally being honest with me. Don't worry. You won't see me again after tonight." I turned to my mother. "I'm sorry for having caused father to hate me."

She reached up and laid her fingers on my cheek. "You'll always be my son, and I am proud of you, Zachary, and of Saga. Your father will eventually come around, but not before you're long gone, I'm afraid."

"Thank you, Mother."

I inclined my head at both of them, then turned on my heels and left, feeling their eyes on my back. Delia and Richard intercepted me, and the conversation was much less strained.

By the time we said our goodbyes and left, well after midnight, I felt pity for my father, who'd let his dislike of my choices long ago fester into hatred over the decades. I hoped mother was right, and he'd get over it, but I wasn't going to hold my breath. Besides, I doubted I'd ever come back once we left Mykonos. Home was the sovereign star system of Caledonia now.

# — Forty-Eight —

Secretary General of the Commonwealth Brodrick Brüggemann, who'd been staring out the tall windows at a leaden Lake Geneva under a lowering sky, turned to face his silent cabinet, seated around a long, oval table. Their bleak expressions mirrored the weather as they variously looked at their readers, at the windows, or at each other. None of them dared meet Brüggemann's furious gaze.

"It's illegal," his voice thundered over the silent assembly. "Illegal. The constitution of the Commonwealth does not allow star systems to unilaterally secede, let alone colonies belonging to Earth or one of the Home Worlds. I want options to stop this nonsense at once."

The incendiary subspace message from Mykonos announcing the secession of the OutWorlds and colonies had arrived an hour earlier, just as the SecGen and his cabinet members were enjoying their weekly breakfast meeting. Needless to say, the original agenda had gone out the window, replaced by a hastily thrown-together briefing from the SecGen's chief of staff.

Andreas Bauchan, Director General of the Sécurité Spéciale, leaned forward, elbows on the table, hands joined. Technically, he wasn't a member of the SecGen's cabinet, but Brüggemann had, in recent times, made Bauchan a sort of adjunct at the latter's subtle prodding.

"As I see it, sir, you have but a few options. One of them would be to walk back your earlier rejection of the constitutional convention's demands and say you'll see that they're enacted by the Senate and the sovereign star systems provided the convention walks back its declaration of secession."

The Deputy Secretary General let out a snort of derision. "I think that ship has sailed, Andreas. Besides, it would merely open the way for further blackmail by the OutWorlds."

Bauchan inclined his head toward her.

"As you say, Madame Deputy. Another option would be to challenge the right to secede and foment discord on the OutWorlds, putting the matter in doubt among the general population. It might tip the balance on a few worlds, and the rest will come back into the fold when enough of them see their coalition dwindling. In fact, I recommend we do so no matter the chosen option. But we should concentrate our efforts on the most vulnerable to unrest, meaning Wyvern, Dordogne, Scandia, Cascadia, and a few other major star systems."

Brüggemann studied Bauchan for a few seconds, then gave him a brusque nod. "Make it happen, Andreas. Anything else?"

"Prevent secession by force. Once again, concentrating our efforts on the most vulnerable star systems."

"With what?" The Secretary of Defense asked. "Didn't we just hear that Caledonia, where Fleet HQ is located, voted for secession? At least half of the Armed Forces will side with the secessionists, if not more, simply because they're OutWorlders. I daresay the senior Navy and Marine Corps commanders in the systems Andreas just mentioned will take their orders from the secessionists and resist any attempts to reimpose Earth's rule. Not that we will easily field formations loyal to us that are powerful enough to overcome secessionist units in more than a handful of star systems while keeping our own secure from retaliatory attacks."

"No." He shook his head. "Preventing secession by force is not a valid possibility at this time. At least not until we figure out how the Fleet will react."

Bauchan inclined his head again. "And so it is. Which leaves one last choice. Accept the secession of the OutWorlds and the colonies. Negotiate the best terms possible, especially regarding the Armed Forces, then work hard to undermine this Federation of theirs. We might pick off a few of the border star systems in time."

"Or not," the Deputy Secretary General said. "My instinct is to declare war on the secessionists, but we're rather helpless until we know how the Fleet shakes out."

Brüggemann turned away from the cabinet table to stare out the windows again.

"Yes, we are," he finally admitted. "Very well. Andreas, unleash whatever you must to cause trouble in the OutWorlds while we step back and watch this debacle unfold. If they've renounced the Commonwealth, then they're legitimate targets."

After a long silence, Brüggemann said, "I would dearly like to know how this happened. How did a handful of malcontents on the OutWorlds grow into a secessionist movement trying to shatter the Commonwealth without our knowledge?"

Even though Brüggemann kept his back to the cabinet table, he knew all eyes were now on Andreas Bauchan, whose organization should have foreseen the recent events.

"It was perhaps not a handful of malcontents," the latter finally replied. "But a more widespread sentiment that has been growing in the shadows for years. Well, not always in the shadows. There have been plenty of times in recent years when OutWorlds and Earth were at great odds, be it publicly or behind the scenes. We merely underestimated the depth of the sentiment."

"Merely?" Brüggemann turned around to face his spymaster. "Merely? I would have planned my reply differently if we had known they would call for secession once we rejected their demands."

Bauchan's left shoulder twitched in a half-shrug.

"I think anything less than a full acceptance of their demands would have triggered the same result. In fact, the more I think about it, the more I'd venture that the result of the OutWorld secession was baked into the convention.

Somehow, the OutWorlds secretly negotiated their collective break with the Commonwealth ahead of time. And all it must have taken was a handful of the influential star systems to lead the way. The rest fell into step. And," a sick smile briefly lit up Bauchan's face, "the Fleet was surely in cahoots with them from the beginning because secession becomes easy once you know you have all the military power in the OutWorlds on your side."

"In other words, we were blindsided. You — my chief of Security Intelligence — were blindsided."

"Yes, we were, Mister Secretary General," Bauchan admitted.

"Then why should I keep you on as director general of the Sécurité Spéciale if no one in your organization saw it coming?"

Bauchan's smile returned. "Because you won't find anyone better suited to deal with the situation, sir."

Brüggemann locked eyes with Bauchan for a few moments. "Maybe. But find out how your people missed this."

Andreas Bauchan left the cabinet meeting deep in thought, trying to figure out how the entire Sécurité Spéciale missed a plot by dozens of sovereign star systems intent on breaking away from the Commonwealth. And not only the Sécurité Spéciale but also its unofficial auxiliary in a large swath of the OutWorlds, especially the Rim Sector — the Deep Space Foundation. And that began to bother him. The Deep Space Foundation had been so close to the political pulse in the Rim and the neighboring sectors and provided invaluable intelligence since he made an alliance with Britta Trulson, the Foundation's representative on Earth. Why had she suddenly failed at this most crucial time?

Once back in his office, he tried calling her, but to no avail. The Britta Trulson he'd known for the past two years had vanished.

A very different woman boarded a shuttle from the Geneva spaceport to the Terra orbital station a few hours later and walked aboard a liner headed to Wyvern, her job on Earth done.

# About the Author

Eric Thomson is the pen name of a retired Canadian soldier who spent more time in uniform than he expected, both in the Regular Army and the Army Reserve. He spent his Regular Army career in the Infantry and his Reserve service in the Armoured Corps.

Eric has been a voracious reader of science fiction, military fiction, and history all his life. Several years ago, he put fingers to keyboard and started writing his own military sci-fi, with a definite space opera slant, using many of his own experiences as a soldier for inspiration.

When he's not writing fiction, Eric indulges in his other passions: photography, hiking, and scuba diving, all of which he shares with his wife.

Join Eric Thomson at http://www.thomsonfiction.ca/

Where you'll find news about upcoming books and more information about the universe in which his heroes fight for humanity's survival.

Read his blog at https://blog.thomsonfiction.ca

If you enjoyed this book, please consider leaving a review with your favorite online retailer to help others discover it.

# Also by Eric Thomson

## Siobhan Dunmoore

No Honor in Death (Siobhan Dunmoore Book 1)
The Path of Duty (Siobhan Dunmoore Book 2)
Like Stars in Heaven (Siobhan Dunmoore Book 3)
Victory's Bright Dawn (Siobhan Dunmoore Book 4)
Without Mercy (Siobhan Dunmoore Book 5)
When the Guns Roar (Siobhan Dunmoore Book 6)
A Dark and Dirty War (Siobhan Dunmoore Book 7)
On Stormy Seas (Siobhan Dunmoore Book 8)

## Decker's War

Death Comes But Once (Decker's War Book 1)
Cold Comfort (Decker's War Book 2)
Fatal Blade (Decker's War Book 3)
Howling Stars (Decker's War Book 4)
Black Sword (Decker's War Book 5)
No Remorse (Decker's War Book 6)
Hard Strike (Decker's War Book 7)

## Constabulary Casefiles

The Warrior's Knife
A Colonial Murder
The Dirty and the Dead

## Ashes of Empire

Imperial Sunset (Ashes of Empire 1)
Imperial Twilight (Ashes of Empire 2)
Imperial Night (Ashes of Empire 3)
Imperial Echoes (Ashes of Empire 4)
Imperial Ghosts (Ashes of Empire 5)

## Ghost Squadron

We Dare - Ghost Squadron No. 1
Deadly Intent - Ghost Squadron No. 2
Die Like the Rest – Ghost Squadron No. 3
Fear No Darkness – Ghost Squadron No. 4

www.ingramcontent.com/pod-product-compliance
Lightning Source LLC
Chambersburg PA
CBHW072007190726
48293CB00001B/197